Also available from Headline Liaison

Sense
and Sensuality

Louisa Campion

HEADLINE
Liaison

First published in 1997
by HEADLINE BOOK PUBLISHING

A HEADLINE LIAISON paperback

10 9 8 7 6 5 4 3 2 1

ISBN 0 7472 5578 4

Typeset by
Letterpart Limited, Reigate, Surrey

Printed and bound in Great Britain by
Cox & Wyman Ltd, Reading, Berks

HEADLINE BOOK PUBLISHING
A division of Hodder Headline PLC
338 Euston Road
London NW1 3BH

Sense
and Sensuality

ONE

Julia Calvert paced the floor of the drawing room at Cumberley, the flounced skirts of her blue muslin morning dress swirling around her slender ankles with each step.

'I'm sorry, Isabel, but I feel it's my duty to remain here until I receive some definite word,' she told her cousin.

'You've been living alone for almost two years now,' Isabel reminded her. 'What's the point of being buried alive in the depths of the countryside, when you could be enjoying all the amusements of civilization in town?'

'My neighbours call on me from time to time. I read, I play the pianoforte and I ride,' Julia defended herself.

She went over to the window and stared out at the gardens and parklands bathed in bright spring sunshine. Her china-blue eyes were troubled and she absently smoothed her golden curls as she listened to her cousin.

'But those are such dull pursuits. Return to town with me tomorrow and take your proper place in society,' Isabel urged her. 'Do you not yearn to go to balls, rout parties, concerts and the theatre again?'

'Of course I do!' cried Julia, going to join Isabel on the sofa. 'But I feel it would be wrong of me.'

Isabel Marchmont regarded the young woman next to her steadily. 'You are not yet twenty,' she pointed out, 'but you have to all intents and purposes eschewed the world and the manifold pleasures it offers. Do you intend to continue in this way for the rest of your life? Tell me the truth,' she continued, 'do you not lie in your lonely bed at night, aching for a man's arms around you, his member buried deep inside your sex?'

1

Julia sprang to her feet and went over to the window again. 'You must know I do,' she replied in a low voice.

'Then return to London with me. It grieves me to think of you sequestered here. You need not open the town house – you must know it would delight me to have you as my guest for an indefinite period. No one would think ill of you, for what could be more natural than that you should take up residence with me?'

This wasn't the first time that Isabel had descended on Julia for a visit and tried to persuade her to quit the quiet and isolation of the countryside. This time, however, she had openly voiced her intention to remain at Cumberley until Julia acquiesced.

The entrance of a servant to announce the arrival of one of Julia's neighbours effectively interrupted their tête à tête and shortly afterwards Sir Henry Bartrum was ushered into their presence.

A burly, well-bred widower in his late thirties, Sir Henry was Julia's nearest neighbour and rarely a week passed without him calling.

He greeted them both and settled himself into a chair, a gleam of admiration in his eyes as he surveyed the two women. They made a pleasing picture even to the most demanding of observers.

With her porcelain-pale skin and delicately chiselled features, Julia Calvert was possessed of the type of ethereal, golden beauty which many other women were unable to forgive her for.

Happily her cousin Isabel, a strikingly attractive dark-haired woman some eight years her senior, was not of their number. She was possessed of an elegantly curvaceous figure, lustrous dark hair and heavy-lidded grey eyes. A certain languorousness to her movements hinted at the essential sensuality of her nature, which the opposite sex were not usually slow to discern.

'How long do you propose to remain in the neighbourhood, Lady Marchmont?' Sir Henry asked Isabel.

'Until I can persuade Julia to return to London with me,' she replied, adjusting the demi-train of her lilac silk gown to greater advantage. 'Perhaps you'll take pity on me and dine with us tonight – otherwise she and I may fall out, as I'm determined not to take "no" for an answer.'

Her eyes wandered briefly over his well-muscled legs, shown to advantage by his riding breeches and highly polished top-boots, then returned to his face.

'With the greatest of pleasure,' he said. 'But I fear that I would intrude.'

Julia cast an indignant glance at Isabel for proffering the invitation without consulting her first, but good manners prompted her to say, 'Do say you'll come – it would be most agreeable to have you join us.' She was unable to resist adding, 'And anyway, my cousin might die of boredom if she's deprived of male society for twenty-four hours.'

He bowed in her direction. 'I can see I have no alternative but to accept.'

He stayed for half an hour, chatting easily on a variety of topics and then left them, promising to return for dinner.

'A good-looking man,' commented Isabel, a cat-like smile on her face.

'Do you think so? I hadn't noticed,' replied Julia indifferently.

'When he visits, do you never imagine him throwing you down on the sofa and pleasuring you?' asked Isabel. 'His wife has been dead these two years, so no doubt he misses the comforts of the matrimonial bed.'

Julia flushed and averted her face.

'No gentleman worthy of the name would behave in such a way,' she retorted.

'Perhaps not, but I think I know the male sex far better than you. It would be well nigh impossible for any virile, healthy man to be alone with you and not wish to make love.'

'Sir Henry is aware of my circumstances and respects them.'

'I'm sure that with only a little encouragement he could be prevailed upon to forget them,' pointed out Isabel.

'Well, I'm not about to offer him any.'

'Do you have no interest in him at all?'

'None,' replied Julia in a decided tone. 'I have no interest in any man, except Charles.'

After luncheon Isabel retired to her room to rest, declaring that she was still tired after her journey the previous day. Julia ordered her horse to be saddled and went up to her bed-chamber to change into her green velvet riding habit, then picked up her gloves and riding crop and went outside.

Maybe it was Isabel's visit, or maybe it was because it was spring, but she was plagued by a restlessness she couldn't shake off. She mounted her bay mare and, once she'd reached the open parkland, urged the horse into a gallop. She rode for a couple of hours and then headed for home at a more sedate pace.

Perhaps she *should* go to London, as Isabel wanted her to. She had, after all, been a long time alone.

As she came to the top of a rise, Cumberley came into view and she reined in the mare and studied the lovely old house, its windows aflame in the afternoon sunshine. Truly it was a magnificent building – large and imposing, but with too much charm to be forbidding. Built from honey-coloured stone some two centuries previously, it was now smothered in ivy on one side, almost to the roof.

It looked just as it had that day Charles had originally brought her here and she'd seen her future home for the first time. Little had she known then that all too soon she would be living here on her own.

She rode back to the house and went up to her bed-chamber where, helped by her maid, she changed her clothing and tidied her guinea-gold hair. She went to find her cousin who was lounging on a sofa in front of the fire in the drawing room.

'I beg you – say you will journey to London with me tomorrow,' Isabel greeted her, 'or I declare I'll expire from boredom.'

'You would have been most welcome to ride with me,' Julia pointed out.

'I hate to ride in the country – there's nothing but mud and dirt,' commented Isabel. 'Come and sit by me – I wish to talk to you seriously.'

Suppressing a sigh, Julia obeyed her.

'Charles has been gone now these last two years,' began Isabel. 'I say this with the greatest reluctance, but I think that if he were coming back, he would have got word to you somehow.'

The faint pink bloom in Julia's cheeks paled and she bit her lower lip.

'He is coming back – I know he is,' she insisted.

'The journey to the colonies would have taken him but three months, his business there only a few weeks. You expected him to return some eighteen months ago but he did not and no one has seen him or heard from him since he journeyed into the interior.'

'There could be many explanations for that,' protested Julia.

'The most likely one is that some accident befell him and he died. I'm sorry to speak so bluntly, but I feel I have to make you face the facts.'

Julia leapt to her feet.

'You have no right to talk to me of such things. If Charles were dead, I would know it!'

She hurried from the room and up to her bed-chamber, where she threw herself down on the bed and wept.

TWO

If Sir Henry noticed that Julia was pale and subdued over dinner, he gave no sign of it. He treated both ladies with equal gallantry and was so eager for their company again that he lingered for only a few minutes with the port decanter after they'd left the dining room.

Ill disposed for further conversation, Julia seated herself at the pianoforte and played some of her favourite pieces while Isabel and their guest enjoyed what appeared to be a mutually satisfying flirtation.

During her first season Isabel had had the good fortune to catch the eye of the very wealthy Lord Marchmont and shortly afterwards had married him with great ceremony. The fact that he was not in the first flush of youth did him no disservice in her eyes.

When he died only three years later, she genuinely grieved for him for twelve months, before casting off her mourning and rejoining society. Since then many had sought her hand, but she made no secret to Julia that the independent life of a wealthy widow suited her very well and she had no intention of ever marrying again.

Her lovers, however, were legion and she discreetly pursued the pleasures of the flesh whenever the fancy took her. To Julia, it appeared that the fancy took her cousin now as Isabel lowered her heavy-lidded grey eyes flirtatiously and then tapped Sir Henry on the wrist with her painted ivory fan.

Isabel was wearing a wine-red silk gown with a low décolletage and short, puffed sleeves. It was lavishly trimmed with lace and the high waistline was emphasized by a tasselled belt through which she had tucked the end of her train. Elbow-length gloves covered her creamy forearms and she had rubies at her neck, ears and on one wrist.

Julia finished playing and closed the lid of the pianoforte. She rose to her feet and crossed the room.

'I find myself very fatigued and I think I'll retire,' she told them. 'Sir Henry, there is no need for you to take your leave. Indeed you would be doing me a great service if you stayed and kept my cousin company for a while longer, otherwise she'll do nothing tomorrow but complain of the early hours we keep in the country. If you'll both excuse me.'

Sir Henry leapt to his feet and kissed her hand, then bowed her from the room with a gallant flourish. Isabel waved a languid hand in her cousin's direction, but her grey eyes sparkled with anticipation.

As soon as Julia had left the room Isabel beckoned to him and said lazily, 'It seems you must entertain me. Are you equal to the task, do you think?'

'Undoubtedly,' he assured her, falling to his knees in front of her.

Slowly, an inch at a time, he raised the scalloped hem of her silk gown until her shapely calves in their silk stockings were exposed, then bent and kissed them fervently. She leant back against the cushions, a faint smile curving her mouth as he worked his way gradually up to her knees.

When her lacy garters came into view he groaned and bent his head to press his lips to the bare flesh above them. He kissed and nibbled his way upwards until he came to her loose-legged silk drawers.

He raised his head, entreaty on his face and she smiled her acquiescence. He slid his fingers upwards until they encountered the soft, dark hair of her fleece. He stroked it ecstatically and she lay further back against the cushions and parted her thighs.

He delved eagerly between them until his fingertips encountered the slick, velvety folds of her vulva. He felt the heat and wetness of her sex and with his other hand tore at the buttons of his pantaloons.

A shadow crossed her face at his haste and she murmured, 'There is no occasion for hurry. Pleasure me with your hand first.'

He obeyed her, probing her deepest, most hidden places and caressing the slippery slopes and valleys of her private parts. She moaned softly as he made contact with the throbbing bud of her clitoris and, laying her hand over his, showed him what movements gave her the most pleasure.

She felt the delicious, hot tingling spreading outwards from the stiffening nub and opened her legs even further. He continued to stroke her until she stifled a low cry and came, her voluptuous body racked by spasms of deep-seated, heady pleasure.

He drew out his rigid member and would have entered her immediately, but she took it in her hand and caressed it, causing it to harden even further. It felt like silk-encased steel, the glans a dark, swollen purple, a drop of moisture already forming on the end.

She lifted her legs onto the sofa and he mounted her, guiding the engorged tip of his phallus up the leg of her drawers. But it became caught in the silken folds of the flimsy garment and she raised her bottom so he could draw it down her legs, laying bare her dark fleece and the creamy skin of her thighs and belly.

Isabel gasped, then gasped again as he entered her and began to thrust in and out. His hands found her breasts and freed them from the low-cut neck of her gown. Full and ripe, they had umber nipples, hardened now to taut points.

He caressed them avidly, covering them with his hands and then bending his head to take one sensitive peak in his mouth. He sucked at it, flicking it with the tip of his tongue, as she moved beneath him, her hips shifting in an erotic, undulating rhythm.

She came again just before his urgent plunges quickened in pace to pump his boiling juices into her in a series of last pleasurable thrusts.

He lay on top of her for a few moments, breathing hard, then, always the gentleman, rolled to one side. Isabel smiled languidly and lazily adjusted her disordered gown, then swung her feet to the floor and indicated the decanter of wine set on a side table.

'Some refreshment would be most welcome,' she told him. He fastened his pantaloons and went to pour them both a glass of wine.

He seated himself beside her while they chatted in a desultory manner, but his eyes kept straying to her ripe, white breasts, most of which were on display.

Aware that his interest was rising anew, Isabel hid a smile. Her own considerable appetites were far from satisfied and she was not displeased to see the desire in his eyes as he looked at her.

'You're the most beautiful woman I've seen in many a day,' he told her. 'I plan to visit London soon – may I call on you?'

'By all means,' she assured him. 'And I feel certain that Julia will welcome you as I do.'

'Do you think you'll get her to return with you?' he asked, taking a deep drink of his wine.

'I'm determined on it.'

'It has to be said – she's most awkwardly circumstanced. Neither a wife nor a widow. Do you believe Charles Calvert to be dead?'

'I regret to say that I do. Now my problem is to get her to accept it. I'm reluctant to cause my cousin any grief, but until she does accept it, her life is in limbo.'

'It won't be easy, she speaks of him as though his return is just a matter of time,' he commented, his eyes again lingering on the ripe swell of her breasts.

Glancing down, Isabel saw that his member was making a noticeable bulge in the front of his pantaloons. She laid a gloved hand on it and caressed it until it hardened into full tumescence. Rising to her feet she strolled over to a brocade armchair and bent over the back.

Unhurriedly, she raised the skirts of her gown until all her legs were exposed to his hungry gaze. She heard him swallow and clear his throat as she drew the skirts up to her waist, giving him an uninterrupted view of the full moons of her curvaceous bottom.

'Madam – I declare that's a sight a man would kill for,' he

said in a hoarse voice. She parted her thighs so he could feast his eyes on the intricate crimson folds of her sex and looked over her shoulder at him.

'Come – take me again,' she invited him huskily.

Upstairs in her bed-chamber Julia tossed and turned, unable to sleep.

Damn Isabel for her interference. She wouldn't accept that she might never see Charles again – couldn't accept it.

She'd been aghast when only six months after their marriage he'd informed her that he had to leave on a mission to the colonies in the service of the crown and would be away for some time. She'd begged him not to go and when he'd told her that refusal was unthinkable, had pleaded with him to take her with him.

But she'd known from the look on his face that it was hopeless and he was determined to travel alone.

The truth was that not only did she love him with all her heart, but she'd become addicted to the pleasure he gave her whenever they were closeted together.

Prior to their wedding he'd restricted his caresses to kissing her, but even that had lit a fire in her sex beyond anything she'd ever experienced before.

Afterwards, in the long dark nights in the privacy of their marriage bed, he'd coaxed a response from her body she could never have imagined in her most erotic dreams. She'd been in a sated daze for months, heedless of anything else, always living from one hot, breathless encounter to the next.

The thought that she might never again feel his hands on her, skilfully caressing her to a state of readiness, was unbearable.

When at last she slept, her repose was disturbed by dark and feverish dreams.

She was at a ball, sumptuously gowned in white shot-silk embroidered with silver leaves, her golden hair arranged in artless ringlets with white flowers deftly inserted among the curls.

She danced every dance until some impulse led her to

excuse herself to her latest partner and seek solitude in the orangery.

She wandered among the potted palms and exotically-hued flowers, pausing to inhale the sweet scent of a gardenia. She plucked one white, velvet-petalled flower and tucked it into the square décolletage of her gown and then, sensing she wasn't alone, looked around.

But there was no one in sight and unable to shake off the uneasy thought that she was being watched, she slipped behind a bank of greenery and went to gaze outside over the moon-silvered lawns. The scent of gardenia hung heavily in the air as she thought she heard a footfall behind her, but once again when she turned her head sharply, she was still alone.

The music wafted in from the ballroom and she gave herself up to dreamy contemplation of the shadowed gardens. Another sound – this one much closer – made her start, but before she could look round again someone seized her from behind and she was pulled against a lean, hard body.

A hand wound in her hair prevented her from catching a glimpse of her captor and forced her to look at the floor.

To her horror the man splayed the palm of his other hand flat against her stomach and moved it in insidious, caressing circles. Heat flared through her belly and her legs trembled as he explored the smooth contours of her slender figure through her diaphanous gown.

His hand glided over her hip, then slid softly upwards to trace a fleeting caress over the upper slopes of her breasts. His palm was cool and smooth and he smelt faintly of eau-de-Cologne.

Julia's legs were trembling so much she felt they could hardly support her and she had no option but to lean back against him. She felt his lips against the nape of her neck then the hand which was wound in her hair was withdrawn, but she was too weak and shocked to turn and see who her assailant was.

She felt him lifting the skirts of her gown at the front and then he slid his hand down inside the ivory silk of her pantalettes. She should have wanted to die of mortification, but instead a surge of desire so strong she could hardly breathe swept over her.

Her eyes fluttered closed and stayed that way as he toyed with her golden floss, gradually slipping lower until the tips of his fingers brushed the damp curls veiling her most secret parts. When his fingers made electrifying contact with her slippery flesh and eased themselves into the slick channel between her outer sex-lips, she moaned softly and was immediately mortified by her own response.

She could feel her own warm juices trickling stealthily downwards, as if in league with him to facilitate his movements. One probing finger found its way between her inner sex-lips and then to her shame slid deep inside her feminine core.

Her lower body felt as though it were on fire, although oddly enough his hand still felt cool against her over-heated, throbbing flesh.

He explored her thoroughly, working two fingers inside her and then swivelling them lazily around. Perhaps it was her trembling legs, or perhaps it was something primitive deep within her, but she found herself bearing down against his hand, wanting the unbearably intimate stimulation to intensify.

He eased her thighs apart and then massaged her vulva, causing the most delicious sensations to course through her. He turned his attention to the throbbing little knot of flesh between her inner sex-lips and stroked it gently.

She heard a gasping, panting noise and knew that it was she herself behaving in such an unseemly way. Her hips began to move to the same rhythm as his fingers as the tingling sensation increased.

The inside of her thighs was damp and became damper as she worked her hips like a woman possessed.

Suddenly, there was a great explosion of heat and the world shattered around her like a bubble bursting. In that moment she was certain that the man was Charles and joy suffused her entire being.

She felt as though if she could just open her eyes, she'd know for sure by looking at his reflection in the darkened glass. But her eyelids felt heavy and it was some time before she could get them to open.

But instead of finding herself in the orangery, her skirts above her waist and Charles behind her, she was alone in her bed at Cumberley, her own hand between her thighs.

Misery swept over her as she lay staring into the darkness of her bed-chamber.

It had just been a dream. Charles was gone and if Isabel were to be believed, he might never be coming back.

THREE

Julia awoke in the morning miserable and depressed. Although there was nothing she felt more like doing than pulling the covers over her head and staying in bed, the recollection of her duties as a hostess forced her to rise at her usual time.

Isabel didn't come downstairs until late morning and one glance at her was enough to inform Julia that her cousin had enjoyed more than Sir Henry's conversation the night before.

She had the unmistakable air of a satisfied woman. Her creamy skin glowed and her dark hair looked sleek and shining as she descended the stairs in a high-waisted saffron silk morning gown with a vee-neck and long, tight sleeves. It was embellished with knots of amber ribbon and had a flounced hem which showed glimpses of her slippers of Denmark satin.

'Did you sleep well?' Julia greeted her.

'Pretty well. You look heavy-eyed – are you ill?'

'Sick at heart would be closer to the truth,' Julia admitted. Isabel put an arm around her and drew her into the library.

'You have been thinking about what I said?'

'Nothing except that, if I am to be honest.'

'Forgive me, my dearest cousin, but I feel the period for false hope is over. It's time to face up to the most likely eventuality and start living your life again.'

'That's easy to say. I have been waiting all this time, telling myself that soon Charles would return to me. If I can no longer believe that, then life has little point.'

Isabel took Julia's hands in her own.

'There is *every* point. The day will come when you will

believe so, but for now I think that the more distractions you have, the easier it will be. Say you'll return to London with me.'

'This is Charles' family home – I'm not sure I can bear to leave it.'

'You won't be leaving it forever, you can come back any time you wish,' pointed out Isabel. 'And anyway, the town house has also been in Charles' family for generations.'

'We spent little time there. We came here immediately after our honeymoon and remained here until the day he left.'

'Then it's time you had a change. Come to London with me and if you find it unbearable I can hardly stop you retiring to the country again.'

Privately Isabel vowed that she would spare herself no exertion in her cousin's entertainment, so Julia would have no opportunity to brood.

Julia looked around the library, aware that every time she entered it she thought of Charles. It was the same with every room in the house. Perhaps she would be better off staying with Isabel – at least for a time.

'Say you'll come,' Isabel urged her. Julia took a deep breath.

'Very well,' she capitulated and Isabel enfolded her in a scented embrace.

'We'll have a wonderful time – you'll see,' she promised. 'I'll go and tell my maid to pack at once. We'll leave first thing tomorrow morning.'

'I can't leave so soon,' protested Julia. 'I'll have dozens of things to arrange first.'

'Nonsense – that's what your staff are for. All you need do is order your maid to pack your clothes.'

After some argument, Isabel reluctantly agreed to delay their departure for two days and then went jubilantly off to tell her own maid.

Just as they were sitting down to lunch, a lavish basket of fruit was delivered together with a magnificent bouquet of flowers.

Extracting a card from among the fruit, Julia said, 'From

Sir Henry. The fruit is for me and the flowers for you. He begs us to dine with him tonight, do you wish to accept his invitation?'

'Assuredly,' said Isabel.

'I'll send word back with his manservant.'

It was the first time Julia had dined anywhere but at Cumberley since Charles had left and she wore one of her more formal evening gowns.

In rose-pink gauze, split down the sides to show her ivory silk slip, it was trimmed with ivory lace and embroidered with seed pearls around the hem and the short puffed sleeves. A Norwich shawl was draped over her arms and her hair had been dressed in ringlets with a pearl circlet pinned to it.

In his determination to provide a dinner fitting for his guests, Sir Henry had ordered a feast enough for ten people. The soup was followed by three courses, each consisting of at least a dozen dishes.

The table was presided over by an elderly aunt of Sir Henry, who lived in the neighbourhood and acted as his hostess whenever he entertained. Julia partook sparingly, but Isabel allowed their host to press her to dish after dish.

The second course included a roasted Davenport fowl, a boiled leg of lamb with spinach, a country roast ham, baked fish in white sauce and a pigeon pie. Several dishes of vegetables and some broiled mushrooms accompanied this modest repast and Julia had eaten more than enough by the time the dishes were removed.

They were replaced by a sirloin of beef, fillets of turbot in béchamel sauce, a cold partridge, fricassée of chicken, an omelette, pancakes and yet more vegetables.

By the time the last course was served, Julia couldn't eat another mouthful and looked in dismay at the apple pie, cakes, sweetmeats, preserved fruits, jellies and creams being placed on the table. Eventually she nibbled politely on a sweetmeat while Isabel ate a dish of Rhenish cream with every appearance of relish.

After dinner the three ladies retired to the drawing room

but were joined within a very short while by Sir Henry. Tea was served and they conversed for some time, but Julia was very aware of the amorous glances being exchanged between Isabel and their host.

She was not at all surprised when he cleared his throat and announced, 'I promised to show Lady Marchmont the picture gallery. Would you care to accompany us, Mrs Calvert?'

Correctly interpreting Isabel's expression, Julia declined and instead, at their hostess's request, agreed to play the pianoforte.

As he escorted Isabel up the wide flight of stairs leading to the first floor, Sir Henry turned to her.

'Throughout the day I've thought of nothing but yesterday evening. I've been hard and ready since I awoke this morning.'

Glancing around to ensure that they were not observed, Isabel ran her hand over his crotch and felt the rock-hard bulge under the stockinette of his pantaloons.

'So I apprehend,' she murmured. 'Are we likely to be disturbed in the picture gallery?'

'I gave very specific orders to the contrary.'

The gallery was lit by several branches of candles which flickered over the oak-panelled walls and the well-fed faces of Sir Henry's ancestors.

But Isabel was given little time to admire the portraits because he pulled her into his arms and kissed her passionately. His broad chest felt hard and muscular against the soft orbs of her breasts and he clasped her bottom with one large hand and kneaded and squeezed it avidly.

They kissed for some time and then he stepped back and scooped her breasts from her emerald-green satin gown so they were on full display.

'I'd like a portrait of you looking like that,' he told her in a thickened voice.

'Or perhaps like this,' she suggested sweetly, gliding to a table and sitting on the end of it. While he watched mesmerized, she drew up her skirts to expose her stockings with their frilly garters and then kept on raising the hem until it was above her waist.

Sir Henry looked as though he were about to lose

17

consciousness as he saw that beneath her skirts she was naked. No drawers or pantalettes veiled her dark, silken fleece or the crimson folds of her vulva.

He opened his mouth to speak but no sound came out. Slowly, she opened her legs and let him feast his eyes on her labia and the whorled entrance to her hidden chamber.

His hand went to his fly, but that wasn't to Isabel's liking.

'Come – kneel before me,' she bade him. He obeyed her and she caressed the back of his head, toying with his short, wiry hair. 'I wish you to pleasure me with your lips and tongue,' she told him.

He looked taken aback, confirming her belief that he had never done such a thing in his life. But she was determined that if he wished to make love to her, he must first comply with her request.

She thought for a moment that he was about to refuse, but his desire for her overcame his reservations and he moved closer and bent his head. He kissed her dark floss and then tentatively pressed a kiss on her outer labia.

Emboldened, he worked his way over her vulva and then touched the soft bud of her clit with the tip of his muscular tongue.

'Yes,' she breathed. 'That gives me particular pleasure.' He licked the shaft several times and then stabbed at the head, making her squirm with delight on the polished table-top.

His mouth felt wonderful against the sensitive tissues of her sex-flesh and she continued to encourage him verbally as he pushed his tongue experimentally into her quim.

Gathering confidence as he went on, he plunged it as far into her inner chamber as it would go and then used his hands to hold her open so he could gain even greater access.

This type of stimulation was one of Isabel's favourite methods of climaxing and she began to wriggle in his grasp as she felt her satisfaction coming closer.

'Harder . . . lick harder,' she moaned as he flicked at her swollen little nub and then took it gently between his lips and sucked.

She felt the heady rush of pleasure sweeping over her and jammed his face hard between her thighs, rubbing herself shamelessly against him until the convulsions dwindled to a faint, tingling heat.

He rose to his feet and mopped his dripping face with a handkerchief.

'For a favour given there shall be a favour returned,' she murmured huskily and, flipping her emerald-green skirts back around her ankles, she sank to her knees in front of him. She unbuttoned his fly and took out his organ, marvelling at the ramrod-hardness of it as she explored it.

Her breasts were still hanging immodestly out of her gown and he covered them with his hands and toyed with her nipples as she opened her lips and let the first two inches of his phallus slip between them.

She knew instinctively that this was no new thing to him and that some other woman had pleasured him in this way before. He groaned as she sucked on his member, let it slip from her mouth and then took it back in again.

With her gloved hand around the base she commenced an erotic dual action, making the throbbing shaft harden even more.

She sensed his impending eruption and released him, then took her time about arranging herself on her back on the table with her thighs apart and her knees bent.

He plunged into her and began to drive in and out while she held onto the sides of the table to prevent herself from sliding off it to land in a heap on the floor. She wound her legs around his waist and used them to guide his movements.

Above them his ancestors gazed down indifferently at the lascivious scene being enacted under their eyes. Isabel worked her internal muscles and felt another climax gathering. She redoubled her efforts, wanting to come before Sir Henry achieved his own satisfaction.

She wasn't sure how long they'd been in the picture gallery, but she suspected it was longer than the dictates of politeness allowed.

He exploded into her with a deep, heartfelt groan and she followed him a few seconds later, driven over the edge by his last frantic thrusts.

They lay together without speaking, the only sound their

19

breathing and the guttering of the candles. Sir Henry withdrew from her and buttoned his fly.

'My only regret is that we must rejoin the others before our absence occasions comment,' he said. 'If you wish to tidy yourself before descending to the drawing room, I've had a bed-chamber readied for your use.'

He conducted her to the door and then waited at the head of the stairs for her. Isabel washed herself in a bowl of warm water and then deftly tidied her hair and smoothed her gown.

So accustomed was she to illicit dalliance and repairing her appearance afterwards, that when they rejoined the others no one looking at her would have suspected that only a short while before her hair had been escaping from its pins and her skirts had been bunched wantonly around her waist.

FOUR

The journey to London in Isabel's well-appointed carriage was as comfortable as such a long journey could be, but even so Julia was weary by the time they reached Marchmont House. She was in low spirits and already regretted having let Isabel persuade her to leave Cumberley.

The noise and dirt of the city depressed her after the peace and fresh air of the countryside and when they arrived she acquiesced to Isabel's suggestion that she go straight to the bed-chamber which had been prepared for her.

Hot water was carried up the stairs to fill a bath tub placed in front of the fire, then after she'd bathed she climbed into bed where she was served a light supper.

Isabel came to say goodnight, already attired in her night-gown.

'I thought you would be eager to go out and seek some fashionable amusement after your sojourn in the country,' commented Julia sleepily.

'It was a tiring journey and I'm not in good looks because of it. Tomorrow will be soon enough after a long sleep. Stay in bed as long as you wish in the morning.' Isabel kissed her on the cheek and glided gracefully from the room.

Even in the quiet London square where Marchmont House was situated, the noise seemed to Julia to go on all night. She slept fitfully and her repose was interrupted by more disturbing dreams.

She felt dispirited and was still in bed drinking a cup of hot chocolate when Isabel swept in towards eleven o'clock looking radiant.

'How did you sleep?' Isabel enquired.

'Not very well,' she admitted.

'I thought perhaps you might wish to buy some new gowns. Something new in one's wardrobe is always such a tonic.'

'Perhaps, but not today,' replied Julia listlessly.

'Maybe you're right and you should spend the day resting. Tonight is the Langrishes' ball and we shall celebrate your return to society by attending. Anabel Langrishe is an old friend of mine. I'll send her word that you are staying with me and I know an invitation will be immediately forthcoming.'

'Thank you, but I don't have the slightest wish to attend a ball.'

Isabel stared at her cousin in consternation.

'Not wish to attend a ball? But everyone will be there.'

'I'm sorry, Isabel, but I think perhaps it was a mistake for me to come here.'

'My dear Julia, that's nonsense. You're just feeling low after that long and tiresome journey yesterday. Spend the day in bed resting and I'm certain you'll feel better by this evening.'

But far from feeling better, by evening Julia was shivering and feverish. Isabel was dismayed to see that her cousin was ill and immediately sent for the apothecary. He prescribed a draught, said that he didn't think it was a matter for serious concern and promised to call again the following day.

For the next couple of weeks Julia lay drifting in and out of sleep, aching in every limb and unable to partake of anything more nourishing than a few spoonfuls of soup every once in a while. She was glad that she slept so much because whenever she was awake she was unable to stop the tears from cascading down her face.

Isabel was extremely concerned and called for a second opinion, but it didn't differ materially from the first and with that she had to be content.

Julia was plagued by dreams of Charles, some of which were highly sexual in content, adding another dimension to her sense of loss. But some of her erotic dreams featured an unknown man – the same who'd made so free with her person in her dream about the orangery.

One night she dreamt she was attending a dinner and was waiting in the drawing room for the man who was to take her in. A large party was gathered there, the women all elegant in elaborate gowns, the men correctly attired in frock coats, tight breeches, silk stockings and pumps.

She herself was wearing a lovely gown of figured lace over daffodil-yellow silk, with a richly embroidered train of the same colour. A diamond-studded opera comb sat amid her golden curls and she carried a pretty painted fan in her gloved hand.

Her hostess led her partner over to her and presented him. He bowed low and she made her curtsey, but because the light was behind him and his face was in shadow, she was unable to see him properly. She only knew that he was tall, broad-shouldered and dark and that she felt she should know him.

They were the last couple to enter the dining room, but instead of leading her to her seat, he led her to the head of the table and moved behind her.

She was shocked to see him pick up a knife and use it to slash her train free from her gown. It fell to the floor in a gleaming yellow pool of silk and then he set about slicing her lace gown from her until it lay in ribbons, leaving her standing in just her yellow under-dress.

She seemed powerless to stop him and no one seated at the table made any attempt to come to her aid. On the contrary, they all watched avidly, the eyes of both men and women gleaming hungrily in the candlelight.

He placed the knife on the table and she hoped her ordeal was over, but worse was to follow. Grasping the back of her under-dress just below the high waist, he tore it from her in a brutal gesture which left her naked except for her gloves, stockings, tightly laced bodice and pantalettes.

The bodice, which after the fashion of the time was held up by shoulder straps, exposed almost all of her breasts. It raised and pushed them together to give her the high bosom necessary to show off a gown to greatest advantage, but it was

23

not designed to be worn in a public place with nothing over it.

To make matters worse, he scooped her breasts from it as easily as if they were oranges in a bowl, so that they were fully exposed above the garment. Julia felt a warm flush of mortification stealing over her pale cheeks as everyone's attention was riveted on her porcelain pale orbs and rose-pink nipples.

Amazingly, he then pulled out her chair for her and she sank into it, almost swooning from shame. At least she was now hidden from the waist down, but it was small comfort as it appeared she was expected to eat her dinner with her breasts on display.

He took the chair next to her and the tureen of soup was brought round. Conversations sprang up around the table, but most people were still staring at her. When the tureen reached her she shook her head, but he took the ladle and helped her to some anyway.

She became aware that she was still holding her fan and opened it with the intention of hiding her breasts from the intrusive stares of the other people around the table. But he reached across, twitched it lazily from her grasp and tossed it to the other side of the room.

To Julia it was an endless meal, particularly as between courses he fondled her carelessly. She almost leapt from her chair in shock the first time she felt his hand glide over her almost naked breasts, smoothing over the satiny skin and then toying with her nipples.

The presence of the bodice must have hindered his pleasure because he removed it impatiently, before resuming his caresses.

Her cheeks crimsoned as slowly, the two peaks hardened into taut points. She was deeply ashamed of herself for responding to his touch, but he handled her sensitive flesh so surely that to her intense embarrassment an insidious squib of arousal began to smoulder in her very core.

He caressed her thighs over the fine muslin of her pantalettes and then let his hand stray up to the swell of her mound, before cupping it and leaving it there as he ate a wedge of pigeon pie.

Heat seemed to be flooding into her groin where he touched it, spreading upwards and outwards until all her senses were aflame. She trembled as he began to stroke her pubis, trembled and hated herself because she discovered she wanted him to touch her yet more intimately.

She was to get her wish because suddenly, with one deft tug, he undid the ribbon holding up her pantalettes and the delicate garment fluttered downwards to lay bare her hips and belly.

A further impatient tug by her tormentor and her golden fleece was visible, but happily only to him as she was hidden below the waist from the others by the table.

He stroked her floss as though it were a nervous little animal, but soon his searching fingers were slipping lower and into the secret furrow of her sex. With a great effort of will she jammed her thighs together, then bit her lip and held her breath as he pushed them firmly apart. He delved briefly into her vulva, as if assessing her state of readiness, then got to his feet.

All conversations stopped as he addressed the assembled diners.

'Prepare yourselves to observe something of great interest.'

Julia was completely unprepared for what came next. He seized her around the waist and lifted her so she was standing on the table, then ripped her pantalettes from her so that her only garments were her gloves, silk stockings and kid slippers.

If she had been embarrassed before, now she was shamed to her very soul. Her tormentor positioned her with her legs widely parted and then touched her throbbing clitoris with the tip of his forefinger.

'See how this hidden jewel responds to stimulation.'

He stroked it in a stealthy, arousing movement which soon had her sex moistening in treacherous response. He caressed both sides of the shaft and then concentrated his attention on the head, which was so sensitive that she automatically flinched away.

But he placed his other hand firmly on her backside and kept her pelvis arched forward to give everyone an even better view of what he was doing.

There was a tickling sensation on her inner thigh and looking down, she saw that a tiny thread of moisture was trickling downwards, mute testament to the strength of her arousal.

'See how wet she is. See how her little jewel swells and grows hard as I touch it,' he drawled. Despite his cultured diction Julia was reminded of a showman at a fair urging the gawping crowds to watch a performing animal do tricks.

But even so she was gasping with need, wanting more than he was giving her, and when he slid two fingers inside her while continuing the stimulation with his thumb, she found herself bending her knees and bearing down on his hand.

It was agony and it was ecstasy. Her hips jerked and her breasts bounced as she sought satisfaction. The people around the table began to clap in time to her movements while perspiration filmed her forehead and gathered in beads between her breasts.

He thrust another finger inside her and her internal muscles clenched and unclenched rhythmically. With a sudden high pitched cry, barely audible over the clapping of the audience, she came; her entire body convulsing helplessly into spasms of the most decadent erotic pleasure.

She slumped to her hands and knees on the table top and was only dimly aware that the man was unbuttoning his breeches. A massive erect phallus sprang out and slapped smartly against his belly. He stood at the head of the table and, seizing her by the hips, pulled her backwards until her naked derrière and swollen, dripping vulva were just inches away from his organ.

She could feel the heat from it as he positioned it at the furled, crimson entrance to her sex and then strangely, she heard Isabel's voice saying, 'She's fallen out of bed – help me get her back in.'

Julia's eyes fluttered open to find herself crouched awkwardly on her hands and knees beside the bed. She was half helped, half lifted, back onto the goose-feather mattress and then the covers pulled up over her.

'Shh, be still,' murmured Isabel. 'Be still and go back to sleep.'

FIVE

Julia's recovery was slow and she was so pale and thin that Isabel had her chef prepare endless different delicacies in the hope of tempting her cousin's appetite.

Although Julia was soon well enough to dress and sit downstairs, she resisted all of Isabel's attempts to get her out of the house.

Isabel encouraged her friends to call in the hope that their company might entertain Julia, but she seemed fatigued by the effort of making conversation.

One morning she was resting on the sofa in the blue drawing room when the butler announced a visitor she hadn't met before, Richard Wortham.

Isabel was conferring with her housekeeper and, having asked the butler to inform his mistress that she had a caller, Julia prepared to receive Mr Wortham.

When he was shown in she was taken aback by his beauty. He looked to be about her own age and was tall and slender with silky silver-gold hair which framed a sensitive, high-cheekboned face. Thick, dark lashes veiled eyes the colour of slate, and he was immaculately dressed in a navy-blue cuta-way coat with silver buttons, worn with breeches and top boots.

He made his bow and presented her with a small posy of primroses.

'I hear you have been indisposed,' he said, crossing one lean, booted leg elegantly over the other. 'I hope you're now fully recovered.'

Julia answered politely, but she was conscious of an unnerving flush of excitement rising slowly through her body. Instead of feeling slow and sluggish as it had for a long time, her blood felt as though it had begun to fizz through her veins and there was a not unpleasant sensation of heaviness in her belly.

They were joined by Isabel before they had the chance to exchange more than a couple of sentences.

Richard kissed her hand and she patted him on the cheek saying, 'Richard is my late husband's nephew. Have you two met before?'

'No, never,' replied Julia, her voice not quite even.

'I've been out of the country for many years,' he told her.

'Richard's father was the ambassador to Portugal,' Isabel explained. She shot a searching glance at her cousin and then at Richard.

'How very much alike the two of you look,' she commented. 'You could almost be brother and sister.'

It was true, but as Julia looked at him she realised to her surprise that her feelings were anything but sisterly. The strength of the physical attraction she felt for him had taken her completely unawares. She suddenly felt alive for the first time since Charles had left.

She was barely aware of what the others were talking about and only spoke herself to reply haltingly to any direct questions.

'Do you ride, Mrs Calvert?' he asked her.

'Yes, usually, but not at present.'

Isabel cast a shrewd glance at them both.

'I've been trying to persuade Julia to take the air in the park,' she told him. 'She needs fresh air to put the roses back in her cheeks after her illness.'

'Perhaps I could take you for a drive in my curricle,' he suggested. 'The trees are in blossom in the park and make a beautiful sight.'

About to refuse, for she knew not what reason, Julia was pre-empted by Isabel.

'What a wonderful idea,' she said warmly. 'Tomorrow afternoon, perhaps?'

'It would be my privilege,' he assured her. He picked up his hat and cane and rose to his feet to take his leave.

As soon as he'd gone Julia said, 'You might have let me answer for myself.'

'Certainly not,' was Isabel's serene reply. 'You would have refused his invitation and you have been languishing about the house too long. The company of such a charming young man and a drive around the park will do you nothing but good.'

The following day Julia found herself taking particular trouble with her appearance and had Jenny, her maid, arrange her hair in feathery curls upon which to set her favourite blue-ribboned bonnet.

She dressed in a gown of deep delphinium-blue over which she wore a velvet pelisse of a much darker hue. Kid gloves, half boots, a reticule and a parasol completed her outfit.

Isabel came into her bed-chamber just as she was pulling on her gloves. She surveyed the younger woman critically and then smiled her approval.

'You look lovely,' she complimented her. 'You may see me in the park because Captain Moore is to take me driving.'

'Captain Moore? Do I know him?'

'I don't think so, but if our paths cross I shall certainly introduce him.'

It was a beautiful spring day, warm and sunny with just a hint of a balmy breeze. As they drove through the busy streets in Richard's stylish curricle Julia felt more alive than she had in some considerable time.

His close proximity made her feel slightly breathless and she had to admire the competent way in which he handled the reins.

She'd forgotten how beautiful Hyde Park could be in spring and laughed delightedly when a flurry of pink almond blossom settled around them like pastel snowflakes as they passed under its spreading branches.

She found Richard easy to talk to and his company more agreeable than she could have believed possible. They encountered several of her acquaintances walking or riding and he obligingly pulled up each time to allow her to greet them.

No one mentioned Charles, for which she was thankful – she wasn't sure that she could face talking about him yet. She could only assume that Richard knew of her circumstances as he was a relative by marriage of Isabel's.

She mustn't think about Charles. She must put him resolutely from her mind or she would go into a decline.

They were soon hailed by Isabel, as richly dressed as always in figured amber silk, being driven by a darkly handsome officer in a scarlet tunic, white breeches and gleaming top boots. He reined in and doffed his bicorne as Isabel introduced them.

Julia knew at once that he was Isabel's lover and had to admit to herself that he was a very attractive man.

'Captain Moore has offered to reserve a box for us at the theatre tomorrow night,' Isabel told her. 'Shall we accept?'

'You'll join us, Wortham?' The captain included Richard in the invitation. 'We'll have supper afterwards.'

Richard looked questioningly at Julia.

'I'd be delighted to come,' she said after a moment's hesitation.

Richard accepted with alacrity, then they parted company.

As Isabel watched them drive off, she turned to Captain Moore.

'You've just succeeded in doing something I've failed to do.'

'What's that?' he asked, glancing at her and letting his amorous gaze linger on the firm swell of her breasts before turning his attention back to his horses.

'Getting my cousin to accept an invitation to go out in the evening.'

'Damn shame about Calvert,' he commented. 'But it's a waste of a beautiful woman for her to lock herself away.'

'My opinion entirely,' agreed Isabel. 'I wouldn't have thought Richard was her type, he's about as different from Charles as it's possible to be. But it pleases me greatly to see her taking an interest in life again.'

Captain Moore drove to a quiet corner of the park and said, 'There's a pretty little path through the trees over there. Shall we walk?'

She smiled at him, her eyelids dropping briefly over her grey eyes, her lips curved in an anticipatory smile.

'Let us do that. The narcissi are in full flower and deserve that we should admire them.'

He helped her down and threw the reins to his groom with orders that the man should walk the horses. He offered Isabel his arm and they strolled down the path until they were hidden from view by the banks of rhododendrons.

He stopped, took her into his arms and kissed her passionately. One gloved hand slipped into the bodice of her dress and fondled her ripe breasts, drawing them from the low-cut neck of her gown so the warm breeze played over them and stiffened the crinkled brown nipples.

He bent his head and took one taut nipple between his lips and nibbled on it softly. Isabel felt an answering tug in her groin and her head fell back as he pulled her closer to him so she could feel the hard bulge of his manhood under his breeches.

He lifted her skirts at the front and feasted his eyes on her shapely legs, then slid his hand behind her to explore the lush contours of her buttocks through her silk drawers.

'You excite me more than any woman I've ever known,' he muttered hoarsely.

He backed her against the trunk of a silver birch and secured her skirts around her waist by tucking them into the sash of her gown. He drew her drawers down her legs and she stepped out of them. Inhaling deeply, he held them to his face before putting them in his pocket.

He stripped off his gloves then his hand glided between her legs to massage her vulva, his palm soon slippery with her copious juices. Isabel's breathing was already ragged and her breasts heaving as he continued to stimulate her.

He toyed with her sex-flesh, tugging gently on her distended labia and then rubbing her throbbing bud with the knuckle of his forefinger and squashing it against her pubic bone until she was gasping with excitement.

She unbuttoned his fly and took out his magnificently erect penis. She paused to admire the heavily-knobbed end and run her finger over the glans before guiding it to her sex.

He seized her by her curvaceous hips and then thrust inside her in one long, smooth movement. She was pressed back against the tree as he pierced her to her very core again and again, his movements gathering speed as they coupled urgently.

Isabel trembled violently as she felt the heat building in her groin and wayward waves of pleasure washed over her. His rod was so strong and smooth, filling her completely and making her gasp and moan.

Neither of them tried to make it last – there was too much danger of interruption – and within a few minutes Isabel felt her entire body convulsed in hot, racking spasms of sheer erotic delight as she gave herself over to a long drawn out climax.

He quickened his movements, jamming her back against the tree trunk and kneading and caressing her breasts as he made three last plunges and groaned loudly before erupting into her.

They clung together for a few seconds and then Isabel's head turned as she heard voices. They parted rapidly and she threw her skirts hastily down around her ankles and smoothed her hair.

Captain Moore was just as swift to render himself present-able and by the time a middle-aged couple came into view, they were already strolling decorously away down the path.

SIX

Julia was increasingly conscious of Richard's hard thigh against hers as they continued to drive around the park. She kept glancing sideways at his aquiline profile and then at his strong, slender hands holding the reins.

She imagined his hands on her breasts, touching her gently, stimulating her to intense arousal with delicate caresses. She felt her sex-flesh quickening and swallowed, hoping he couldn't guess in which direction her wayward thoughts were turning.

There was a pulse beating a hectic tattoo in her quim and she shifted uneasily on her seat, trying to block out the erotic images which were whirling unbidden through her mind.

When eventually he drove her home she invited him in, reluctant to have the afternoon end so soon.

They sat in the drawing room and conversed, but their conversation was disjointed and they both fell silent.

'I—' began Julia.

'Do—' said Richard. There was an awkward pause and then he rose to his feet saying, 'I must go.'

She stood up too and as he passed her on his way to the door, in the grip of what later she could only think of as madness, she wound her arms around his neck and kissed him.

He made an inarticulate noise and for a few seconds she thought he was going to pull away, leaving her totally humiliated. But then he put his arms around her and, holding her as if she were made of china, kissed her back.

It was a sweet, heady kiss which seemed to go on forever. His lips were warm and gentle against hers and his hand moved over her back in the lightest of caresses.

For the first time since she'd watched Charles ride off down the drive, never to see him again, she felt a lightening of her despair. Combined with her swiftly mounting sexual arousal it was a heady feeling.

A sound from the door made her pull away, but not in time to stop Isabel taking in the scene and smiling enigmatically.

Richard swept them both a bow and made his departure without saying a word, leaving Julia to sink into the sofa, feeling weak and confused.

Isabel was regarding her quizzically and overcome by a welter of conflicting emotions, Julia buried her face in her hands.

'Goodness – what on earth's the matter?' asked Isabel in concern.

'What must you think of me for behaving so shamelessly?' wailed Julia.

Isabel sat next to her on the sofa and squeezed her hand. 'That I'm absolutely delighted to see you taking an interest in life again.'

'I don't know what came over me – I must have been mad.'

'Nonsense.'

Julia began to weep and Isabel put her arm around her shoulders, saying, 'It's time you started to live again, you are only young and have seen so little of life. You went from the schoolroom to the marriage bed within a matter of months and then so soon afterwards, were condemned to a life of total seclusion. If you decide to take a lover who would blame you? Certainly not me. Make the most of it and enjoy yourself. Richard is handsome, sensitive and virile – he should make a magnificent lover.'

When Julia didn't reply, Isabel went on, 'I loved my husband but he was taken from me and if I seek solace in the arms of different men, I do not believe that to be wrong. Take your pleasure where you can find it, for who knows what tomorrow might bring.'

'Won't . . . won't people talk?'

'Undoubtedly, but as long as you are always discreet, no one will blame you. Most of the married women in society have lovers. That in itself is never considered worthy of censure. Being caught out is the only crime. In public behave with circumspection, under this roof you may do as you choose.'

'But what if I've shocked Richard?'

'I saw the way he looked at you. Believe me – the only thing on his mind will be how soon he can be alone with you again.'

It seemed that Isabel spoke the truth because the following day he sent her a bouquet of flowers and a book of poetry together with a note which assured her how much he was looking forward to seeing her again.

Julia suddenly decided that none of her gowns were fit to be seen in and, accompanied by her cousin, visited a fashionable shop on Bruton Street.

The gowns were entrancing and she bought three, together with some silk stockings, a shawl from Lyons and a hooded evening cloak of rich black velvet lined with pearl-grey silk. She would have moved on to another shop and bought more, but Isabel said that they should return home and rest if they were to enjoy the evening to the full.

For their visit to the theatre, Julia chose to wear a delicious confection of amethyst tulle with a beaded sash of matching silk and a spider-gauze train. From her jewel case she chose an amethyst necklace and bracelet and her maid pinned three white ostrich feathers into her golden hair with an amethyst clip.

'You look beautiful, absolutely beautiful,' Isabel complimented her when she descended the stairs followed by her maid carrying her new black velvet cloak.

Isabel herself looked magnificent. Her gown was of silver brocade with tight wrist-length sleeves slit to show the white satin lining. It had a low décolletage which displayed her creamy cleavage to great advantage. She was wearing diamond ear drops and a diamond tiara sparkled dazzlingly against the burnished sheen of her piled-up dark hair.

'What an attractive quartet we shall make,' Isabel commented happily, making a last-minute adjustment to her hair in the gold framed mirror in the hallway. 'Both you and

Richard with your golden beauty, my darkly handsome captain and myself. I'm so glad that you aren't a brunette – I think I should be much less fond of you.'

This made Julia, who was feeling extremely nervous, laugh out loud. Captain Moore arrived to escort them to the theatre and paid them both extravagant compliments as he helped them into his carriage.

Richard was waiting for them in the foyer and offered Julia his arm as they made their way slowly through the crowds to their box. There was little opportunity for private conversation until they were seated. Isabel insisted that Julia and Richard take the two seats in front and Julia had to stare straight ahead, certain that if she looked down she would feel dizzy, they seemed so high above the stage.

As soon as Isabel and Captain Moore had begun a flirtatious exchange, Julia thanked Richard for his gifts.

'I would like to give you so much more,' he murmured. He lifted her hand to his lips and kissed it. Immediately Julia felt a frisson of sheer eroticism feather up her arm and down her spine to her sex.

He turned her hand and kissed the palm, pressing his lips against it with such passion that she was glad she was sitting down, otherwise her legs might not have supported her.

A ripple of anticipation running through the audience indicated that the play was about to begin. Julia sat back on her seat but made no attempt to remove her hand from Richard's.

The play was a light-hearted, frivolous piece of work and required no great effort to follow the plot. Which was just as well because Julia was constantly distracted by having Richard rub her palm lightly with his thumb, or toy with her fingers.

At the interval Isabel and Captain Moore went to greet some friends while Julia and Richard remained in the box and enjoyed a glass of champagne each.

The sparkling wine, the excitement of being out in the fashionable world and Richard's close proximity made Julia experience a sense of exhilaration long missing.

It was a heady feeling and she watched the second act without really taking in much of the action. After the final curtain they left the box and went to join the other theatre-goers in the foyer to wait for their carriage.

Supper was at a fashionable hotel and accompanied by more champagne. Captain Moore had ordered in advance so their table set in an alcove was ready for them and they were served within minutes of arriving.

Julia was just laughing at something Richard had said, when she became aware that she was the focus of someone's attention. Glancing across the room, she saw glaring at her a middle-aged woman with prominent teeth, thick brows and a puce complexion which clashed with her magenta turban.

Puzzled, Julia looked away. She caught Isabel's eye and murmured, 'Who's that woman over there at the table by the fireplace?'

Isabel surveyed her briefly and then a shadow crossed her face as she replied, 'That's Lady Berwick.' When Julia looked none the wiser she added, 'Charles' aunt.'

Instantly Julia's pleasure in the evening was destroyed. She remembered her now. She'd only met the woman a couple of times and had thought her ill mannered and unpleasant. Throughout the meal she was conscious of the older woman's scrutiny and was uncomfortably aware of how the situation must appear.

When the people in Lady Berwick's party began to disperse to their carriages Julia prepared herself for the inevitable confrontation. Attended by her daughter, a stout girl with her mother's protuberant teeth, Lady Berwick sailed majestically across to them.

'I thought my eyes must be deceiving me,' was her abrupt greeting. 'What are you doing here, Miss?' She completely ignored Julia's companions, making Julia wince at her ill breeding.

'I think you know my cousin, Lady Marchmont,' she said faintly. 'May I also present Captain Moore and Mr Wortham.'

Lady Berwick looked as if she'd much rather not acknowledge them, but she inclined her head briefly before continuing, 'Pretty behaviour with no one knowing if my nephew is dead or alive.'

Seeing Julia flinch, Isabel said sweetly, 'My cousin Julia is here only at my most earnest request. I thought she had been too long secluded in the country and persuaded her to come to town for a short stay. When my nephew, Mr Wortham, arrived back from Portugal around the same time, I decided to get up a small family party.'

'Family party indeed! And to what branch of your family does Captain Moore belong?'

'My mother's cousin married one of the Northumberland Moores.' There was nothing in Isabel's face to indicate whether this was true or not. Before Lady Berwick could reply she continued, 'And which of your delightful daughters is this? Maria, isn't it?'

Lady Berwick nodded coldly.

'And is this your first season, Maria?' enquired Isabel, her voice dripping honey.

'No, my third,' the girl whispered, her eyes cast down to the floor.

Isabel's eyes widened. 'Indeed?' she said, a whole world of meaning in her voice.

'We must be going – come, Maria,' snapped Lady Berwick and to Julia's intense relief, stalked off.

The captain, who had been looking amused, said, 'What was that about?' Seeing that Julia was pale and distressed he poured her another glass of champagne before topping up the other glasses.

'Lady Berwick wanted Charles to marry Maria, but as the girl takes after her mother in looks and her father in temperament, Charles wasn't interested. Lady Berwick kept pushing her under his nose, but with the most shameless ingratitude he chose to marry Julia, for which Lady Berwick has never forgiven either of them. Maria has been out for three seasons and received no offers, a fact which is a source of some embarrassment to her mother.'

Under the cover of the tablecloth Richard found Julia's hand and squeezed it sympathetically.

'Just out of interest,' said Captain Moore, '*did* your mother's cousin marry one of the Northumberland Moores?'

'Now I come to think of it, it was one of the Northumberland Meadowes – an easy mistake to make,' admitted Isabel, smiling wickedly. The captain burst out laughing and kissed her hand.

'Come, don't let the unpleasant woman spoil your pleasure in the evening,' Isabel urged Julia, rising to her feet. 'Let us return to my house for one last glass of champagne.'

SEVEN

The hall of Isabel's house was lit by a dozen flickering candles in two candelabra. She and Julia went upstairs to allow their maids to relieve them of their cloaks while the butler fetched a bottle of champagne for their guests.

As soon as the sparkling wine had been served and the four of them were ensconced in the drawing room, Isabel told her staff that they could go to bed.

Julia found that she was trembling, but whether from nerves or anticipation, she wasn't sure. They chatted about the play while they sipped their drinks and then Isabel exchanged a meaningful glance with Captain Moore and rose to her feet, holding out her hand to him.

'We'll bid you goodnight,' she said, pausing to kiss Julia's cheek. The captain bowed with his usual gallant flourish, then they left the room.

Julia was overcome by confusion and didn't know where to look, but Richard stood up, removed the glass from her hand and pulled her gently into his arms.

It felt like heaven to be held and kissed after so long without the caresses she'd taken for granted in the brief idyllic months of her marriage.

He kissed her for what seemed like a blissful eternity, his lips persuasive against her own, his tongue eventually flickering between them and finding hers. His hands traced gentle arabesques over her back and pressed her ardently against him so she could feel the strength of his arousal.

In those long minutes, Julia felt her agony and her pain about Charles' failure to return slipping into the remotest depths of her consciousness.

Richard's lips traced a path down her neck to the soft skin of her décolletage, upon which he pressed burning kisses. She heard him groan softly as his lips made contact with the upper slopes of her porcelain-skinned breasts. She felt seared by the heat of his desire for her and knew that she couldn't deny him – she would only be denying herself.

They sank together onto a sofa and he slipped his hand down the front of her gown to stroke her breasts until she could feel the urgent pulse in her sex twanging like the wires on her pianoforte.

She knew that warm moisture was forming in her private parts and trickling downwards until the crotch of her pantalettes was damp. He began to unhook her dress, his sureness of touch making it obvious he'd performed this service for a woman before.

He helped her out of the amethyst gown, her slip and her bodice, before lifting her so she was lying on the sofa. He divested himself swiftly of his coat and then joined her.

She reached for him and they kissed again, while he slipped his warm hand between her thighs and swallowed when he felt the dampness there. He tugged on the ribbon that held her pantalettes closed, laying bare her belly. He knelt beside her and she felt the silken brush of his silver-gold hair over her skin as he kissed his way to the swell of her mound.

She raised herself when he grasped the waist of her last covering against immodesty and he drew her pantalettes down her slender legs.

He parted her thighs so she was open and exposed to him and then caressed her sex-lips with infinite tenderness. Lightning bolts of sensation shot through her as his forefinger found her clitoris and stroked it steadily, slipping easily over her hot, slick flesh.

He eased two fingers inside her throbbing core and explored her velvety wetness, then unbuttoned his fly and mounted her. She closed her eyes and gasped as she felt the hard, smooth end of his phallus butting up against the entrance to her quim.

She gasped again when he slid it inside her a little way and

41

then paused for a few moments before continuing with the intoxicating penetration which had her clutching his shoulders and moaning.

He took his time, treating her as though she might break, and only when he was satisfied she was enjoying his movements did he speed up and commence a smooth, controlled thrusting, his hands finding her breasts and stroking them.

Julia wound her legs around his thighs and moved under him, pushing her pelvis eagerly upwards to meet each thrust. But his self-control was obviously more tenuous than it appeared, because suddenly he let out a long groan, his movements quickened and he erupted into her like a long-dormant volcano.

He buried his head against her shoulder and lay there for a few moments, before easing out of her and saying, 'That was wonderful – you're so very beautiful.' He lay to one side of her and took her in his arms, one hand lying idly on her breast.

He began to toy with the rose-pink nipple, watching it as it stiffened into a taut point.

Julia enjoyed his caresses, but she hadn't yet achieved her own satisfaction and her little nub still throbbed urgently. She took his hand and guided it diffidently between her thighs.

He located her bud and rubbed it gently, his fingers making a slight squelching sound among her slippery tissues. It was an intoxicating feeling, lying abandonedly in his arms, naked except for her silk stockings and kid slippers while he pleasured her.

A faint roaring in her ears and a sensation of moist heat sweeping her body preceded her climax, then she clamped her thighs tightly over his hand, cried out and came in a series of spine-arching spasms which left her weak and trembling.

Physically sated she smiled sleepily and snuggled closer to him. He stroked her hair and then kissed her hand, saying softly, 'I must go.'

'Must you?' she asked, not unwilling to seek her bed herself, but reluctant to part from him.

'Yes, I have to go out of town tomorrow, but I hope to be

back by the evening to attend the ball at Clareminster House. I assume you've been invited?'

'I don't know – I'll ask Isabel.'

Although invitations arrived at the house on a daily basis, Julia had not until now felt the slightest interest in them, but suddenly it seemed infinitely desirable that she should attend.

Richard helped her back into her gown, eased himself into his jacket and they went quietly into the hall where they kissed one last time, then he left and Julia made her way to bed.

She slept better than she had in a long time, not waking up until after ten. She was conscious of a languorous ache in her thighs and a slight tenderness of her sex-flesh as she stretched luxuriously.

She breakfasted in bed and then rang for hot water for a bath. Through the window she could see that it was a sunny spring morning and the fresh, bright green of the newly unfurling leaves on the trees in the square gardens was touched with gold.

As soon as her bath had been filled her maid pinned up her hair, then she shed her muslin nightgown and stepped into the steaming water. Her maid took her amethyst gown away to press it and Julia lay back in the tub.

There was a tap on her door.

'Who is it?' she called.

'Isabel. May I come in?'

'Certainly you may.'

Isabel entered the room tying the ribbons of a white lace robe over a nightgown so diaphanous that Julia could see the outline of her cousin's shapely legs through the fine fabric.

Isabel's lustrous dark hair was hanging down her back and her grey eyes wore a look of languid contentment.

'How lovely you look in your bath,' she greeted her. 'I'm sure Richard would give much to see you like this.'

The hot water had given Julia's usually pale skin a rosy glow which intensified the china-blue of her eyes. Isabel knelt by the tub and, taking the sponge from Julia, rubbed it

43

with the cake of lily-of-the-valley scented soap and began to wash her back.

'How was last night?' she asked. 'Although from your appearance I'd guess that it went very well.'

'What do you mean?' asked Julia, blushing.

'You look less drawn, less haunted, than I've seen you these last two years. Many men think that physical pleasure isn't important to women, but we know differently.'

She lathered Julia's shoulders in lazy circles. 'The tension I've felt in you has abated somewhat. Was Richard a pleasing lover?'

Julia blushed even more.

'Very,' she murmured. Then in a sudden rush of uncertainty she turned her face to her cousin.

'Tell me that I have not done wrong. I would have waited until doomsday for Charles to come back if I'd had the slightest reason to hope, but now I fear that you are right and that he lies in his grave on foreign soil and I shall be forever without him.'

Isabel put her arm around Julia's slender shoulders and hugged her.

'Believe me because I know – when there seems to be nothing that will ease the empty anguish of the heart, it is possible to lose oneself in physical pleasure and let it be a balm to suffering. Don't return to the country – stay here with me and find solace where you can.'

The two women embraced and then Isabel passed Julia a dainty lace handkerchief to dab her eyes with.

'Richard plans to attend the ball at Clareminster House tonight. Tell me – are we invited?' Julia asked.

'But of course. Do you wish to go?'

Julia nodded as Isabel went on, 'It's a masked ball so we'll need silk dominoes to wear over our gowns as well as masks. I think there are some in one of my closets – I'll have my maid look them out.'

'A masked ball?' repeated Julia. 'I've never been to one – they were completely forbidden before I was married and afterwards we were at Cumberley.'

Isabel ran the sponge down Julia's arm and then dipped it

in the water and squeezed it to send rivulets of soap suds over her shoulder.

'Masked balls are not generally considered to be *bon ton* and only the laxest of mothers would allow their unmarried daughters to attend because there is too much scope for licentious behaviour.'

A wicked, cat-like smile curved her lips. 'We, however, may do as we please. Unmasking is at midnight so we can always leave before then if you wish to remain anonymous. For myself I am greatly looking forward to it.'

EIGHT

Clareminster House was ablaze with light when they finally drew up in front of it, having been waiting in a long line of carriages as each in turn disgorged its occupants. Flambeaux blazed in holders on either side of the door and the illumination from several hundred candles poured out of the windows.

A royal blue carpet had been unrolled so that the ladies could alight and walk up the steps with no risk of soiling their dainty dancing slippers.

Captain Moore, one woman on each arm, escorted them into the mansion. Isabel was wearing a crimson domino over her gown, the hood down around her shoulders, but with a black velvet mask concealing her identity.

Julia's domino was the palest sky-blue and she too wore a black velvet mask. As they waited for Captain Moore to fetch them some refreshments, Isabel said idly, 'How will we recognize Richard?'

'He sent me a note telling me he would be in a Prussian-blue domino and would meet me in the library at ten. He didn't think he could arrive before then as he's been out of town today.'

'Listen – the orchestra is striking up. As soon as the captain returns, let us move into the ballroom and see how many of our acquaintances we can spot.'

A few minutes later they stood watching the dancing while Isabel kept up a running commentary on their fellow guests.

'See, there's Elizabeth Westbourne and if I'm not very much mistaken she's dancing with Thomas Althorne. She wanted to marry him but he was too poor to be acceptable to

46

her parents. She married Lord Westbourne instead and he's rumoured to be wildly jealous and will barely let her out of his sight – I wonder if he knows she's here?'

Elizabeth Westbourne was a delicately built woman with a few locks of gleaming honey-coloured hair spilling out from under the hood of her raspberry-pink domino.

'Westbourne's attending a political meeting tonight,' Captain Moore informed them, 'so my guess is that she's slipped out to meet Althorne here.'

'Who could blame her? Westbourne's an oaf,' commented Isabel. 'There are a lot of unsavoury rumours about him and they say he beats her. I hope it isn't true. Oh, look, there's Jamie McMasters – it doesn't matter how far forward he has his hood, one glimpse of that carroty hair and everyone knows it's him.'

'It could be his brother, Douglas,' pointed out Captain Moore.

'No – he's several inches shorter.'

A tall man in a purple domino approached them and bowed to Julia.

'Will you dance with me?' he asked simply.

Julia curtseyed and murmured, 'I'd be delighted,' and was immediately waltzed off around the room.

She didn't lack for partners and by ten o'clock was so out of breath that she was happy to excuse herself and leave the ballroom to go in search of Richard.

All the time she'd been dancing, she'd found she was looking for a glimpse of a Prussian-blue domino, in the hope that he'd arrived early.

The library was deserted and she pulled a book down from a shelf and leafed idly through it, aware that her heart was beating faster in anticipation of their reunion.

The door behind her was pushed open and she turned, smiling expectantly, only to find that it wasn't Richard – it was Elizabeth Westbourne, the girl with the honey-coloured hair whom Isabel had pointed out earlier.

Elizabeth seemed to be in some distress. She leant back against the door, her hand at her throat, her eyes behind her mask swivelling wildly around the room.

'Can I help you? Are you ill?' asked Julia, coming forward.

'I . . . yes . . . I don't know. He must not find me!' gasped the girl. Her forearm was visible and on it Julia could see some livid purple bruises. 'I think he saw me come in here!' she added frantically.

Guessing that Elizabeth was being pursued by her violent husband, Julia wanted to help. Unfortunately the only door into the room was the one they were standing by. There was no other way out. Thinking fast she said, 'Quickly – switch dominoes with me.'

With a trembling hand Elizabeth undid the ribbons holding her pink domino closed and passed it to Julia who handed over her own blue one.

'If you get behind the curtains, he won't see you.' Julia indicated the heavy red velvet curtains half drawn at the windows and Elizabeth darted behind the one nearest the door.

Julia hurried to the far end of the library and into a shadowy alcove where she stood leafing through a book, her face turned away from the door.

A few seconds later it was flung open.

'You deceitful little slut!' rasped a voice from behind her. 'How dare you leave the house without my permission! You'll pay for this as soon as we get home!'

Julia heard a heavy footfall across the floor and then felt herself being grabbed roughly by the shoulder as he swung her round, his hand raised to strike her. Behind him she saw Elizabeth glide from behind the curtains and out of the door. She drew herself to her full height, wrenched his hand from her shoulder and said icily, 'What is the meaning of this, sir?'

Lord Westbourne was a thick-set man of about forty, with bloodshot eyes and a high complexion. He was also apparently not possessed of particularly quick wits, because, obviously unable to believe the evidence of his own eyes, he ripped her mask off and only then appeared to accept that she was not, in truth, his wife.

For a few moments she thought he was going to hit her anyway, his other hand was still raised and she saw violence in his eyes. Then he muttered furiously, 'I beg your pardon, madam. I mistook you for someone else.' Turning away he blundered from the room.

Julia sank trembling into a chair and then nearly jumped out of her skin when from somewhere above her she heard the sound of applause.

Peering upwards into the shadows, she saw something she hadn't noticed before – a narrow gallery around the wall about seven feet below the ceiling, which gave access to the volumes stored at that great height.

A tall figure descended the spiral staircase in one corner of the room, his black silk domino billowing around him as it was caught by a draught.

Julia caught a glimpse of long, hard, muscled legs and narrow hips before the cloak settled back around his ankles as he reached the floor.

'You are to be congratulated, madam – that was quick thinking on your part.'

'Who are you?' she demanded, unnerved by his unexpected presence when she'd believed herself to be alone. 'What were you doing up there?'

'Just inspecting some of our host's rare books.' He sat on the over-stuffed arm of the chair opposite hers and stretched his long legs out in front of him. His hood had fallen down revealing hair as dark as night, streaked in places with silver. His eyes behind his mask glittered in the candlelight and she felt at a great disadvantage because he could see her face but she couldn't see his.

'You should have made your presence known,' she told him coldly.

'Why? It was a most amusing interlude.'

'I'm glad you thought so. No doubt you would have found it even more amusing if that vile man had struck me.'

'No. I should have found that tiresome because I should have felt obliged to intervene.'

She glared at him as she stood up, put her mask back on and pulled her hood over her guinea-gold curls. On her way to the door she paused in front of him for a parting shot.

'I'll leave you to your solitude, sir. Perhaps further

entertainment might come your way in the form of a trysting couple to spy on.'

As soon as the words were out of her mouth, Julia regretted them. It would have been much more dignified to have left the room and waited for Richard outside, rather than to have stayed and bandied words with this annoying stranger.

'Do I deduce that a tryst was what brought you here?' His eyes roamed insultingly over her body as he spoke. 'Then where is your lover? I assure you that *I* should not have kept you waiting.'

He rose to his feet and she thought he was about to go and leave her in possession of the library, but instead he ran the knuckle of his forefinger down the smooth skin above her breasts through the opening of her cloak. She gasped in outrage and then froze in shock as he bent and kissed her hard on the mouth.

What she wasn't prepared for was the surge of white-hot arousal which flooded her body. One of his arms went around her as he deepened the kiss and his other hand slid into the bodice of her gown to commence a practised caress of her breasts.

She was instantly on fire. Flames licked in her sex and she had to cling to his shoulders to stop herself from buckling at the knees.

Without meaning to, she found herself returning his kiss and then moaned as his cool fingers found her nipple and stroked it lazily until it pushed against the silk of her gown like a small thimble.

She could tell that he had become as speedily aroused as she had, because she could feel the hard ridge of his manhood against her hip. Unthinkingly she rubbed herself against it, aware that wanton, wayward juices were already rendering her quim wet and slippery.

The urgent tingling of her clitoris was driving her wild. Since last night, every time she'd thought about Richard the sensitive nub of flesh had pulsed and throbbed until she'd almost succumbed to a desire to touch it herself and have a climax by her own hand.

She'd only stopped herself by thinking that it would be

more enjoyable to wait until Richard could slip his fingers between her thighs and give her the same pleasure he had last night.

But now her need was so urgent that she couldn't wait a moment longer. The stranger was stroking her belly over her dress and somehow he'd undone the strings of the pink domino because it lay in a puddle of raspberry silk around her feet.

She was leaning against the back of the armchair and she held her breath as he massaged her belly in a way which made her want to grab his hand and jam it whorishly between her thighs.

His fingers brushed the swelling of her mound and she moaned again and parted her legs for him. If he was surprised by her abandoned behaviour he gave no sign of it. He felt between her thighs and then, palm upwards, massaged her vulva in a way that had her bearing down on his hand, too aroused to care what he thought of her.

He raised her skirts, dragged her pantalettes around her ankles and then lifted her so she was perched on the broad back of the over-stuffed armchair, the leather cool beneath her bare bottom. She had no choice but to hold onto the chair or risk tumbling backwards in an undignified flurry of skirts.

He pushed her thighs apart and then, much to her surprise, bent over and kissed her lingeringly on her inner sex-lips. She went rigid with shock at the intimacy of the caress and then heard her own whimper of pleasure as he stabbed his tongue rhythmically against her clitoris, his saliva mingling with her own copious juices.

She came immediately, clinging onto the chair and crying out, barely aware that he was unbuttoning his fly.

She caught a glimpse of a hugely erect penis and then he pierced her to the heart of her slippery sex-core, holding her around the waist to prevent her being pushed off the chair.

Nothing could have been more different from last night's coupling. Where Richard had entered her slowly and gently, the stranger drove into her with single-minded vigour.

Each fierce thrust made her cry out and every one worked

51

her nearer to another delirious climax. She could feel the leather under her becoming wet as the tangible proof of her arousal trickled relentlessly out of her.

She kept her eyes closed because whenever her eyelids fluttered open, she saw his own sloe-dark eyes glittering with a feral intensity through the slits in his mask.

With each thrust she was impaled on his member which cleaved swiftly and smoothly into her yielding flesh. She felt completely out of control of her own satisfaction, a china doll in his strong grasp.

She climbed higher and higher up the spiral of arousal until he gave a half-suppressed groan and then pumped his juices into her in a boiling, ferocious flood. It pushed her over the brink and she came herself, digging her nails into the leather armchair and moaning loudly as a torrent of pleasure washed over her and nearly drowned her with its intensity.

He pulled abruptly out and had adjusted his clothing before she found the strength to open her eyes. She was just in time to watch him make her a mocking bow and then he strode from the room, his black domino swirling around him.

She was left alone, his juices dripping from her widely parted thighs, naked from the waist down and with her vulva on full display for anyone who chanced to enter the room to see.

NINE

It was another twenty minutes before Richard arrived, profuse in his apologies for his tardiness. By then Julia had tidied her clothing and just about regained her self-control. She didn't know whom she felt more furious with – herself or the black-dominoed stranger.

How could she have been so lost to propriety that she'd allowed him to make love to her only minutes after meeting him? They hadn't even been introduced.

When Richard did eventually join her in the library, she decided on balance to say nothing about the incident involving Elizabeth Westbourne and her husband – it was probably better to remain discreet. She certainly didn't want anyone to know about the subsequent events and that a total stranger had made amorously free with her. She'd just have to hope that their paths didn't cross again.

But when Richard took her in his arms and tried to kiss her, she was ashamedly aware that her body was still dripping with another man's juices and pulled away.

'What is it?' he asked with some concern.

'I . . . I'm feeling somewhat fatigued. I . . . must have danced too long.'

He led her solicitously to a chair and sat her down, saying, 'I'll find Isabel. You should return home immediately – you must have overdone it too soon after your indisposition.'

He left the room while she strove to compose herself before he returned with Isabel, who took one look at her cousin's flushed face and agitated demeanour, then sent Captain Moore to summon the carriage.

She bathed Julia's forehead with cologne and then the four

of them went out to the carriage. Once back at Marchmont House, Richard took his leave, saying that he'd call the following day. Isabel helped Julia upstairs before leaving her in the care of her maid and returned to Captain Moore, who was sipping a glass of wine.

'Is she much indisposed?' he enquired, standing up as she came into the room.

'No, just tired, I think. If she seems unwell tomorrow I'll send for the apothecary again.'

He nodded and then pulled her into his arms murmuring, 'Let's retire to your bed-chamber.'

'In ten minutes or so – let's give the servants time to go to bed.'

'I don't think I can wait that long.'

'You must,' she told him, smiling provocatively.

'Must I?' he asked, raising one eyebrow and then going over to the door and locking it. 'And I repeat, I don't think I can wait that long.' He unbuttoned his fly and his phallus sprang out, erect and ready enough to verify his statement.

He caught her around the waist and drew her over to a wooden upright chair with carved arms. He sat on it, turned her so her back was to him and flipped her skirts up. Under his urgent fingers her drawers fluttered to the carpet and then he eased her creamy buttocks apart and ran his tongue down the cleft between them until it reached her sex.

Isabel moaned softly and bent forward, opening her thighs so he could tantalize the plump, moist tissues of her vulva with his wickedly flickering tongue. He strummed delicately at her membranes and then kissed one firm buttock and then the other. He bit gently into the silken flesh, sucking at it hard enough to leave a pink mark when at last he withdrew his mouth.

He branded its twin in the same way before pulling her down until he'd positioned her above his member. She gripped the arms of the chair to steady herself as she felt the smooth head nudging eagerly against the furled entrance to her hidden chamber.

She lowered herself slowly, taking it in an inch at a time, her internal muscles clenching around it until she was penetrated to her very core. He grasped her hips as she began to ride him, her well-rounded haunches an alluring sight as she moved above him.

A knock on the door made them both suspend their urgent movements and freeze.

'Who is it?' Isabel demanded, her annoyance at the interruption evident in her tone.

'It's me, Jenny – Mrs Calvert's maid, Lady Marchmont.'

'What do you want?'

'Should I sit up with Mrs Calvert or go to bed? You didn't say.'

Beneath her, Isabel felt Captain Moore shaking with silent laughter. Telling herself that she must get the housekeeper to speak to the girl the following day and instruct her in the ways of the household, Isabel called, 'Go to bed. Mrs Calvert will ring if she needs you.'

'Yes, Lady Marchmont.'

Isabel let Captain Moore's organ slip from her and moved away from him, her gown falling back down to conceal her naked bottom.

'We can go to my bed-chamber now,' she told him. His eyes gleamed with anticipation as he buttoned his fly and rose to his feet.

Once upstairs he shed his clothes and stretched out on the bed while Isabel seated herself at her dressing table and absently smoothed her hair.

'Come to bed,' he urged her. When she didn't reply he propped himself up on one elbow.

'What is it?' he asked.

'I'm concerned about Julia.'

'Julia will be fine, she danced too long and tired herself – that's all.'

'I hope you're right.'

Captain Moore left the bed and went to stand behind her. He busied himself unfastening her gown and then slid his hands into the front of it and caressed her breasts. He bent to kiss her neck, murmuring, 'Your thoughts should be of me – not your cousin.'

When she merely smiled vaguely he lifted her into his arms

and carried her over to the bed where he removed her gown without ceremony and tossed it carelessly to the floor. He covered her voluptuous body with his own and kissed her hard, his tongue sliding into her mouth and demanding a response.

He pushed a hand between her thighs and found the swollen centre of her pleasure. He manipulated it deftly, until she was moaning with need and her hand found his own organ and squeezed it.

Hot, tingling carnality washed over her in waves, making her tremble beneath him. She arched her back and bit her lip as he continued with his determined stimulation, set on driving all thoughts from her head except their love-making.

Heat built in her groin and then exploded into a release that had her clutching his shoulders and gripping his hand between her thighs as she gave herself up to the waves of sheer erotic sensation washing over her.

He withdrew his hand and then entered her in one unhindered thrust before bending his head to take a hard, umber nipple between his lips. Her bottom undulated on the bed-cover as he began to plunge in and out of her, caressing her breasts, her hips and her thighs.

It was a long and satisfying coupling and Isabel came again before Captain Moore rolled to one side of her and lay with his eyes closed. After a few minutes his even breathing indicated that he'd fallen asleep. Isabel regarded him silently for a few moments and then slipped off the bed and poured herself a glass of wine from the decanter on the table. She returned to his side and then tossed half the wine onto his detumescent manhood.

He cried out, leapt off the bed and made a grab for his dress sword, only to sheath it again as he realized she was not in fact an assailant. Isabel raised the glass to her lips and smiled at him.

'How very ungallant of you to fall asleep,' she murmured.

He unbuckled the sheathed sword and smacked her lightly across the buttocks with it.

'I think I may be even more ungallant and make your delectable bottom smart. Do you realize I could have hurt you? Never play such a trick on me again.'

Isabel pouted and bent over the bed, her derrière thrust towards him. She wriggled it provocatively in his direction.

'Do so if you wish – anything is better than having you fall asleep on me.'

He smacked her playfully a couple more times, then ran the tip of the leather sheath down the cleft between her buttocks and moved it over the slippery bud of her clitoris.

Isabel suddenly felt as if her whole body was on fire as the lewd and unaccustomed stimulation sent hectic messages of renewed arousal coursing through her veins. She parted her thighs more widely and began to pant, unable to hide her excitement.

Captain Moore saw her reaction and rubbed her harder, the wet leather making an obscene squelching noise as it moved over her swollen nub.

He began to slide it backwards and forwards between her thighs, keeping the pressure on her most sensitive spot. She bore down, gasping and crying out as she came with a swiftness which surprised both of them.

He withdrew the sword and hit her across the bottom with it again, before putting it down, seizing her from behind and driving into her.

She thrust urgently back against him, her backside making a smacking sound as it made contact with his thighs. Her moans echoed around the room as he shafted her tirelessly, one hand slipping in front of her to massage her mound roughly.

She came again, her back arching and her body going rigid as delicious carnal pleasure suffused her whole being. Captain Moore made several last staccato thrusts and then emptied himself into her before they collapsed onto the bed together in a tangle of limbs.

TEN

The following day Julia felt physically better, but still inwardly disturbed by her wanton behaviour. Somehow, in the course of only a few days, she'd had carnal knowledge of not just one, but two men.

She was ashamed of herself but even worse, whenever she thought about either Richard or the black-dominoed stranger, she was aware of a libidinous lick of lust high up in her sex which made her body feel hot and her private parts moist.

She'd always believed that her eager physical response to her husband had been because she loved him, but now it seemed that virtually any man could touch her and arouse her.

She considered confiding in Isabel, but although she was aware that her cousin took as many lovers as she pleased, Julia still baulked at exposing her own debauched behaviour.

As soon as Jenny told her that Isabel had ordered her breakfast, Julia went to see her cousin. She found her propped up in bed against a pile of downy pillows wearing a fetching lace cap which matched her lavishly be-ribboned lace nightgown.

Isabel was sipping a cup of chocolate, a slight smile curving her mouth. Her gleaming dark hair fell around her shoulders in glorious disarray and a wayward lock curled into her creamy cleavage.

She greeted Julia fondly, enquired after her health and seemed reassured when her cousin assured her that she felt much better.

'You look as if there's something on your mind,' commented Isabel as Julia fidgeted with a scent bottle and then sank into a chair by the window.

'Do I?' asked Julia, who thought she'd succeeded in concealing her agitation.

'What is it? You can tell me, whatever it is.'

Casting around in her mind for some reason to explain her lack of composure, Julia lighted on the first thing that presented itself.

'It's . . . it's Charles' aunt, Lady Berwick. Now that she knows I'm in town I really ought to call on her, but I dread doing so.'

'If you do call on her, she'll spend the entire duration of the visit being unpleasant. Family obligations can be so tiresome – let me think for a minute.'

Isabel leaned back against her pillows while Julia stared out of the window at the spring sunshine and wondered if she could face seeing Richard again after she'd played him false with another.

'I know,' announced Isabel, sitting up and putting her empty cup on the bedside table. 'We shall call and leave our cards when we know she's out.'

'How will we know that?'

'I shall despatch one of the servants to keep watch. When she and her ill-favoured daughter are safely out of the way, we'll order the carriage and proceed there immediately. If she returns the call, I'll give orders that she's to be told we're not at home.'

Julia burst out laughing at Isabel's inventive scheme for dealing with a troublesome problem.

'That won't stop her reviling me if our paths should chance to cross in public,' she pointed out.

'True, but it will be much easier to escape,' said Isabel serenely. 'I thought the reason for your disquiet might be something to do with the fact that when we arrived at the ball last night you were wearing a pale-blue domino, but when we left it had been transformed into a pink one. How that happened I really cannot imagine, but it is my earnest wish that you should enlighten me.'

Julia flushed, wondering how she could have overlooked the fact and realized that Isabel couldn't fail to have noticed.

She decided she might as well tell her cousin the truth about switching dominoes with Elizabeth Westbourne, but omit any mention of the masked observer of the scene and the subsequent lascivious events.

Haltingly, she described what had happened and how Lord Westbourne had come close to striking her. Isabel sat bolt upright in bed, an expression of consternation on her face.

'No wonder you became unwell. But why did you not tell me this before we left the ball last night? I'm sure Captain Moore would have been more than happy to teach the oafish man better manners.'

'I . . . I didn't want any attention drawn to the incident. I'm sure he would have made his wife suffer if he'd been taken to task.'

'That's probably true,' said Isabel thoughtfully. 'How sorry I feel for that poor woman. But there is little point in dwelling on what cannot be helped. Now, how shall we amuse ourselves today?'

Richard paid an early call and was so solicitously charming and concerned for her health and well-being that she soon felt easy with him again.

He proposed that they go riding in Richmond Park, a suggestion Julia acquiesced to with some eagerness. While sequestered at Cumberley, her daily rides had been her greatest consolation and already it seemed a long time since she'd last been on horseback.

The only drawback was that she had no horse in London, but Isabel announced that she'd recently purchased a pretty grey mare which she herself only rode occasionally and which was at Julia's disposal for the duration of her visit.

It was a pleasantly warm spring day and Julia was glad to leave the hustle and bustle of London behind them. Richmond Park seemed blissfully quiet and verdant in contrast. As soon as the opportunity presented itself she urged her mare into a gallop and gave herself up to the enjoyment of the exercise. She knew that galloping was frowned on in

Hyde Park, so she wanted to make the most of it while she could.

Richard kept abreast of her, his silver-gold hair ruffled into disarray by the wind, his slim figure showing to advantage on horseback. Julia found her eyes drawn to the way his tight-fitting breeches moulded themselves to his firmly muscled thighs and buttocks and found that her mouth was getting dry.

Eventually they reined their horses to a halt.

'You ride very well,' Richard complimented her, his eyes roaming over her and lingering on the swell of her breasts under her green velvet riding habit.

'So do you,' she replied. 'Did you ride much in Portugal?'

'Almost every day,' he said, dismounting and tethering his horse to a low hanging branch of a tree. He held up his arms to her and she slid gracefully into them, enjoying the sensation of slithering down his hard body until her booted feet touched the grass. He bent his head to kiss her, but the mare whinnied at that moment and tried to sidle away, forcing Julia to leave Richard to attend to her mount.

She tied her to a tree and then rejoined him. Their kiss was long and passionate and she could feel the burgeoning thrust of his manhood against her as his mouth sought a response from hers.

After what seemed like an eternity he drew away, saying hoarsely, 'We must stop. To be with you here like this, to touch you, to kiss you, makes me want you so badly that I can scarce control myself.'

Julia's pulses were racing and her senses reeling. Her desire for him made her reckless. Taking his hand she led him away from the open parkland and in among the trees.

'There's no one around,' she murmured. He looked startled and then as if he were afraid he'd mistaken her meaning. 'We could make love here,' she continued.

'Here?' he echoed. 'But . . . but someone might come along and find us together.'

'We haven't seen anyone since we entered the park.'

She took his hand and guided it to her bosom, letting him feel the firm swellings of her breasts through the soft stuff of

61

her habit. He groaned and stroked them until her nipples formed hard points against his palm.

He kissed her again, sliding his hand into her bodice and toying with her crinkled areolae, while his other hand caressed her backside.

A light breeze stirred the trees and the sunlight filtered down through the green canopy of interleaved branches above them. Richard left off caressing her for long enough to unfasten the front of her bodice and expose her pink-tipped orbs, before bending his head and kissing one nipple.

He drew it gently into his mouth and flicked at it with his tongue. An answering gathering of moisture in her sex made her moan and reach for his manhood. She caressed it lingeringly through his breeches which seemed on the point of bursting as it grew to even greater rigidity beneath her touch.

Unable to stop herself, she fumbled with his buttons and took it in her hand. It felt smooth and warm and throbbed as she caressed it. He groaned and lifted her in his arms, then laid her on the grass.

He pushed the skirts of her habit up to the waist and then undid her pantalettes. She cried out with pleasure as he slipped a hand between her thighs to explore the soft, slippery contours of her vulva. She parted her legs and closed her eyes as he probed her gently with two fingers, moving them in and out of her silken tunnel.

Her arousal was unmistakable as honeyed juices covered his hand until it was as wet as her private parts. He knelt between her thighs and guided his engorged shaft to the welcoming crimson folds of her sex.

In the urgency of her arousal, Julia completely forgot she was lying in a woodland glade in Richmond Park and that should anyone find out about this reckless dalliance, her reputation would be ruined.

The only thing on her mind was the almost desperate desire she felt to lose herself in the intoxicating excitement of this carnal embrace. As he entered her, his manhood filling her completely, she pushed her pelvis demandingly upwards.

They commenced an ardent coupling on the grass. She wound her legs around his thighs as he thrust in and out of her with increasing urgency. Each deep stroke sent hectic messages of pleasure coursing through her and her swollen bud felt as though it were about to explode.

She angled her pelvis to gain the maximum stimulation from the encounter and then at last felt the delicious surge of heat through her body that preceded her climax.

As it swept over her he erupted with an inarticulate groan, flooding her with his hot juices and then pulling out and rolling to one side, before gathering her in his arms.

They lay in silence for a while, then Julia gradually became aware of the damp striking up through her riding habit and got reluctantly to her feet to rearrange her clothing. She peered doubtfully over her shoulder at the crumpled velvet of her muddied skirt.

'I'll have to tell my maid I took a fall,' she commented ruefully, picking a burr from where it had attached itself to her hem. 'Could you brush me down please, Richard.'

He obligingly tried to brush off some of the mud, but only succeeded in making it worse. 'At least we don't both look as though we've been dragged through a hedge by a runaway horse,' she said, struggling to tidy her hair. As he'd been above her, Richard had emerged from the encounter with only a creased neckcloth to mar the elegance of his clothing.

As they rode back towards town, Julia was very conscious of the swollenness of her sex and the dampness of her pantalettes, which made the ride somewhat uncomfortable, but served as a reminder of the pleasure she'd just enjoyed. She bade Richard goodbye as soon as he'd seen her safely back to Marchmont House, with a promise to meet him later at an evening party held by a friend of Isabel's.

As Julia had anticipated, Jenny expressed consternation over her supposed fall and sent for water for a hot bath for her mistress, then fussed over the ruined habit.

'I don't think it'll clean up,' she said. 'But I'll take it away and see what I can do. Perhaps steaming it over a kettle will do the trick.'

When Julia had bathed and dressed in a blue satin robe, she stretched out on a day bed in front of the fire and fell asleep, to be awakened by Isabel in the early evening.

'I needn't ask if you spent the day pleasantly,' Isabel said, sinking into a chair opposite her. 'You were smiling in your sleep.'

Julia stretched and eased herself into a sitting position.

'And you – how did you pass the day?' she enquired.

'Lunch with a friend, dalliance with Captain Moore and the purchase of two new hats,' she announced. 'Sadly Captain Moore is on duty tonight so I've invited an old friend, Lord Myersham, to escort us. Will Richard be there?'

'Happily, yes. What shall you wear?'

'Perhaps the jonquil twilled silk, or the peach frosted crêpe. Lord Myersham joins us for dinner.'

She left the room in a swirl of scented skirts leaving Julia to lie back on the day bed and dwell on Richard's myriad charms.

Their coupling in the wood had been exciting in the extreme. As she recalled the feeling of his hands on her breasts and the delicious sensation of his shaft forging its way deep within her, she felt herself becoming breathless and her bud began to tingle again.

Her hand slipped into the front of her robe and then between her thighs to coax the flaccid little sliver of flesh into renewed arousal. But as she stroked herself she found that her thoughts were no longer of Richard, but of the black-dominoed stranger and the assured way in which he'd pleasured her.

She remembered being perched precariously on the back of the armchair, her skirts shamelessly around her waist, her thighs wide apart, as he'd used her like some common strumpet.

Her hand moved faster over her tingling nub and then, just as she dwelt lasciviously on the heady climax he'd brought her to, she came with a barely suppressed moan and lay back, panting.

She could only fervently hope that he was not a regular guest at the parties and dinners she would be attending herself. The thought that he might be there and recognize her, while she herself remained unaware of his identity as her seducer was too embarrassing to contemplate.

ELEVEN

It was after midnight when the carriage pulled up by a crumbling, ivy-covered wall in the shadows of a thickly leaved oak tree. The carriage's sole occupant stepped out and after a muted exchange with the driver, waited until the vehicle had driven away and was out of sight.

A long hooded cloak concealed her identity as, keeping close to the wall and barely visible in the darkness, she made her way around a corner until she came to a creaking wooden door half concealed by overgrown bushes.

Glancing around to make sure she was not observed, she pushed it open and closed it behind her. A stone-flagged path wound through trees and undergrowth, then skirted a small lake before leading to a semi-derelict mansion.

No lights showed at any of the windows and the only sounds were the rustlings, squeakings and occasional cries of the many species of birds and beasts which had made the house and grounds their home.

The woman stopped at a door set into the decaying wall and knocked on it. It swung silently open and just as silently she slipped inside and it closed behind her.

'Welcome,' said the man who'd opened it to admit her. He had dark red hair and was wearing tight-fitting breeches tucked into supple, black leather boots with a white lawn shirt which was partially unbuttoned to reveal glimpses of his firmly muscled chest sprinkled with reddish hair.

He carried a riding crop which he tapped against one boot as the woman divested herself of her cloak and hung it from a peg on the wall of the cavernous stone-flagged chamber in which she found herself.

Under her cloak she was wearing a simple white silk gown fashioned from strips of fabric which were stitched together at the neck, just below her bosom and at the hem. It was apparent to any observer, even in the flickering light from two flaming torches set in metal brackets on the wall, that beneath the gown she was naked except for her stockings and garters.

As she moved the strips of silk fluttered around her to reveal intoxicating glimpses of her creamy skin and voluptuous curves. Her dark hair was pinned up and fell in glossy waves around a face partially hidden by a black velvet mask, but the sensual fullness of her lips was clearly visible as were her firm jaw and the elegant lines of her neck.

'And what is your pleasure tonight?' the man asked her, casually using the riding crop to part the silk over her left breast to reveal one puckered brown nipple. He touched it delicately with the end of the crop as in a low voice she told him.

Like her his identity was concealed by a mask through which he surveyed her carefully as she spoke.

'Follow me,' he said at last and preceded her from the room and along a narrow passage, then up a winding flight of worn stone steps.

He paused to open a sagging door which led into a small chamber which contained only four crimson velvet curtains, hanging from the ceiling to form an enclosed space about three feet square.

The curtain facing them had been drawn open to reveal a fancifully carved throne-like chair around four feet high with two steps in front of it. The man helped the woman climb the steps and then sit on the chair with her slippered feet placed on two foot-rests set wide apart.

The chair seat had a circle cut from it, and as she sat down the strips of silk forming her skirt fell apart so that her derrière and private parts were accessible to anyone crouched in the hollow base beneath. The man drew the curtain in front of her so she was enclosed in the velvet chamber and a few seconds later he extinguished the flambeaux on the walls. She was plunged into total darkness and waited breathlessly as she heard him leave.

It was some time before there came the sound of the door opening again and several people entered the room. No one spoke, but she could tell that they were arranging themselves around the velvet chamber.

She was aware that her sex was slick with moisture formed in lascivious anticipation of what was to come. She bit her lip to stop herself exclaiming when something brushed against her vulva, something soft and feathery which tickled and which made her want to squirm around on her seat.

Moments later a hand groped for her breast through the gaping strips of silk and caressed it roughly, pinching her nipple and then massaging it in an arousing circular movement. Another hand – a much smaller one – began to stroke her thighs, smoothing over her silken skin and working gradually upwards from her knees. Soon there were hands all over her, touching, caressing and fondling her; some gently, some roughly.

The person beneath her continued to tantalize her swollen sex-flesh with what she guessed to be a bunch of ostrich feathers. The touch was arousing but not satisfying and she was almost relieved when after quite a while, it stopped and was replaced by what felt like a soft brush.

It could have been a child's hair brush or the type used to sweep crumbs from a tablecloth, but whatever it was the bristles were long and silken and when it was drawn softly over her private parts, it was an intensely pleasurable experience.

Her pubic fleece was brushed forwards and then backwards, after which fanciful curlicues and circles were traced over her dripping sex, making her shiver with delight.

Whoever was beneath her held her outer sex-lips open and worked the brush deep into every niche and crevice, then swept it over her tingling bud over and over again. After that it was used to stab rhythmically upwards over every inch of her vulva, until the whole area was suffused by warm, tingling heat. The brush was removed and there was a prolonged pause before something else was substituted.

She couldn't be sure but she suspected it was a riding crop

and wondered if it was the man who'd admitted her who was crouched below her. The thought excited her even more and she wriggled as she felt the crop drawn along the outer rim of her vulva.

He probed her sex-flesh with it, parting the swollen folds and delving into the furrows between them. She felt the end make contact with her clitoris and then he commenced a stealthy stroking movement which made her gasp and catch her breath.

She was well aware that it could just as easily be a woman stimulating her – there were undoubtedly at least a couple of members of her own sex fondling her through the slits in her revealing gown – but she'd found the red-haired man particularly attractive and hoped it was him.

Having so many people pleasuring her at the same time was a wonderfully decadent experience and one she was savouring to the full. The pressure on her tingling bud had become more pronounced and she was aware that her copious juices had drenched whatever was being used to stimulate her, because she could hear the slight squelching noise it made as he worked it over her slippery flesh.

She found it difficult to keep still and wriggled harder, but the crop was withdrawn from her clitoris and then it landed squarely across her vulnerably exposed buttocks in a warning tap that made her cease her movements and sit still. She was aware that to continue to squirm would be an open invitation to further chastisement which would become increasingly severe if she went on wriggling.

She knew that many people craved the contrast between pain and pleasure, but she wasn't one of them and with a great effort of will remained still. The stimulation of her clitoris continued until she was clutching the arms of the chair and trying not to moan out loud.

Her body was suddenly assailed by a tingling heat and then she came, crying out into the darkness as she convulsed into orgasm.

For a few moments she was only dimly aware that something was sliding into her inner chamber. Her internal muscles clutched at it as it moved in and out of her in a way that threatened to send her toppling directly into a further climax. If it was a riding crop, the handle was now being used to penetrate her and stimulate her velvety membranes.

It was an intoxicating sensation to feel it slipping smoothly in and out of her while at the same time she could feel a warm mouth on one breast, sucking and licking at her nipple so seductively that urgent tremors of arousal were shooting down to her sex to increase the delicious sensations the unknown lover below her was evoking. The rest of her body was being stroked and caressed into ecstasy by other hands, so that no part of her went untouched.

But it was the attention being paid to her quim that aroused her most. The sureness of touch and knowing familiarity with which she was being handled made her determined to have further intimacy with whoever it was – man or woman.

As the handle continued to slide in and out of her she began unthinkingly to work her hips and then stopped abruptly as she was slapped stingingly across the buttocks.

To add to the myriad sensual sensations assailing her body, her clitoris was suddenly drawn into a warm mouth and stimulated rhythmically with a muscular tongue. She convulsed into another long-drawn-out climax and sagged weakly against the back of the chair.

As if to some silent cue the hands touching her were withdrawn and she heard people leaving the room, just as the crop was withdrawn from her sex with an obscene sucking sound.

From behind her out of the darkness she heard the deep voice of the red-haired man and felt her sex-flesh quicken as she realized it *had* been him stimulating her from below.

'What is your further pleasure?' he asked.

'You – here and now,' she said huskily.

She could just make out the pale fabric of his shirt as he moved in front of her and lifted her from the raised chair as easily as if she weighed no more than the ostrich feathers he'd wielded earlier.

He turned her around and bent her over the throne so she was standing on the higher of the two steps. He stood on the

69

lower one and brushed aside the filmy silk strips veiling her derrière. She gripped the arms of the chair and then gasped as she felt him thrust into her, piercing her to her very core.

He was ramrod hard and forceful in his movements, plunging in and out of her until she was unable to stop herself moaning deliriously. His hands found her heavy breasts and caressed them feverishly as his manhood forged its way to the very end of her velvety tunnel and then just as swiftly withdrew.

Time lost all meaning for her as she felt another climax building. The pressure in her belly and groin was almost unbearable, but she savoured the last moments of anticipation until she was swept away by a deluge of pleasure which left her weak and shaking.

He still hadn't finished with her and grasped her by the hips to stop her sagging exhaustedly against the chair. Making a last effort she thrust her bottom back against him and then cried out as he quickened his pace and pumped his juices into her in a hot surge of release.

As soon as he'd achieved his satisfaction he withdrew and she heard his booted feet striding from the room. She turned slowly around and sat back on the chair, waiting until some strength returned to her limbs.

As soon as she felt able to, she stepped down and adjusted her clothing as best she could. She was aware that throughout the crumbling mansion any number of debauched scenarios were taking place and that she would be most welcome to join in any of them, or to request any further service that she craved.

But she felt sated and her limbs had the heavy languorousness which made her wish to seek her bed. She walked silently along the passageways and down the stairs until she regained the chamber where she'd left her cloak. She passed several people on the way, all masked, but acknowledged none of them.

With her cloak around her and the hood pulled forwards to hide her hair, she left the house and made her way through the gardens to the road and around the corner to where her carriage was waiting.

TWELVE

Wholly engrossed by her affair with Richard, Julia was barely aware that spring had become summer with long, light nights and balmy evenings.

She saw him several times a week and he escorted her to many of the social events to which she was invited. With some satisfaction, Isabel observed that her cousin had regained the bloom which had deserted her these last two years.

One warm June evening they were at a card party given by some friends of Isabel. Julia was standing by the open doors leading to a terrace talking to Richard and sipping a glass of wine. A flurry of movement from the entrance attracted her attention and she saw with a sinking heart that Lady Berwick had just entered with an entourage consisting of three of her daughters, her sister and her son.

It was the first time Julia had seen her since their encounter after the evening at the theatre with Isabel, Richard and Captain Moore. All her pleasure in the party deserted her and she was tempted to slip through the doors onto the terrace and remain there until Lady Berwick had gone into supper.

But further reflection told her that such an action would be cowardly in the extreme and that the only dignified option was to stay and face the inevitable confrontation with what composure she could summon.

'Richard, I beg you – please go and talk to someone else,' she said in a low voice.

'Why do you wish me to do that?' he asked, puzzled.

She nodded in Lady Berwick's direction and he squeezed

her hand in perfect understanding before obediently bowing and leaving her.

After greeting her hostess Lady Berwick scanned the room and as soon as her gaze landed on Julia, she sailed determinedly towards her. Julia found she was trembling, but she tried to smile serenely as Lady Berwick greeted her by saying in an accusatory tone, 'I see you're still indulging your own heedless pleasure, with no thought for my poor nephew – have you no shame?'

Julia felt her cheeks burning as heads turned to look at them, but she managed to say, 'Good evening, Lady Berwick. I hope I find you well.'

'As well as can be expected given the gossip your conduct is causing and the embarrassment it has brought me.'

Throughout her stay with Isabel, Julia had met with nothing but kindness from most people who were aware of her awkward circumstances, and if her liaison with Richard was causing gossip, she was unaware of it.

'I . . . I . . .' she stammered, ready to sink into the ground with mortification.

'I can barely hold my head up for the humiliation of such a scandal in the family,' snapped Lady Berwick. A rustle of skirts to one side of her made her look round to see that Isabel had joined them and was smiling with infinite sweetness as she prepared to join the fray.

'Indeed? I'm surprised that word of it has reached your ladyship,' she purred. 'You must keep your ear very close to the ground to know about your son's gambling debts. But I would have thought that scandal was too strong a word for it – embarrassing no doubt, but you must be used to it by now in your family.'

As both Lady Berwick's loose-living son and husband were notorious for their ability to lose astonishing sums of money at the roll of a dice, and even more notorious for not being able to pay their gambling debts, this had the effect of making her thick brows snap together. She cast a look at her son which boded ill for his immediate future before saying, 'That was not what I was referring to.'

'You have *another* scandal in your family?' enquired Isabel, raising her own dark eyebrows. 'You have my deepest sympathy. I shall not embarrass you by asking which of your other relatives has caused you humiliation. You are very brave to venture into society while living under such a cloud. Come, Julia – we have been invited to make up the numbers at Lady Wilde's table.'

She drew Julia away while, with a face like thunder, Lady Berwick left the room followed by her family party. Julia squeezed Isabel's arm gratefully.

'Thank you,' she whispered.

'It's the first time I've seen all her children together,' commented Isabel. 'I think they must be the most ill-favoured brood in London; they're quite startling en masse, aren't they?'

Julia really had to exert herself not to laugh out loud. It was true that nature had not been kind to them, but too bad of Isabel to mock them for something they couldn't help.

'It's a matter for debate whether the hereditary physiognomy is less well suited to the daughters or the son,' continued Isabel unrepentantly. 'I hear that not only is the son – Gerald I believe he's called – addicted to gambling but to women as well. But as he is possessed of as little personal charm as he is good looks, it costs him a considerable amount of money. I wonder if his mother knows about his regular visits to a house of ill repute.'

'I doubt it very much. Where did you come by such information?' Julia was curious to know the origin of the gossip.

'I have my sources,' replied Isabel with an enigmatic smile. 'That woman will never forgive you for having married Charles. I hear he bailed the family out of debt on several occasions and if he'd married Maria as Lady Berwick intended, she'd now have had unlimited access to his money through her daughter. It's little wonder she's unable to be civil to you. Come – Lady Wilde awaits us.'

It seemed that the evening was to be an eventful one because later, when Julia went out onto the terrace for some air, she was joined by a sweet-faced young woman with honey-blonde hair.

'Mrs Calvert,' the woman greeted her. Julia had thought she was alone and was lost in a reverie. She swung round in some surprise.

'Yes?'

'Do you remember me?'

'I'm sorry – have we met?' Julia replied, not recognizing her.

'Forgive me if I'm mistaken, but I think our paths may have crossed at the masked ball – I'm Elizabeth Westbourne.'

'Yes of course, but how did you know it was me?'

'I'd noticed you with Lady Marchmont earlier that evening. I knew who she was even in a mask – she's so striking. When I saw you together tonight I knew you must be the woman who rescued me.'

'I hope that you . . .' Julia's voice trailed off as she tried to think of some tactful way of indicating that she hoped Elizabeth's oafish husband had not beaten her.

'I wanted to thank you for helping me. It's on my conscience that I left you to face my husband's wrath – I hope he didn't hurt you.'

'When he realized I was a stranger to him he could only apologize and take his leave.'

'That relieves my mind greatly,' said Elizabeth. 'It's also on my conscience that I still have your blue domino.'

'It doesn't matter,' Julia assured her. 'Besides, I have your pink domino.'

'If you'll permit me to, I'll call on you and return it. I believe you're residing with Lady Marchmont.'

'Yes, I am. I'd be delighted to have you call on me, as long as it won't cause you any problems.'

Elizabeth grimaced. 'Lord Westbourne has political aspirations and when he learns that I'm visiting the house of a woman as well connected as your cousin, he will have nothing to say against it.' There was a pause and then she added, 'I heard about your husband and I'd just like to say how sorry I am.'

'Thank you,' murmured Julia.

Elizabeth smiled at her and flitted off, the train of her pale gauze gown flowing behind her in the gathering dusk.

★ ★ ★

Julia didn't dare leave the party with Richard, so she and Isabel returned to Marchmont House alone. Captain Moore had had another engagement and for once Isabel had decided against finding another man to escort her.

She'd seemed subdued for the last few days and as the carriage bore them home, Julia ventured to say, 'Is anything the matter, Isabel?'

'Only that Captain Moore's regiment is removing to Bath very soon.'

'Really?' said Julia in dismay. She'd grown to like him very much and thought his imperturbability and dry sense of humour suited her cousin very well. 'Will you miss him?'

'I will indeed – particularly in my bed. Now I must look around for another lover and it will be hard to find one who suits me so well.' She sighed before continuing, 'It's easy to find men who wish to make love to me, but those who know how best to give a woman pleasure are few and far between.'

'I'm sorry,' murmured Julia, squeezing her cousin's hand.

'It is pointless to repine. I must bid him goodbye and move on.' Isabel settled herself more comfortably on the seat and turned her head to look out of the window.

Perhaps because she'd not been able to spend any time alone with Richard, Julia's sleep was disturbed by dreams as dark and disturbing as they were erotic.

She dreamt that she was cantering through the woods near Cumberley when a man riding a black stallion came out of the trees and blocked her path. In the dim green light filtering down through the interleaved branches, she could see that he was dressed completely in black and his hat was pulled down, casting his face in shadow.

A hectic frisson of alarm tingled down her spine as she reined in her horse and came to a halt in front of him.

'I've been waiting for you,' he greeted her. 'You're late and now you must pay the price for your tardiness. Dismount and tether your horse.'

Trembling in every limb she did as he bade her, her hands in their kid riding gloves fumbling as she tried to secure her mount to a low-hanging branch.

He watched her impassively, until she turned to face him again.

'Disrobe,' he ordered her.

She had no will to resist him. Slowly, she removed her top hat and then began to undo her starched white cravat. Her habit was of wine-red velvet and she tried in vain to reach the fastenings, but they were behind her and she was unable to undo more than the top two. Her maid was usually on hand whenever she dressed or undressed to render whatever assistance was necessary.

He made an impatient gesture and she felt constrained to say, 'I . . . I can't reach them.'

Without a word he dismounted and walked over to her, tucking his riding crop under his arm and stripping off his gloves. She felt his warm breath on the back of her neck as he undid her habit and then it fell to the ground around her. Keeping her back to him she stepped out of it and then hesitated.

'Remove everything.' His voice was deep and harsh and his tone indicated that he would brook no argument. Slowly, still with her back to him, she undid the buttons on her waistcoat and laid it on the habit. Her white lawn shirt with a lace frill down the front followed and then her bodice.

'And the pantalettes.' His voice was implacable. Her face flushed with shame, she tugged reluctantly on the ribbons holding them up. They slid down her bare legs to expose the naked curves of her hips and bottom and although she wasn't looking at him she was horribly aware of the way in which he was appraising her.

She jumped as she felt his hand gliding down her back to rest possessively on her rump. He fondled it briefly, running his fingers down the cleft between her buttocks, before taking her hand and leading her over to his mount.

He lifted her onto the stallion, then swung up behind her, before urging it into a trot. Automatically she wound her hands in the horse's mane and thought how strange it felt to be riding astride rather than side saddle.

Her bare thighs gripped the stallion and she tried not to

think about how curiously erotic it was to be riding naked. Her breasts were bobbing up and down with each movement and she bit her lip as the man behind her clasped them in his hands and caressed them as they continued through the wood.

The warm wind fanned the colour in her cheeks and blew her hair, which had escaped from its pins, out around her. Her companion stroked her thighs and then her pubic floss until she realized that her arousal was now greater than her fear of what was to come.

He slowed the horse to a walk and then turned her around to face him. She saw that he'd undone his fly and that his member, hugely erect, was slapping against his belly with each step.

Holding onto his shoulders and placing her legs over his thighs, she managed to position his engorged organ at the slippery entrance to her quim. She tried to lower herself slowly onto it, but was defeated by the horse's movements and it was suddenly sheathed to its fullest extent in one abrupt motion.

She found she was holding her breath, afraid that the size and fully aroused state of his manhood would hurt her, but she felt her internal muscles relaxing and intense pleasure building with each step the horse took.

The ride seemed endless, throwing her up and down on the shaft skewering her so pleasurably while he caressed her breasts with one hand and kept hold of the reins with the other.

At first he kept the horse to a walk, but as their coupling became increasingly urgent, the pace increased to a trot, then a canter and then a gallop.

The heat in her groin grew to an unbearable level until her whole body was red-hot, despite her nakedness. The sensations suffusing her as she moved up and down on him were more intense than anything she'd ever experienced in her life.

She seemed to be trembling on the brink of climaxing for an eternity and then just as she knew she was about to crest that ecstatic wave, the stallion suddenly reared up, unseating them both and sending her flying through the air.

Julia sat bolt upright in bed, her body bathed in perspiration and her heart beating frantically. As realization dawned that it had just been a dream, she sank miserably back against the pillows, a dull frustrated ache in her belly.

THIRTEEN

Two days later Elizabeth Westbourne called as she'd promised and returned the blue domino she'd borrowed. It was a warm day and they sat together under a chestnut tree in the garden.

Although Julia would never have raised the subject of Elizabeth's unhappy marriage, she was quite happy to listen sympathetically as Elizabeth haltingly touched on the topic herself.

'I feel I owe you an explanation for my behaviour on the night of the masked ball,' she began, taking a sip from her glass of lemonade.

'No explanation is necessary,' Julia assured her.

'You must have thought it odd that I was fleeing from a man you know to be my husband.' Elizabeth put her glass down and twisted her fingers nervously.

'The truth is that he's very jealous and possessive. Unless it suits him to have me with him, he prefers me to stay at home in the evenings. I am . . . I am not happy with him and sometimes if I expect him to be absent until late I slip from the house and meet . . . a friend. I understood my husband to be attending a political meeting on the night of the ball and thought I would steal a couple of hours of pleasure.

'Imagine my horror when I saw him across the other side of the ballroom. He noticed me at that same moment and made his way towards me. I knew that if he caught me he would punish me and if you hadn't intervened he would have found me in the library.'

'Do you think he suspected we'd switched dominoes?' asked Julia.

'I only arrived home about ten minutes before he did, but it was enough time for me to have disrobed and to be in bed feigning sleep. He must have believed that he'd made a mistake because after standing over me for a few minutes he left my bed-chamber and didn't refer to it the following day.'

'Forgive me – but have you no family or friends who can protect you from him?'

'He is my husband,' said Elizabeth simply. 'He is a wealthy, influential man and my family brought pressure to bear on me to marry him. My husband's money paid off my father's debts and now allows my family to live in considerably less straitened circumstances than previously. I would not for all the world distress them by telling them of what I have to bear.'

Julia thought that as Lord Westbourne's contemptible treatment of his wife seemed to be common knowledge, Elizabeth's family must choose not to be aware of it.

'My only consolation is that there is someone else I am very much in love with. The few hours we are able to spend together from time to time sustains me through the darker periods of my life – in that way I am fortunate. But you have known unhappiness much greater than mine. I should not be burdening you with my problems, but I felt I owed you an explanation.'

Julia sat in silence for a few moments before saying, 'I too have found consolation for the grief I have suffered – am still suffering. There is nothing I would not do to bring my husband back to me, but I now feel that all hope is in vain and that he perished on foreign soil and is lost to me forever. My . . . liaison serves to distract me.'

At that moment Richard appeared from out of the house and came down the terrace steps to join them, sweeping them a graceful bow as he reached them.

'I told the servant he had no need to announce me. I hope I didn't presume.'

'No – not at all,' said Julia, taking his hand. 'Come, join us. I believe you know Lady Westbourne.'

'Of course – your servant, ma'am.' He seated himself opposite them and lounged gracefully in the chair. Julia thought again how strikingly attractive he was as the bright sunshine on his thick, dark lashes cast romantic shadows under his eyes and accentuated his high cheekbones.

They chatted for a few minutes and then Elizabeth rose to take her leave. When Julia returned from seeing her to the door, Richard had his eyes closed and his face turned to the sun. He opened them as she seated herself.

'The strength of the sun reminds me of Portugal,' he told her.

'Do you miss it?'

'In some ways. It was a very different life. At this time of day everyone would be taking a siesta, or meeting their lovers behind shuttered windows to enjoy a couple of hours of dalliance in a darkened room.'

Something in his tone of voice made Julia sense that he too had enjoyed many afternoons in this fashion.

'Did you have . . . a mistress?' she asked him.

'Would you mind if that had been the case?'

'No – how could I?'

'Some women would.'

'Well I don't. Tell me about her – was she very beautiful?'

'Very,' he said reminiscently. 'A dark, sultry beauty with a figure that made men want to worship her and a temper that made them quail.'

'Who was she?'

'The wife of a high-ranking Portuguese diplomat. Sancia was considerably older than me but no less beautiful for that. She could have had any man she wanted and I could never understand by what stroke of good fortune she chose me.'

Julia could understand it. With his patrician good looks and elegant figure, Richard must have seemed very different from the Portuguese lady's fellow countrymen.

'Were you lovers for long?' she murmured.

'About a year. We would meet most afternoons at a house belonging to a friend of hers who was out of the country. Sancia had a key and we would rendezvous there for illicit dalliance. I was a raw, callow youth when she took me as a lover – she made a man of me.'

'Do you think of her still?'

He took Julia's hand and kissed it. 'Not anything like as often as I think of you,' he said gallantly. 'For the first few months it was tremendously exciting, she was a very passionate woman with a great capacity for carnal enjoyment. Although she often flew into a temper, it was short-lived and then she would throw herself on me, virtually tear my clothes off and we would make deeply satisfying, ardent love.'

'You must miss her,' commented Julia, half wishing she hadn't expressed any curiosity in her predecessor.

'I'm realistic enough to know that our liaison was never meant to last. Towards the end of our affair her rages became worse and more frequent until she spent more time shrieking at me than enjoying my love making.

'Once she threw a vase at me that split open my head and another time she stabbed me with a pair of embroidery scissors. It was only a matter of time before she told me it was over. She had already begun to tire of me before my father was recalled to England, but immediately after I told her I had no alternative but to return with my family, she spent most of her time violently berating me. She declared that I was spurning her and tried to fell me with a silver candlestick.'

'How terrible,' said Julia, her eyes round.

'I feared she would kill me and had to wrest it from her, then she raked my face with her nails and threw herself on the bed, weeping violently and declaring she would end her life. That was the last time I saw her, but a friend of mine who still lives there wrote to say that within a week of my departure she was seeing the youngest son of one of Portugal's most aristocratic families. I suspect she'd already chosen him as my successor even before she knew I was leaving. But I prefer to remember her as she was at the beginning, tender and passionate by turns.'

He took Julia's hand as he spoke and, turning it palm upwards, kissed it fervently. The touch of his lips sent the blood racing through her body and made her sex-flesh quicken. She realized that she wanted him very much, but at that hour of the afternoon the servants were tending their allocated tasks within the house and it would be difficult to find anywhere to be alone without drawing attention to themselves.

'Come walk with me,' she invited him, rising to her feet. They strolled along the well-tended pathways which wound through the garden, with Julia pausing to inhale the scent of her favourite white roses which were clustered around a rustic arch leading from the formal garden to the shrubbery.

Once in the shrubbery they were hidden from the sight of anyone in the house and Richard immediately slid his arm around her waist, turned her towards him and kissed her.

Through the thin stuff of her almond-green muslin gown she could feel how swiftly his arousal mounted. She pressed herself against him and he stroked her back, tracing the supple line of her spine and then letting his hand slide down to clasp the firm curves of her bottom.

She was instantly on fire and taking his hand led him to a small pavilion swarming with yellow and pink honeysuckle in the furthermost corner of the garden. The only sounds were the lazy humming of the bees and the distant notes of the fountain on the terrace.

They kissed again and Richard slid his hand into the front of her gown to stroke her breasts reverently. His fingertips glided over her nipples, teasing them into firm points.

He pulled her gown downwards and scooped out one ivory-skinned orb, then pressed his lips to it. Julia leant back against the wall and gave herself up to the sensations his warm mouth was arousing. He wound his tongue around one velvety nub, flicking at it and caressing it, making her sigh with pleasure.

The soporific heat of the afternoon and their seclusion in the dim, shadowed interior of the pavilion imbued the situation with a dreamlike quality.

Julia ran her hands across his shoulders over his tight-fitting coat. He paused in his attentions to her breast for long enough to divest himself of the garment and lay it on the floor, then he pulled her against him, moulding the pert contours of her backside as he recommenced pleasuring her. He stroked her bottom through the fine fabric of her gown, then he lifted her into his arms and laid her on his jacket.

He kissed her slowly, an inch at a time, then began to draw the skirt of her gown upwards. When he'd raised it to her waist he slipped a hand inside her pantalettes. His touch intoxicated her and she moaned softly as he stroked her golden fleece.

The pantalettes restricted his movements and he tugged at the ribbon fastening them, before drawing them down her legs while she raised herself partially off the ground to help him. When she was naked from the waist down, he gazed at her for a few moments and then groaned.

'You're so exquisite . . . so beautiful,' he murmured, caressing the soft floss veiling her hidden delta. She felt the warm breeze playing around her private parts and opened her legs to him. He stroked the silken folds of her vulva with great delicacy, then lightly stimulated the half-hidden bud of her clitoris with his forefinger.

Lying on her back with her legs splayed, Julia closed her eyes and enjoyed the erotic sensations his touch was evoking. Little thrills of pleasure coursed waywardly through her veins making her limbs feel heavy and languid.

There was no room for anything in her consciousness except her enjoyment of their illicit lovemaking in the pavilion. As Richard stroked it, her clitoris gradually became swollen and more prominent and her sex lips unfurled around it like the petals of a flower in the afternoon sun.

She moaned again and her hips began to move to the same rhythm. Her entire body seemed suffused with heat as he worked her ever upwards in a wayward spiral towards the ultimate satisfaction.

With a hastily suppressed cry she came, and felt waves of sheer carnal enjoyment wash over her, leaving her weak and sated.

She opened her eyes to see Richard unbuttoning his fly. She gasped as he entered her slowly and with great tenderness, then wound her legs around his thighs as he began to move in and out of her. She caressed the firm muscles of his back through his shirt, her pelvis pushing upwards to meet each smooth thrust.

In the sultry warmth of the afternoon they moved together

in a languid rhythm, stroking and caressing, kissing and licking, enjoying the taste of each other's damp skin. It seemed a long time before Julia felt herself hovering on the brink of fulfilment and then Richard's pace quickened until his thrusts became piston-driven and he erupted into her just as she came again herself, clinging to his shoulders as she arched against him.

He buried his face in her breasts and they lay silent except for the faint sound of their quickened breathing. At last he withdrew and got to his feet, before helping her up.

Julia stepped back into her pantalettes and tidied her clothing, looking with some dismay at the crumpled state of her gown. There were moss stains on the back and a damp patch on her skirt, but there was little she could do about it except hope she could gain the sanctuary of her bed-chamber without encountering anyone.

They walked back through the garden hand in hand. On the terrace he kissed her hand and murmured, 'I adore you,' before taking his leave.

FOURTEEN

'I think I shall give an evening party,' announced Isabel as she sat at her dressing table while her maid arranged her hair. Julia was perched on the window seat watching her cousin. She was wearing a ballgown of frosted peach gauze over peach satin trimmed with tiny knots of matching ribbons. She fanned herself gently with her painted Chinese fan as she considered the suggestion.

'Do you think it would be . . . appropriate?' she murmured.

'Just a small party for a few close friends,' said Isabel airily. 'Perhaps some dancing and a light supper.' The maid made the final touches to her mistress' hair and then stepped back. 'Very good,' said Isabel approvingly. 'Thank you – you may go now.'

Isabel's gown was a rich willow-green silk with an impressive ruched train and a wide embroidered sash. Emeralds gleamed at her throat and ears and an emerald-studded comb was pinned in her dark hair.

She turned to appraise her cousin's appearance and nodded slightly as she took in the sparkle in Julia's eyes and the colour in her cheeks.

'You are in particularly good looks tonight,' she commented. 'The peach is most becoming on you. Shall we see Richard later?'

'Sadly, no. He has to attend a dinner at the Portuguese Embassy. Will Captain Moore be joining us?'

'He'll be here directly after dinner to escort us.'

'When does his regiment leave for Bath?'

'In a week's time.' Isabel's lovely face darkened slightly but then she smiled again. 'He is pressing me to agree to visit him there. He has suddenly become an exponent of the many attractions Bath has to offer and seeks to tempt me with tales of the gaiety I may hope to enjoy.'

'Will you go?'

'Perhaps. Shall we go down to dinner?'

The ball they attended that evening was a lively affair. As she danced with Captain Moore Julia kept glancing around the room, wishing Richard was present.

'I'm sorry to see that my sparkling conversation isn't holding your interest,' Captain Moore teased her. 'I just made a joke you didn't even smile at.'

'I'm sorry,' she said, 'do please repeat it.'

'Alas the moment is past. However, to make up for your lack of attention perhaps you would render me a small service.'

'If I can,' Julia told him.

'Would you encourage Isabel to come visit me in Bath – the impending separation fills me with dread. Unless she comes to me, the most I can hope for in the future is the occasional snatched two days whenever I can get leave. I hope that you'll come as well – and Wortham too if he wishes.'

'I've never been to Bath,' said Julia. 'I should like to see it. I'll give the scheme my encouragement but Isabel is a woman who goes her own way.'

'Don't I know it,' he commented wryly.

Julia danced every dance, flirting gaily with her partners, while wishing Richard was there. But she knew she would see him the following day and was determined to enjoy herself.

The ballroom had four double windows each of which opened onto a small balcony overlooking the garden. Feeling the need for some fresh air, Julia stepped out onto one and stood looking out at the night sky. A lemon-coloured moon was rising and as she watched a swathe of thick, puffy cloud drifted over it and hid it from view.

She was just about to go back inside, when someone stepped out to join her. Turning round she was surprised to see a total stranger beside her and even more surprised to see that he'd drawn the royal-blue velvet curtains over the window as he stepped through them, hiding them both from view of anyone inside.

'We meet again,' he greeted her. 'I was hoping that we would.' In the darkness she didn't recognize him, but assumed he must have danced with her earlier that night.

'I . . . I was just about to go back in,' she said, wondering why she suddenly felt so nervous. Her heart had started beating at what felt like twice its normal rate and she found she had difficulty in catching her breath.

'Not yet.'

The words were spoken with such utter certainty that she was taken aback. About to push past him to rejoin the dancers on the other side of the curtain, she stopped dead as the moon emerged from behind the cloud to cast its pale light on him.

Even though his face had been masked, the silver-streaked dark hair of the black-dominoed stranger was unmistakable.

'Y . . . you,' she stuttered. He made an elaborate bow and then kissed the palm of her hand. She had to fight an urge to snatch it away and was glad that the night hid the warm colour which flooded her cheeks. She felt as though his kiss seared her skin, branding it with his mark, putting a stamp of possession on her.

She tried to withdraw her hand but he wouldn't release it.

'I must go,' she said in a low voice, reluctant to struggle with him. He moved towards her and she stepped back to find the parapet of the balcony behind her, preventing her from retreating any further. His broad-shouldered figure blocked the way to the windows and she caught just a whiff of eau-de-Cologne as he lifted her chin and kissed her.

Immediately and very alarmingly, she was on fire. Just the touch of his mouth on hers had her aching for a more intimate caress. In the grip of some madness she couldn't begin to comprehend, she swayed towards him and he pulled her against him and deepened the kiss.

Horrifyingly she could feel warm moisture already gathering in her private parts and a tingling itch began to pulse high up in her sex. In some distant part of her mind she was aware that if anyone pulled aside the curtains and saw them, her reputation would be in shreds.

After kissing her for what felt like an eternity, he released her and she leant back against the parapet panting like an animal, weak with desire for him. The tingling itch was now an all-consuming throbbing which made her feel desperate for satisfaction.

He reached out and fondled her mound through her peach gown in a lewd caress. She knew she should stop him before this went any further, but she felt powerless in his presence and in her wanton lust.

Worse was to follow; he pulled up the front of her gown and probing fingers slid into the delta between her thighs. Her pantalettes were already damp and she heard him make a faint sound of satisfaction as he encountered the silent testament to the strength of her arousal.

She was shocked to the core of her being when he gripped the waistband of her pantalettes and ripped them from her. It passed fleetingly through her mind that the scenario being enacted was very similar to the one which had occurred this afternoon, except that where Richard had caressed her with gentle tenderness, this man's touch was anything but.

He seized her by the waist and turned her so she was bent over the parapet, then pushed one hand in front of her to fondle her breasts. He dragged her gown up at the back and dabbled in the moisture between her thighs, then slid two fingers high up inside her and swivelled them around.

She could feel her juices trickling over his hand, then down the inside of her thighs as he worked his fingers in and out of her. She found herself bearing down against them, desperate for his touch on the hot throbbing bud of her clitoris. He withdrew the two fingers and rubbed the taut little nub deftly, until she choked back a cry while she felt a molten heat explode within her as she came.

She gripped the edge of the parapet as he nudged her legs further apart with his thigh. A second later she felt the hard smoothness of his member plunging strongly into her and then he commenced a measured thrusting that had her grinding her bottom into his thighs, almost sobbing with the desire to experience another ecstatic release.

She was dimly aware that the moon was shining down on their lascivious coupling and wondered if she was in the grip of moon madness that she was behaving so recklessly.

Each of his thrusts pierced her yielding sex-flesh to the very core and she was aware that her silken membranes were clutching at his organ and intensifying her own pleasure.

Suddenly, his movements ceased as abruptly as they'd begun and he froze in position. She realized immediately what had made him stop – there were voices only a yard away on the other side of the curtain.

Julia caught a woman's voice saying something about a breath of air then the stranger who a moment before had been shafting her so vigorously, abruptly withdrew. He dragged her gown back around her ankles and while she watched, dazed and incredulous, swung himself over the parapet and vanished from sight.

Seconds later the curtain was pulled back and she was joined by two women, both fanning themselves vigorously. She just about retained the presence of mind to step to one side so her ripped pantalettes were hidden under her skirt, but more than that was beyond her.

'Forgive me, but are you feeling ill?' one of the women asked her.

'It's just the heat,' she managed to murmur. 'I'll be fine in a moment.'

'Such a crush,' agreed the woman. She took a bottle of cologne from her reticule and sprinkled some onto a hand-kerchief which she pressed to Julia's forehead.

'Thank you – that's much better,' said Julia, trying fur-tively under the cover of her skirt to kick her ruined pantal-ettes off the balcony. It would undoubtedly cause some comment when they were discovered the following day, but as no one would know to whom they belonged, it hardly mattered. As soon as they'd fluttered off, she managed to say, 'Thank you, I must go and rejoin my cousin.'

She smoothed her gown and then passed through the curtains back into the ballroom, assuming an air of serenity she was a long way from feeling.

FIFTEEN

However much she might have been thrown into confusion after a second encounter with the black-dominoed stranger, Julia was determined not to cause Isabel any additional worry by letting her cousin see how disturbed she was.

She sought the seclusion of an empty room where she tidied herself and then remained until she felt equal to carrying on with the evening as if she hadn't just behaved like a slut of the first water.

Her feelings for Richard went much further than simply carnal desire, although she had to admit the physical aspect of their relationship was very important to her. But she also liked him and respected him and enjoyed all her time in his company.

But the man who'd twice made love to her was a stranger, she didn't even know his name and certainly knew nothing about him. So why did his very presence cause her to throw caution to the winds and let him have her in any way he pleased, regardless of the fact that they might be disturbed at any moment?

She could only be grateful that he'd acted as swiftly as he had in leaving the balcony. In retrospect the idea of being discovered with him taking her from behind just outside a crowded ballroom was too horrifying to contemplate. There would have been a scandal she would never have been able to shake until the day she died.

Lady Berwick's worst fears would have been realized and not all Isabel's influence and connections could have helped her cousin. In all probability she would have had to live abroad, a lifelong exile from society.

She must be on her guard in future, in case their paths crossed again and he had the same devastating effect on her. Even some time after the event she could feel how slick and wet she was just from thinking about the encounter.

Eventually she felt equal to returning to the ballroom, praying that he wouldn't be there because if he was, she felt she would simply die of mortification.

She no longer felt like dancing and instead chatted to some of her acquaintances, until Isabel came to find her and tell her that their carriage had arrived.

As she tossed and turned in bed that night, Julia wondered how wise it would be to ask Isabel if she knew who the man was. But her cousin was very perceptive and Julia was afraid she herself might give something away which would lead to unwelcome questions. She would have to wait for the right opportunity before casually asking if she knew him.

Isabel threw herself into organizing an evening party with her usual sense of style. It was to be no commonplace affair, that she was determined upon.

Julia asked if she could invite Elizabeth Westbourne, which Isabel was quite happy to do, even though she made a moué of distaste at the thought of inviting Lord Westbourne.

'That odious man fawns over me because he thinks I might be useful to him,' she commented, 'but he treats his wife so shabbily. I think I shall invite Thomas Althorne too in the hope that he and Elizabeth might be able to snatch some time together.'

'Are you . . . will you invite Lady Berwick?' asked Julia with some trepidation.

'Assuredly not,' replied Isabel airily.

'Won't she be offended?'

'Hopefully yes and then she won't invite me to any more of her tedious card parties. The champagne served at the last one was decidedly inferior.'

The servants were set to cleaning the already immaculate house including all the chandeliers which were taken down and polished until the crystal sparkled like diamonds. Isabel was in constant conference about matters relating to the forthcoming event and Julia wondered how much of this self-imposed activity was to take her cousin's mind off her impending separation from Captain Moore.

The two women bought new gowns for the occasion and the night before they dined quietly at home and both retired to bed early to get a good night's rest.

Somewhat to Julia's surprise, on the day of the party Isabel remained in bed until lunch time and then rose to eat a light meal before overseeing the last-minute arrangements. She then returned to her room and spent the rest of the afternoon of her day bed resting.

'I've no intention of being so exhausted that I'm unable to enjoy my own party and that by midnight I'm wishing all my guests to perdition,' she commented, gesturing to her maid to lay a shawl over her feet. 'You would be well advised to do the same.'

'Richard is taking me driving in the park,' admitted Julia. 'But I'll insist he brings me back in time to lie down for a while.'

She enjoyed the drive and Richard was his usual attentive self, but somehow Julia found – as happened quite often now – that she was looking for a tall man with silver-streaked dark hair among the people strolling, riding and driving in the park.

That evening she took a long time over her toilette and when her maid had eventually put the finishing touches to her appearance she was pleased by her reflection in the looking glass.

Her gown was of hyacinth blue shot-silk delicately embroidered with silver thread and with a cloth-of-silver train. Sapphires gleamed at her throat and wrists and a filigree silver circlet was pinned carefully into position among the feathery ringlets of her blonde hair.

Isabel looked every inch the *grande dame* in a gown of rich old-rose satin with a swooping neckline which exposed a good deal of creamy cleavage in a manner that verged on the immodest. With her train caught over one arm and her other through Julia's, the two women descended the stairs to dine with Captain Moore and Richard before the first guests arrived.

The musicians were already tuning up and the servants were carrying plates of food into the dining room for the elegant supper to be served later, as the four of them went into the library where a small table had been set by the window overlooking the garden.

Almost as soon as dinner was over the first guests began to arrive and Julia stood next to Isabel and helped her receive them. Elizabeth Westbourne, escorted by her husband, was among the earliest arrivals.

Lord Westbourne looked taken aback when he realized that the woman he'd spoken to so roughly in the library on the night of the masked ball was the cousin of the influential Lady Marchmont and bowed so low over her hand that she hoped he might overbalance and fall over.

She took a couple of minutes to ask Elizabeth how she was while Lord Westbourne paid Isabel fulsome compliments which Julia could tell her cousin found distasteful.

After about an hour Julia's face began to ache from smiling and it was a relief when Isabel murmured, 'I think we may as well circulate – most people have arrived but there are always a few latecomers whom we need not trouble ourselves about.'

Julia was just on the point of going to look for Richard when Isabel placed a restraining hand on her arm. Glancing towards the door she saw two men entering and immediately her stomach lurched. She was aware of a feeling of breathlessness, while somewhere in her female core there started a slow smouldering composed of an intricate mix of anger, fear and lust.

One of the men was in his fifties with patrician features oddly at variance with a decided tendency to portliness. Julia couldn't remember his name, but knew that she'd been introduced to him before. But it wasn't him who'd caught her attention so surely – it was his companion.

There was no mistaking her seducer, the black-dominoed stranger, even if this was the first time she'd seen him face to face in the light cast by dozens of candles.

His sloe-dark eyes were unreadable as they met hers, but she thought she saw a hint of a mocking smile at the corners of his mouth.

94

She was barely aware of Isabel's slight intake of breath as the patrician-featured man – whom she now remembered was Sir William Castle – bent over her cousin's hand and kissed it before saying, 'I believe you know Lord Varsey.'

Isabel inclined her head slightly as he too kissed her hand. There was a long-drawn-out pause before Lord Varsey said, 'I don't believe I've been introduced to your companion.'

'May I present my cousin – Mrs Charles Calvert,' said Isabel, her tone so frigid that Julia shot a startled look at her.

Lord Varsey took Julia's hand and kissed it punctiliously, but although his lips barely brushed her skin she felt seared by them. A hectic little pulse in her sex began to beat a lascivious tattoo and she was aware of a most unladylike desire to reach out and run her hand down his tight-fitting knee breeches where they moulded themselves to his well-muscled thighs.

'Delighted to make your . . . acquaintance,' he said, an ironic edge to his voice which she hoped no one else noticed. 'May I beg the honour of the first dance?'

'I believe my cousin is already engaged,' said Isabel, before Julia had a chance to reply. 'And here comes her partner now.' Richard was making his way through the people in the hall, obviously eager to escort her into the drawing room where the musicians were striking up for the first dance of the evening.

He bowed to both ladies before offering Julia his arm. To her surprise Lord Varsey took the hand she extended towards Richard and tucked it under his own arm.

'Evening, Wortham – I believe Sir William wishes to speak urgently to you on a subject of great import,' he said amiably. 'So I'm sure you won't mind if I take your place with Mrs Calvert for this dance.'

Without giving anyone a chance to reply, he swept Julia off to the drawing room, leaving the two men looking non-plussed and Isabel unusually stony-faced.

The movements of the dance gave them no opportunity to converse for several minutes but when eventually they came together Julia could think of nothing to say. Her partner, however, was not similarly reticent.

'How beautiful you look tonight,' he observed, 'almost as beautiful as when you had your skirts around your waist and your thighs widely parted in the library on the night of the masked ball.'

A flush of mortification stained Julia's cheeks at his words. How dare he make such a direct reference to something he must know she'd rather forget? She would have fled from his presence at once if she hadn't been aware of the comment such an action would undoubtedly occasion.

'You, sir, are no gentleman,' she managed to say from between clenched teeth.

'I don't recollect having claimed to be,' he said. 'But can it be that you labour under the misapprehension that you yourself are a lady?' He smiled as he spoke with a blandness which belied his insulting words. 'No lady would have behaved the way you did last night,' he continued. 'But then, ladies aren't really to my taste – give me a wanton woman who knows what she wants and isn't ashamed to show it, any day.'

The movements of the dance separated them again leaving Julia to seethe with rage as her feet carried her gracefully around the floor.

'You took advantage of me and you know it,' she hissed as they came together for a few seconds. He smiled derisively.

'And the second time?' he queried as they danced down the set. By this time Julia had just about recovered her poise. Schooling her face into an artificial smile, she looked directly up at him for the first time.

'I mistook you for someone else,' she told him sweetly. 'It was rather dark, after all.' He threw back his head and laughed, attracting the attention of several people nearby.

'I went to some not inconsiderable trouble to find out who you were and to arrange for our paths to cross again,' he informed her. 'I didn't want to leave it to chance for the third time. Can it be that my exertions have been in vain and my evening wasted?'

'No, for supper will be most excellent,' she assured him. 'And Isabel serves only the finest champagne. You may console yourself at the table.'

'I even braved the wrath of your redoubtable and lovely cousin by getting Sir William to bring me here tonight. She would never have invited me.'

'Perhaps your manners – or lack of them – are not to her liking.'

'Your voice is as sweet as honey, but your tongue even sharper than Lady Marchmont's – a family trait, perhaps?' he enquired lazily.

'Surely you must be accustomed to such a reaction from the females of your acquaintance?'

She was escorted down the set by the man opposite her, then was able to stand and watch while Lord Varsey danced with the woman facing him. He danced well, his tall, broad-shouldered frame set off to advantage by his waisted frock coat and skin-tight knee breeches. She found her eyes drawn to his groin and swiftly averted them, hoping he – or indeed anyone else – hadn't noticed.

The dance seemed interminable and it was a great relief when at last he bowed to her and she curtseyed as it ended.

'Allow me to escort you back to young Wortham,' he said, foiling her attempts to hurry off by taking her arm. 'There he is against that pillar looking as though he'd like to put a bullet through me.' He stopped suddenly and turned to face her, his eyes boring into hers. 'He isn't what you need at the moment – believe me when I say that.'

'And you are, I suppose?' she flashed.

'Yes.'

Without another word he led her to Richard, kissed her hand and left her.

SIXTEEN

Julia had never seen Richard look so annoyed. 'The nerve of the fellow,' he said angrily. 'How dare he appropriate you like that. What was he just saying to you?'

'He was asking if he could take me into supper but I told him that I was going in with you,' she hastened to placate him and then wondered why. After all, she hadn't gone with the man willingly – he'd left her very little choice.

'What did Sir William want to speak to you about?' she enquired as Richard stared fulminatingly after Lord Varsey's retreating figure.

'A desire to speak to me was obviously as much of a surprise to him as it was to me – I barely know the man. After prevaricating for a few minutes, pretending what it was had slipped his mind, he eventually asked me about Portugal – said he was thinking of visiting the country. The thought had patently never occurred to him before that moment.'

'Who exactly *is* Lord Varsey?' she ventured to enquire. 'I've never heard him mentioned.'

'No one you want to know. I'm surprised Isabel didn't ask him to leave immediately.'

'Why?' she asked in surprise. 'I could tell she doesn't like him, but she could hardly ask him to leave since he'd come with Sir William.'

'Don't have anything to do with him – not tonight, not ever. The set's forming for the next dance – shall we join it?'

The grim line of his jaw indicated that as far as he was concerned the subject was closed. Julia was puzzled by his reluctance to discuss Lord Varsey's shortcomings – she was certain they must be manifold and if she was honest she had to admit she was curious to know more about him.

But she'd no wish to have Richard in a bad mood for the remainder of the evening so she let the subject drop – Isabel was almost certain to mention her unwelcome guest when they discussed the evening the following day.

But despite her best efforts to restore his usual good humour, Richard remained taciturn and unresponsive to her attempts at light conversation and after a while she gave up trying.

The rest of the dance passed in silence and at the end of it she curtseyed formally and then turned on her heel and walked away. If Richard was determined to sulk all evening there was nothing she could do about it, but she wasn't going to let it spoil the party for her.

She felt like a few moments alone and thought she'd go upstairs to her bed-chamber to tidy her hair and splash on some cooling cologne.

In the light of the flickering candles set above her dressing table her face looked flushed as she dabbed her temples and wrists with cologne.

It was a warm night and she felt the need for a breath of fresh air. She stepped through the curtains which separated the alcove of her bay window from the rest of the room and pulled aside the ones over her window so she could open it a few inches.

The sound of her door opening and then closing again made her turn round and look back into her bed-chamber. She was deeply shocked to see Lord Varsey strolling into the room as if it were in his own house.

'What on earth do you think you're doing?' she demanded.

'Following you,' he admitted without a trace of embarrassment. 'I wanted to see you alone, far from prying eyes.'

'How dare you walk into my bed-chamber like that!' she snapped. 'Please leave at once.'

'Not yet,' he murmured, reaching the curtain and stepping through it to join her before closing it so they were alone in the shadowed darkness. His close proximity unnerved her. She swallowed and struggled to hold onto her outrage at his intrusion. He lifted one hand and drew the knuckle of his forefinger down her cheek, then the delicate column of her neck.

'We have unfinished business,' he told her. 'Our last . . . encounter was unfortunately curtailed before it reached a satisfactory conclusion.'

'If . . . if anyone saw you coming in here after me my reputation will be ruined,' she hissed.

'Then let's hope no one did,' he returned affably.

'I insist that you quit my room immediately,' she managed to say, holding onto the last vestiges of her self control as his finger slid slowly down to caress the soft skin of her décolletage.

Her knees trembled and she felt a lewd, demanding heat in her sex. Every nerve-ending seemed to be tingling in carnal expectation as he caressed the soft swellings of the upper curves of her breasts.

It was no good – she wanted him to take her right there in her room, regardless of the possible consequences, but she couldn't allow this to happen a third time – she really couldn't.

'You—' she began, then froze in alarm as she heard her bed-chamber door open again. Her mind racing, she strained to hear some sound which would give her an indication of who it might be. Jenny, her maid, should be downstairs in the room set aside for the female guests' cloaks, attending to any ladies who required assistance with their hair or gowns.

Isabel was unlikely to come looking for her in the middle of the party, so who could it be? A soft laugh and a murmur of voices indicated that it was not one, but two people.

Next to her, Lord Varsey stood as still as a statue, while an overpowering urge to see who it was made her move silently to where the curtain met the wall and put her eye to the chink.

Elizabeth Westbourne and Thomas Althorne were enjoying a passionate embrace just inside the door, her face turned up to his as they kissed with a fervour which Julia found fanned the flames of her own arousal.

If it were possible she was thrown into even more consternation than she had been moments before. If she

100

stepped through the curtains and revealed herself, not only would she embarrass the lovers, but Lord Varsey's presence would become apparent. Although she felt she could rely on Elizabeth's discretion, she knew nothing of Thomas Althorne and whether he too could be trusted to say nothing.

Hoping that the couple's embrace would be brief and that they would quit her bed-chamber very soon, she kept quiet and tried to breathe as silently as possible, difficult when the blood was coursing waywardly through her veins at what felt like twice its usual rate.

'I only dare stay a moment,' breathed Elizabeth, gently freeing herself from Thomas' embrace.

'But I haven't seen you for days,' he murmured, encircling her with his arms again. 'And it may be some time before we can be together again.'

He kissed her, one hand smoothing languid circles over her shoulders, making her press herself against him and caress the back of his neck.

Julia was horrified when he picked Elizabeth up and deposited her on the bed, before joining her there. Surely they weren't going to actually make love?

It seemed they were, because he stroked her hips and bottom avidly before stealthily drawing up the front of her gown to reveal her silk stockings and garters.

Julia felt that her legs would no longer support her and leant her shoulder against the wall, turning her back on Lord Varsey. She almost let out an exclamation of surprise when he too peered through the chink in the curtain just above her head.

She heard him hastily smother a noise which sounded suspiciously like a chuckle and then he dropped to his knees behind her.

He lifted the hem of her gown and she knew she had no way of stopping him without alerting the couple on the bed. He raised it to her waist and tucked it deftly into her sash so its delicate folds wouldn't hamper his movements. A swift tug on the ribbon of her pantalettes made them flutter to the ground, although, too late, she tried to catch them.

Naked from the waist down except for her stockings,

garters and blue satin slippers, she had to stifle an exclamation when she felt his lips on the smooth skin of her buttocks.

He kissed and nibbled each pert swelling, making her bite her lip as she tried not to moan with pleasure. She knew she should stop watching what was taking place on the bed, but somehow she couldn't tear her eyes from the stirring sight.

Thomas drew Elizabeth's breasts from the bodice of her gown and took one deep-pink nipple between his lips. She threw her head back and moaned softly, her hands busy unbuttoning his satin breeches. There was an urgency to their movements totally lacking in Lord Varsey's arousing ministrations.

His tongue found the cleft between Julia's buttocks and licked it delicately before working his way downwards with agonizing slowness. When his tongue reached her sex-flesh and he began to taste her copious honeyed juices, she found herself parting her legs for him. She continued to lean against the wall, her eyes widening as she saw Elizabeth draw Thomas' member from his breeches and use it to stimulate the swollen folds of her vulva.

It felt strangely erotic to be both watching and participating in a furtive sexual encounter. When Thomas slowly sheathed his organ in his partner's yielding sex-flesh, Julia was aware of a renewed flood of moisture trickling from her hidden core.

Lord Varsey's tongue found the shaft of her clitoris and flicked at it wickedly, but as he was behind her he couldn't reach the blunt point. He slipped a hand in front of her and began to stroke it softly, evoking shivers of delight from her.

The lovers on the bed were now moving urgently against each other, his hands clasping her bottom and her thighs wound around his. Their moans were now loud enough to drown any slight moist sounds that Lord Varsey's manipulation of her clitoris was making.

Julia felt the familiar wave of heat sweep over her as she neared her release and thrust her hand to her mouth as she came in a glorious flood of sensation which rippled through her slender body.

Behind her he rose to his feet and a few seconds later she

felt the rigid length of his phallus nudging determinedly between her thighs. It was fortunate that at that moment Thomas reached his climax with a loud groan, because she was unable to stop herself gasping as the hot, hard length of Lord Varsey's member forged satisfyingly inside her.

To keep her balance she had to remove her eye from the chink and turn to face the wall. The strength of her own excitement was now so great that she was completely focused on the sensations evoked by the rhythmic thrusting inside her and for several minutes she forgot everything except her own wanton pleasure.

She moved with him, pushing her hips back to meet each smooth stroke, letting her head drop back against his chest as his lips sought her neck and kissed it hungrily. His hands found her breasts and eased them from her gown, teasing the nipples into hard points and clasping them in his hands.

She came again, biting her cheek so hard to suppress her cries that she could taste her own blood. She was dimly aware of an exchange of words between the other couple and then Lord Varsey erupted into her in a scalding jet of fluid.

She sagged weakly against him and heard the sound of the door opening and someone leaving. As she could hear the rustle of clothing she deduced that one of them – probably Thomas – had left.

With a stealthy movement Lord Varsey withdrew from her and she felt the warm trickle of their mingled juices on her thighs. A moment later she heard Elizabeth leave the room and exhaled with relief.

After swiftly peering around the curtain to ensure that they were alone, she flew swiftly across the room and locked the door, determined not to risk discovery at this stage.

Lord Varsey strolled after her, his clothing tidied, looking remarkably composed for a man so recently in the throes of sexual passion.

He grinned at her, his eyes gleaming in the candlelight.

'At least we managed to bring things to a satisfactory conclusion this time,' he told her. 'I hope next time we can manage to find somewhere to be alone where there can be no possibility of interruption. My house, perhaps.'

Already shame at her own wanton behaviour was beginning to replace the excitement of her recent arousal.

'There will be no next time,' she snapped. She caught sight of her reflection in the looking glass and flushed with mortification. Her breasts were exposed, her gown above her waist and her thighs were glistening with warm moisture.

With an exclamation of annoyance she began to rearrange her clothing and stopped when she realized he was watching with lascivious interest.

'Get out of my room!' she cried.

He crossed the floor, turned her face upwards and kissed her hard on the mouth.

'Until next time,' was his parting shot.

SEVENTEEN

It was several minutes before Julia had washed herself and rearranged her clothing. She would have liked to have stayed in her bed-chamber for much longer, but she knew she had been absent from the party for too long and that it was her duty to return to it and help Isabel with their guests.

As she hurried along the hallway her mind was in turmoil. She hoped fervently that Lord Varsey had left – the thought of having to face him after their recent intimacy made her feel faint.

As she rounded the corner to the wide flight of stairs, she stopped abruptly for there, peering nervously over the banister, was Elizabeth Westbourne.

Suppressing a desire to retreat in confusion, Julia forced herself to move forwards and greet her friend.

'Elizabeth – are you all right?'

'Yes . . . no . . . I'm not sure,' she murmured.

Julia had wondered if she'd be able to meet Elizabeth's eyes after witnessing the intimate scene between her and her lover, but Elizabeth seemed to be thrown in more confusion than she herself was.

'What is it?' she asked.

'Lord Westbourne is at the foot of the stairs talking to someone, but I know he's standing there waiting for me. He's probably noticed my absence and suspects the worst.'

Julia wondered if he'd been standing there when Thomas descended the stairs. If so it might go badly for Elizabeth.

'We'll go down together,' she suggested lightly. 'Let him think you were with me.'

Elizabeth looked deeply relieved as she murmured, 'Thank you.'

As they descended the staircase side-by-side, Lord Westbourne glanced upwards. His face darkened into a scowl at the sight of his wife and then he hastily rearranged his features into a travesty of a smile as he saw her companion.

'My dear – I've been looking for you everywhere,' he greeted Elizabeth. 'Where have you been?'

'I . . . I . . .'

'I was just showing Lady Westbourne a hat I purchased yesterday,' Julia told him mendaciously. 'But we fell to conversing and were much longer than we intended to be. I hope I haven't caused her to incur your displeasure.'

She looked him directly in the eye as she spoke, but he swiftly averted his and she knew he was remembering his threatening words to her when he'd believed her to be his wife that night in the library.

'Not at all, not at all,' he said, the heartiness of his tone at variance with the shifty expression on his face. 'I'm delighted to find you getting on so well. Come, Elizabeth – let me take you in to supper.'

Julia moved among the guests, talking to all those she knew and then danced three dances in succession. One of them she'd been engaged to Richard for, but as he was nowhere in sight she accepted another partner without hesitation. She didn't see Lord Varsey and was relieved that it looked as though she'd got her wish and he'd left.

She felt thirsty and although she knew that the man she'd just danced with would have been happy to get her a glass of champagne, she thought she'd go and see how supper was progressing. Captain Moore strolled into the hall just as she was crossing it.

'I am desolate – Isabel won't eat supper with me,' he greeted her. 'Perhaps you'd like to?'

'I'd love to,' she returned, taking the arm he offered her.

'I thought Richard would have claimed that honour,' he commented as they went into the dining room to find the table covered with a tempting array of the most elegant dishes, all prepared by Isabel's French chef.

'Richard is annoyed with me because Lord Varsey virtually compelled me to dance with him and it was one I had promised Richard,' she explained as they helped themselves.

'Varsey – is he back in the country?' he asked absently, his attention focused on the food.

'Do you know him?'

'Not really – I was abroad with my regiment for an extended period of time and our paths rarely crossed, but I heard he was living on the continent a while back.'

'I received the impression that Isabel doesn't like him,' Julia said, taking a succulent piece of chicken breast. 'She didn't invite him tonight, but he came with Sir William Castle and I got the feeling she wished he hadn't. Do you know why that might be?'

'No idea, I'm afraid,' he said easily, surveying his lavish selection from the cold collation with regret. 'I don't think I can get anything else on my plate – do you have enough?'

'Thank you – yes.'

They repaired to one of the small tables set at intervals around the room and ate in silence for a while. Julia suddenly found she was hungry and consumed her supper with relish, thinking it was a great pity Captain Moore hadn't been able to enlighten her further. He made another visit to the table to replenish his plate and then suggested that they dance.

As they twirled around the room in a waltz she suddenly felt the downy hairs on the back of her neck prickle and glancing behind her saw Lord Varsey leaning against the fireplace watching her, a glass of brandy in one gloved hand.

She was seized by a desire to show him how little he meant to her and responded to a lighthearted pleasantry from Captain Moore by laughing up at him, her blue eyes fixed attentively on his face.

'I'm obviously even wittier than I think I am,' he said a couple of minutes later after she'd greeted a comment from him on the success of the party with a burst of tinkling laughter and a look of adoration. 'Are you teaching Richard a lesson, by any chance?'

'What makes you think that?' she asked, smiling radiantly.

'You don't usually look at me like that. I should warn you that if you keep it up you're liable to turn my head. I'm extremely susceptible to the flattery of a beautiful woman. I think I should also point out that Richard isn't in sight and so your performance – charming though it is – is wasted.'

She saw over his shoulder that Lord Varsey was watching them. He raised his glass to her, the mocking smile back on his lips. She ignored him and pouted winsomely at her partner, her blue eyes sparkling.

A moment later she saw Isabel enter the room and as the dance was just ending she was quite happy to relinquish Captain Moore to her cousin, particularly as she was engaged for the next dance with a handsome naval officer.

He too was the happy recipient of her smiles and considerable charm, so much so that by the end of the dance he was obviously smitten and asked permission to call on her.

She was unfortunate in her next partner, Mr Soames, the husband of one of Isabel's friends. He obviously took her smiles for encouragement to behave freely with her and pulled her much closer to him than she considered acceptable. She attempted to draw away, while trying not to look as annoyed as she felt.

He'd obviously imbibed too freely of the excellent claret being served and the arm around her waist tightened while his hand slipped low enough to clasp her bottom.

Aware that Lord Varsey was still watching her, she kept the smile pasted determinedly on her face as she said, 'You forget yourself, sir, please behave with more decorum.'

His only reply was a leer and a squeeze of her rump. Unable to stand his insupportable behaviour, she freed herself from his grasp and left the room, fuming.

The blue drawing room was thankfully empty and she sank onto the sofa mentally cursing Richard, Mr Soames, and most of all the detestable Lord Varsey.

The sound of the door opening made her look round and then she got hastily to her feet as the man who'd just made free with her came lurching in.

'There you are,' he said, slurring his words. He came over and leant over her, his eyes glazed and the smell of alcohol heavy on his breath. She turned angrily away, but he grabbed hold of her and clumsily attempted to kiss her.

Unwilling to cause a scene by shouting for help, she struggled with him and then in a sudden surge of anger as he pawed at her breasts, hit him as hard as she could across the face.

He let her go and she backed hastily away from him, unwilling to lose her dignity by fleeing from the room. A moment later she wished that she had because although she tried to evade him, he grabbed her roughly and threw her onto the sofa.

'You teasing little hussy,' he said in a thickened voice. 'Don't pretend you're not dying for it.'

She struggled in earnest, but he pinned her to the sofa with the full weight of his body. When he began to fumble with the buttons of his knee breeches she knew she had no alternative but to scream for help – it was either that or succumb to his drunken attentions. She opened her mouth to scream, but he clamped his hand over it.

Without warning his weight was suddenly lifted from her and the next moment he was sprawling ignominiously on the floor. Behind him stood Lord Varsey who shook his head in gentle reproach as her attacker scrambled to his feet.

'You've forgotten your manners, Soames. Now I think you should beg Mrs Calvert's pardon.'

For a moment Julia thought Mr Soames was going to charge at Lord Varsey like an enraged bull, but instead he brushed ineffectually at his rumpled clothing, glaring at the other man.

He tried to walk past him to the door, but found his way barred.

'I think you heard what I said.'

Reluctantly, Mr Soames turned to Julia. 'I'm sorry,' he muttered, scowling at her. Lord Varsey stepped aside and her assailant stumbled from the room.

'And now I suppose you expect me to thank you,' she said, knowing she was being ungracious – he had, after all, just saved her from at best a great deal of embarrassment and at worst the violation of her body.

'Not really,' he returned amiably. 'I don't like the idea of sharing you. I want you to promise me that you'll break off your liaison with young Wortham.'

'Why on earth should I do that?' she demanded.

'As I've just said – I don't like the idea of sharing you.'

'Then don't,' she snapped, stalking across the room to the door.

'Julia . . .' She turned at the unfamiliar use of her Christian name. 'Either break it off yourself or I'll do it for you.' His voice was soft, but she sensed the underlying menace in his words.

He reached out and stroked her hip, a seductive gesture which made her tremble. She told herself that her unguarded reaction was a result of the ungallant treatment Mr Soames had offered her, while Lord Varsey's hand glided across to her belly and circled it, the tips of his gloved fingers just brushing the top of her mound.

Warm, unwelcome moisture dampened the crotch of her pantalettes and she had difficulty in concealing the fact that her breathing had suddenly become laboured. She wanted to take his hand and guide it downwards so it slid between her thighs to toy with her moist intimate parts, until the moisture became so copious that it covered her vulva in a glistening coat of female honey.

She remembered him falling to his knees behind her in her bed-chamber earlier that evening and then lifting the hem of her gown until it was above her waist. She felt faint with desire as she recalled the touch of his lips to the cleft between her buttocks.

He withdrew his hand and she was conscious of a feeling of disappointment which fuelled her rage with him.

'My relationship with Richard has nothing to do with you,' she said from between clenched teeth.

'Then keep it that way by ending it.' He was smiling as he spoke but his eyes were dark and hard as ebony.

Julia swept out of the room and slammed the door behind her to find Isabel standing in the hall listening to something Captain Moore was whispering into her ear. She looked surprised to see her young cousin behaving so impetuously and raised one winged eyebrow.

'What has occurred to vex you?' she asked.

'Nothing of any import,' replied Julia hastily. 'Let's go and see how the dancing goes on.' She edged towards the drawing room, anxious to get Isabel out of the hall before Lord Varsey emerged and made it obvious they'd been closeted together.

'Have you been quarrelling with Richard?' Isabel wanted to know.

'He's been quarrelling with me,' she retorted sourly. At that moment the door to the blue drawing room opened and Lord Varsey sauntered out. He nodded amiably at the three of them and then made his way into the library.

Isabel's face briefly registered consternation, before she turned back to Julia and murmured, '*Most* unwise.'

She drew her cousin to one side and continued, 'He is a man to be avoided at all costs. I'm only sorry that his arrival took me by surprise and I was unable to stop him being introduced to you. I must warn you to have nothing to do with him.'

'Why?' asked Julia.

'We cannot speak of it now. Go, find Richard and make it up with him.'

Isabel turned back to Captain Moore and took his arm, leaving Julia frustrated that her curiosity had not been satisfied.

She vowed that whatever happened the following day, she'd not rest until she found out whatever Isabel knew about the infuriating Lord Varsey.

EIGHTEEN

It was late when eventually all the guests had departed and Isabel and Captain Moore made their way to her bed-chamber. While she disrobed, Captain Moore poured them both a glass of brandy before unbuckling his belt and beginning to remove his uniform.

When she'd undressed she pulled on a nightgown of sheer ivory silk lavishly trimmed with lace, through which the voluptuous curves of her body were plainly visible.

He paused to survey her appreciatively. 'You're so beautiful,' he told her in a thickened voice, his eyes lingering on the generous swell of her breasts and the thrusting points of her umber nipples.

He removed the rest of his clothing while he watched her brushing her hair, seated at her dressing table. Although her back was to him, he could see the mesmerizing movements of her firm orbs in the mirror as she drew the brush through her lustrous dark hair.

When he was naked he walked towards her, his member, a dark brick-red, rearing up against his belly. She turned around on the chair and bent to take the head in her mouth. He stood with his hands on his hips while she flickered her tongue around the ridge below the glans, then strummed her way to the base. She licked the soft spherical swellings of his testicles and then kissed her way back up to the head.

She glanced upwards and saw that his eyes were closed and his face wore an expression of ecstatic appreciation. She slid his phallus into her mouth and commenced a seductive sucking, tugging gently with her lips and then sucking harder so that he groaned and moved his hips.

Isabel used her considerable expertise to bring him to boiling point and then removed her mouth, letting his organ slip slowly from it an inch at a time. He lifted her in his arms, kissed her between the breasts and then carried her over to the bed.

After laying her on it and kissing her hungrily, his member nudging its way between her thighs, he tried to thrust inside her but she twisted away, not yet ready for intercourse.

'No. You lie on the bed on your back.'

He obeyed her and reached for her with eager hands. He caressed her body through her silk nightgown, weighing her voluptuous breasts in his hands and squeezing and fondling her curvaceous bottom.

She knelt to one side of him and he pushed his hand between her legs, finding her slippery sliver of flesh and rubbing it briefly, then lifting her so she was astride him. Usually a considerate lover, tonight he seemed determined to penetrate her as soon as possible.

But that didn't suit Isabel. If Captain Moore had a fault as a lover it was a tendency to drift off to sleep as soon as he'd climaxed, so experience had taught her that her own satisfaction should be sought early on in the proceedings.

A feeling of restlessness consumed her and she pulled his wrists to the top of the bed and lashed them deftly to the headboard with the sash of her nightgown.

'What are you doing?' he asked her, not resisting, but obviously not happy about the way things were going.

'Something you'll enjoy very much,' she assured him, tying the knot as tightly as she could.

'I was just about to do something I enjoy very much,' he pointed out, tugging at his bonds. 'But you stopped me.'

'Relax,' murmured Isabel, stroking his chest and trailing her fingers over his belly.

She sat astride his chest and toyed with his engorged member, making him groan with frustration and his phallus throb hectically, then she moved up the bed and positioned herself over his face. She parted her sex-lips with her hands and showed him the slippery folds of her vulva and the little point of her bud.

'Make me come with your lips and tongue,' she ordered him.

'I'd rather make you come with my cock,' he protested, seeing the satisfaction he craved so urgently slipping further away.

She ignored him and lowered herself to just above his face. With the air of a man doing his duty he plunged his tongue into her as far as it would go and began an oral exploration of her vulva. He was nothing if not thorough and once embarked on the task was obviously determined to do it properly. But soon the scent and taste of Isabel's sex ensnared him and his oral contortions became more enthusiastic.

After licking and nibbling his way over the swollen folds of her sex-flesh, pausing every few seconds to delve into her slick inner chamber, he took her clitoris between his lips and began to suck it. She squirmed around on his face, feeling her pleasure mount and the heady ascent to orgasm begin.

He flicked the tip of his tongue wickedly along the shaft of her bud and then stabbed at the point, making warm eddies of delight give way to hot waves of ecstasy.

Her spine arched and her head fell back on her shoulders as he performed the last swift strokes which sent her tumbling over the edge with a half-stifled cry.

When at last she lifted herself from his face it was glistening with her juices which she wiped tenderly away, before holding a glass of brandy to his lips so he could drink.

'Untie me,' he urged her, but Isabel was enjoying the feeling of dominance that having him lie tethered to her bed was giving her.

'Not yet,' she murmured, positioning herself over his erect phallus and using it to stimulate the swollen, tingling bud which protruded prominently from between the slick tissues of her inner-labia.

It was a deep, dark crimson and she used his member as a simple instrument of delight, rubbing it rhythmically over the dripping point of her clitoris.

She came again very swiftly and then lowered herself onto his shaft and began to move on it, rotating her pelvis and rocking slowly up and down. She used it to give herself pleasure, while he yanked impatiently at his bonds, eager to be free.

'I want to see your breasts,' he said hoarsely.

She let her nightgown slip from her shoulders so it was bunched around her waist and he feasted his eyes on the rhythmic rise and fall of her full orbs, obviously frustrated by his inability to touch them.

She gave herself up to the sheer erotic pleasure of being impaled on his huge organ, able to control their movements while he bucked his hips below her, trying to urge her on to greater efforts.

But Isabel took her time and only when she was ready did she speed up until she was riding him wildly, her hair tumbling over her bare shoulders and tantalizingly half-veiling her breasts.

Captain Moore's strangled cry of satisfaction sounded as though it had been wrested from him by torture as he exploded into a prolonged orgasm.

Isabel's third climax followed swiftly and she moaned loudly, before shakily adjusting her position so she was lying on top of him.

'Untie me,' he begged her as their breathing slowly returned to normal. She let his detumescent manhood slip from her with a last regretful squeeze of her internal muscles and turned her attention to the knots holding his hands secured.

'You've pulled too hard and tightened them,' she murmured, as she struggled in vain to undo the sash. 'You'll have to stay here as my prisoner, awaiting my visits, your sole purpose to pleasure me.'

She felt a renewed quickening in her sex and toyed with the idea of teasing her lover into an erect state again while he was still secured. But there were ugly red marks around his wrists and she was certain that his bonds must be paining him, though she doubted whether he would ever admit it.

At last she managed to free him and he sat up, rubbing his wrists and looking at her broodingly. He picked up his glass of brandy, tossed the rest down his throat and then turned to her and caressed the luscious curves of her rump.

'You've had your fun with me and now you must pay the price,' he threatened her, pulling her back down on the bed.

NINETEEN

Always a late riser, Isabel didn't ring for her maid until after eleven on the day following the party. Julia had been awake since before nine and had told Jenny that she was to be informed as soon as Isabel surfaced.

Julia wasn't in the best of humours. She had eventually found Richard playing cards with some acquaintances, but he'd made no move to leave the card table to speak to her even though the game had ended as she stood there watching.

Later, at the end of the party, he'd come to make his farewells, but she'd merely coldly inclined her head and he'd left without having made any arrangements to see her again. But it wasn't Richard who obsessed her thoughts on this sunny summer morning – it was Lord Varsey.

Now that the opportunity had presented itself for her to find out about him, she wasn't about to let it pass by.

By ten o'clock she was so impatient to speak to Isabel that she nearly went to wake her up, but luckily common sense prevailed and she pulled on her bonnet and spencer and went for a walk around the square instead.

She knew that Isabel wouldn't thank her for disturbing her sleep and she was aware that she had to tread carefully and not let her cousin know how eager she was to find out more about Lord Varsey.

She planned to discuss the party in general terms before mentioning him, in the hope that Isabel would bring him into the conversation and explain why she'd warned her to avoid him at all costs.

Isabel still wasn't up when she returned and so she went

into the library to try to interest herself in a book. But the servants were bustling about setting the room to rights, so it was a relief when Jenny told her that Isabel had just summoned her hot chocolate.

Julia hurried upstairs and tapped on Isabel's door. Her cousin was examining her reflection in a hand mirror, but she put it down as Julia entered in response to her call of, 'Come in.'

'Good morning, Isabel. I hope you slept well – is anything amiss?' asked Julia as she saw Isabel wince as she reached for her chocolate.

'Just my aching muscles,' admitted Isabel airily. 'Captain Moore was on exceptional form last night and quite tired me out.'

She didn't look tired. On the contrary, her creamy skin had a luminous glow and her grey eyes were sparkling, even if she held her chocolate as if the cup were too heavy for her.

'The party went very well, don't you think?' commented Julia, perching on the foot of the bed.

'I believe so,' returned Isabel, not without some satisfaction. 'I feared that we might run out of champagne, but happily we did not. Did you enjoy yourself?'

'I did, but I would have had a better time if Richard hadn't behaved in such a tiresome way.'

'He was still annoyed when he left?'

'Unfortunately yes.' Julia waited, hoping that Isabel would mention Lord Varsey, but she merely sipped her chocolate absently. 'It wasn't my fault that Lord Varsey took his place for the first dance,' continued Julia after a pause. 'I was taken by surprise and could think of nothing to do but go with him.'

'His arrival was as unexpected as it was unwelcome. Don't blame yourself, Julia, he's a man who rides roughshod over the feelings of others and taken by surprise like that as you were, it would have been difficult to refuse him.'

Isabel pushed herself further upright against her pillows and with the air of someone broaching a subject with reluctance continued, 'I know you spent some minutes alone with him in the blue drawing room. I must warn you to be on your guard never to let such a thing happen again – fortunately I don't think anyone other than Captain Moore and myself noticed. I can only regret that Lord Varsey's acquaintance was forced on you, but should your paths cross in the future, a cool nod is all the acknowledgement necessary.'

Julia wondered what Isabel would say if she knew that her cousin's acquaintance with Lord Varsey went way beyond that.

'Tell me about him,' she encouraged Isabel. 'How has he displeased you that you were reluctant to have him at your party?'

Isabel averted her eyes before saying, 'Society is much harsher on women than it is on men. Lord Varsey's offences are many, and had he committed just one of them as a woman he would not have been received thereafter. As it is, there are many ladies in society who will not invite him to their houses, despite his wealth and status. His reputation with women is to say the least unsavoury and no respectable female would risk having her name linked to his.'

'But what has he actually done to offend you?' persisted Julia.

'Some things are best not discussed. I insist that you heed my advice and stay away from him. If he ever asks you to dance again, just say that you are already engaged for all of them. Now, what are your plans for the day?'

'I thought I might send Elizabeth a note to see if she would ride with me.'

Isabel nodded approvingly. 'Very well. It will do no harm if Richard should call to apologize and find you from home. Men are absurdly jealous creatures and although I advise a certain coolness until he has atoned for his foolishness, the sooner you can make it up the better it will be.'

Julia found the exchange unsatisfactory. If Isabel was going to lay down the law about Lord Varsey she could at least give her cousin the details of his transgressions.

'Captain Moore leaves for Bath later today,' said Isabel. 'He will call soon to say his last goodbyes. If you have no objection I plan to lunch with him privately.'

'None whatsoever,' Julia assured her, rising from the bed. 'If you'll excuse me, I'll go and scribble a note for Elizabeth.'

Captain Moore arrived just as she was leaving. He kissed her affectionately and murmured in her ear, 'Remember, I depend on you to bring Isabel to Bath.'

'I'll do my best,' she replied, then set off to meet Elizabeth, who seemed in good spirits.

'Lord Westbourne was delighted to hear that we were to spend the afternoon together,' she said as they rode into the park. 'Usually he makes the greatest difficulty about me seeing anyone, even Mama and Papa.'

Elizabeth was wearing a habit of forest-green French cambric with frogging and epaulettes which gave it a military appearance. Her matching hat was à là Hussar with a curled plume which bobbed friskily with every movement. She rode well on her pretty chestnut mare and Julia noticed more than one admiring glance coming her friend's way.

She herself was in a new riding habit of burgundy velvet with a tightly-fitting jacket over an embroidered waistcoat and frilled white lawn shirt.

She wasn't altogether surprised when they were joined by Thomas Althorne who asked if he might ride a little way with them. She felt the colour rising in her cheeks as she remembered spying on him the night before and watching him sheath his manhood in Elizabeth's yielding flesh. Surreptitiously she urged her horse forward so it was just in front of theirs for a minute or two until her normal colour returned.

Thomas chatted civilly about the party, although he only had eyes for Elizabeth much of the time. They paused to exchange a few words with some acquaintances and then she spotted Richard riding towards them.

She kept her head turned towards Elizabeth to give Richard every opportunity to avoid her if he wished, but he reined in his horse as they drew level and bowed to them.

'May I ride with you?' he asked, looking her in the eye.

'Certainly, if you wish,' she returned coolly.

They fell in behind Elizabeth and Thomas and rode in silence for a few minutes. Julia was determined not to speak if he did not, but eventually he said, 'I must ask you to forgive me for my behaviour last night. I realize on reflection that you were not to blame for Varsey's intolerable presumption. You were not to know either, that he is no fit dancing partner for you.'

'Why is he not?' she asked, hoping that Richard might enlighten her more satisfactorily than Isabel.

'He is not a man whom I would want any respectable female of my acquaintance to associate with. You have not been out in the world for long and I would not wish to sully your innocence with tales of his exploits.'

Julia bit her lip in frustration. Why did everyone persist in treating her like a schoolroom miss? She'd had a husband and now she had a lover, but it seemed that as far as Isabel and Richard were concerned she was a total innocent to be kept in the dark about everything.

It would serve them right if the next time their paths crossed she asked Lord Varsey directly about his dubious reputation.

'. . . tonight?' She became aware that Richard was asking her something.

'Forgive me – what did you say?' she enquired.

'I asked if you were planning to attend the reception at Dover House tonight.'

'I'm not sure,' said Julia abstractedly. 'Captain Moore leaves for Bath today and Isabel may not feel like going out.'

He looked crestfallen, but didn't pursue it until it came time for them to part when he said, 'Do, I beg you, try to be there tonight, or I will think you still haven't forgiven me.'

Julia *hadn't* forgiven him, so she merely smiled distantly and said that it depended on her cousin.

TWENTY

When she returned home Isabel was lying on the *chaise longue* in her room and obviously in low spirits.

'Why do we not visit Captain Moore in Bath and then you will see him again soon?' Julia suggested, mindful of her promise to him.

'Perhaps,' replied Isabel. 'But I suspect that the most sensible thing I could do would be to look around for another lover whose destiny is his own to command. A long-distance affair is of no great interest to me.'

Trying to divert her thoughts to a more cheerful direction Julia asked if they would attend the reception at Dover House.

'I have not the heart for it, but if you wish to go, I believe Emma Soames and her husband are to attend and I'm sure you would be most welcome to go with them.'

Mr Soames was the last person whose company Julia wanted to seek out and she hastily said that she did not care to go herself. Anyway, it would serve Richard right to look for her in vain.

The two women spent a quiet evening alone and both retired to bed early.

Isabel paced her room restlessly, not ready for sleep and trying to resist the temptation to slip out into the night to seek solace somewhere she knew she would be guaranteed to find it.

She sipped a glass of cognac in the hope that it would make her sleepy, but instead it made her uncomfortably aware of the demanding ache in her sex.

Eventually, just before midnight, she sent for her carriage, then locked her bedroom door and opened a secret compartment in the back of her wardrobe and surveyed the garments which hung there.

These were not the richly fashioned silks and satins which befitted her rank, but the most diaphanous of garments, often with immodest slits and holes, which were designed to reveal more of the female form than they concealed.

She chose a black silk chiffon gown of Grecian design, with a low cowl neckline which floated around as she moved to expose most or all of her breasts. There was a split at the front from just above her mound to her knees which offered the casual observer glimpses of her pubic fleece. A matching split at the back served a similar purpose for her derrière.

She pulled a black satin cloak over the gown and fastened it carefully so that no hint of her unusual attire was visible. She went down to her carriage and spent the journey gazing out of the window at the familiar sights of London as she was driven to her destination.

The coachman dropped her by the crumbling ivy-covered wall and she made her way along it, through the gardens and eventually knocked on the door of the semi-derelict mansion.

The man who opened it was slim with light brown hair and narrow hips. He was bare-chested and his only garments were a black silk mask, skin-tight breeches and highly polished top-boots. Isabel, who'd donned her own mask in the gardens, slipped inside and he closed the door behind her, saying, 'Welcome. Do you have any particular requests tonight?'

'Only that I should leave completely satisfied and that my fate should not for a couple of hours lie in my own hands.'

He relieved her of her cloak and indicated by a gesture that she should turn around. She did as he bade and he watched the delicate folds of her gown float around her, exposing her breasts, buttocks and sex for a few tantalizing moments each.

'There are those present tonight who will be happy to accommodate you,' he told her. 'Including myself. Wait here a moment.'

He returned a few minutes later with another man – dark,

thickset and of medium height – who was carrying some lengths of silk cord with tassels on the ends.

'Put your hands behind your back,' the slim man ordered her. He lashed them together with a length of the silk cord and then wound another loosely around her neck so that the tassels brushed her breasts. He took the last length of cord and said, 'Part your thighs,' then fed one end through the slit in the back of her gown between her legs and out of the one in the front where it was seized by the dark man.

'Follow me,' the dark man muttered, tautening the cord. With the slim man behind her holding the other end, she followed him through the door. As they made their way along the stone-flagged passage the two men moved the cord backwards and forwards between her thighs, working it gradually upwards until it brushed her vulva.

It was a depraved sensation to be walking along being stimulated by the entwined strands of silk which at times became caught in the folds of her labia and rubbed arousingly over her clitoris. But they never allowed her more than a few seconds of that particular pleasure, twitching the cord downwards or to one side to free it.

She found she was bending her knees to maximize her contact with it, but the slim man jerked it upwards so it cut uncomfortably into the valley between her outer and inner sex-lips and she was forced to walk on her tiptoes.

He relaxed it after a few moments and she was able to walk normally until they came to a flight of stone stairs. The angle of the ascent meant that the cord ran directly over her clitoris and pressed against her mound over her pubic floss.

A dark, secret heat was building in her sex and it was intensified by the fact that the tassels hanging down her front swished around with each step, brushing over her breasts and nipples like the delicate caress of a lover.

They had to pause at a turn on the stairs to allow a couple to pass them. A woman in a gauze cloak which was open to reveal her bare breasts was leading a masked man, naked except for his boots and shirt, down the stairs by his erect phallus.

While they waited for the couple to pass the slim man slid

his hand between Isabel's thighs and touched her intimately, while the dark man turned to caress her breasts, handling them carelessly but nevertheless making her swallow as her mouth suddenly became dry.

They continued up the stairs until they came to the second floor where they turned down a wide corridor and into a large candlelit room, sparsely furnished with a table and several chairs.

Isabel was led over to the wall and her bound hands briefly freed, then tied in front of her and hooked over a bracket set into the stonework above her head so she had her back to the room. The silken cord, sticky now in the middle where it had soaked up her juices, was drawn from between her legs.

The slim man went over to the table where there was a bowl of grapes, a decanter of wine and several glasses. He poured himself a glass, while the dark man seized Isabel by the hips and compelled her to step back a couple of paces and then positioned her so she was bent forward, her curvaceous backside thrust towards him.

The split in the back of her gown meant that her buttocks were bared and protruded rather rudely through the aperture. The slim man pulled a couple of grapes from the bunch and ate them, his eyes on her bottom while his companion wound the sticky centre of the silken cord around his hand, lifted it and used it to whip her backside with.

Unlike a whip, the sensation of the silk tassels striking her across the buttocks was arousing but not painful, serving only to make her push her derrière further towards him in anticipation of each blow. He lashed her lazily, amusing himself by making the tassels bounce off a different bit of her posterior each time.

It was a delicious feeling, eventually making her bottom feel hot and glowing, but leaving no marks that would still be there in a few hours. Isabel could feel her clitoris tingling and hoped they wouldn't leave it too long before allowing her to enjoy her first climax.

The dark man laid one final blow squarely across the crown of her rump and then unwound the cord from his hand. She was startled when he began to push it, an inch at a time, into her hidden chamber, until several inches were inside her and the tassels dangled obscenely between her legs.

He sauntered over to the table and drank some wine while the slim man took his place behind Isabel. He reached in front of her and found the sliver of her tingling bud which he toyed with for a minute, while she worked her internal muscles in the hope of precipitating a climax.

But he stopped caressing her too soon and fondled her breasts instead. After teasing her nipples to hard peaks of arousal, he unhooked her bound wrists, led her over to one of the chairs and seated her in it. He undid her hands, only to secure each of them firmly to an arm of the chair.

The front of her gown was arranged on either side of her breasts and then he bent his head and took one nipple in his mouth, rolling it between his lips and sucking gently. She closed her eyes and moaned softly while he moved his mouth to accord similar treatment to her other taut point.

Meanwhile the dark man parted her thighs and lifted her skirt to expose her sex, the tasselled cord still dangling from it. He studied the intricate folds of her vulva and then brought the bowl of grapes from the table.

The slim man stopped nuzzling her nipple, positioned himself to one side of her and carefully eased open her sex lips. His companion jerked the cord from her quim with an obscene plopping sound and then detached several grapes from the bunch.

Isabel swallowed as he slid the first one inside her, pushing it as high up into her sex as he could with his forefinger. Several more followed while she consciously relaxed her internal muscles to help him.

Instead of inserting the last one, he popped it in her mouth and she felt a rush of saliva as she bit into the juicy fruit which was echoed by an increase of honeyed moisture around the succulent grapes lodged securely in her sheath.

He fell to his knees and Isabel moaned with delight as he plunged his tongue into her and busied himself with extracting the grapes one by one.

Grape juice mingled with her own juices to render her

inner thighs and the wooden seat of the chair sticky. In between retrieving the grapes he stabbed wickedly at her clit with his tongue.

He captured the last one, withdrew it with a voluptuous swirl of his tongue and swallowed it. He turned his attention to her clitoris and while her sex-lips were still held open by the other man, stimulated it deftly. Isabel cried out as she came, the sound echoing eerily off the stone walls.

She bore down on the seat to prolong the tingling waves of pleasure, barely aware that both men had left her and moved over to the table. They discussed something in low voices and then one of them released her from her bonds and handed her a glass of wine.

She drank thankfully and wondered what was to come next. A few minutes later a blindfolded woman was led into the room, wearing only her stockings, garters and slippers. Her breasts were large and firm with prominent crimson nipples which reminded Isabel of raspberries.

She had wide hips and a narrow waist and her legs looked strong and shapely. The man with her was the red-haired man Isabel remembered from her last visit and she felt herself shifting on her seat as her vulva tingled in excited anticipation.

The woman was lifted onto the table and laid on her back with her legs hanging off the end. Isabel could see her lips were curved in a smile as she opened her thighs and waited for someone to pleasure her.

The red-haired man ignored them all as he unbuttoned his breeches and took out his organ. Isabel recalled the feel of it inside her as he used it to tantalizingly stroke the woman's vulva.

He rubbed it up and down her slippery sex-valley while she squirmed delightedly on the table. Isabel wondered if she was aware that they had an audience, or indeed whether she cared. He slid just the head inside her and then moved his hips to rotate it teasingly.

Suddenly she reached out and grabbed him around the waist, thrusting her pelvis upwards so his manhood slid deep into her. She became like a wild cat, hooking her legs around his thighs and clawing at his back with her nails.

He pinned her to the table with the weight of his body and held her wrists above her head, while shafting her vigorously. She struggled beneath him, jamming her hips upwards as much as she was able, to meet each hard thrust.

Isabel was mesmerized, her eyes never leaving the couple, watching his muscular buttocks in the skin-tight breeches and the woman's urgent response.

It seemed to go on a long time but she couldn't have said how long before he pumped his juices into her with shuddering intensity and she cried out her satisfaction in a long-drawn-out wail of pleasure, then subsided back onto the table and lay still.

The red-haired man pulled out of her and buttoned up his breeches before helping her to her feet and leading her from the room, still blindfolded, their mingled juices trickling down her thighs.

Isabel felt as though her quim was on fire as one of the men beckoned to her. She was bent over the table and her skirt unceremoniously thrown up to her waist. The dark man opened his breeches and she glanced over her shoulder to catch a glimpse of a large, thick phallus with a plum-like glans.

Evidently this was the wrong thing to do because he slapped her briskly across the buttocks, making her flinch. He must have enjoyed it because he slapped her several more times, so her backside smarted. She gritted her teeth, not enjoying it, but knowing that to protest would probably prolong her punishment.

Without warning he gave her what she wanted by plunging his organ into her, filling her up and stretching her to capacity. He began to thrust in and out of her with long, slow strokes which were intensely enjoyable.

The other man sank to the floor between her widely parted thighs and began to flick at her clitoris with his tongue. The two sources of pleasure seemed particularly enjoyable after her previous discomfort.

Her sex-flesh quickened around his member as he pumped steadily away. She could feel her climax mounting, spurred on by the deft strokes of the other man's tongue.

She came again, her internal muscles clenching around his phallus and then moaned in protest as he pulled out of her. But the slim man took his place and there was barely a break in the rhythm as he too began to shaft her while his companion sat between her legs and stroked the still throbbing bud of her clitoris with his forefinger.

Isabel lost track of time as she came again and again, taken in turn by the two men. At last she cried 'No more!' as her clitoris had become so sensitive from the number of orgasms she'd sustained, that further stimulation was painful.

The man penetrating her immediately quickened his pace and then erupted into her, while the other man wickedly squeezed the swollen, aching nub of flesh between his fingers and made her come for a final time.

She lacked the strength to rise from her position bent over the table, but the slim man lifted her upright and helped her to her chair. Another glass of wine and she was ready to leave.

She was escorted back to the chamber where she'd hung up her cloak and then they left her alone. She was just fastening it around her when another man came in. He was masked but she recognized him immediately and hastily drew up her hood and turned her face away.

'We meet again,' he greeted her, catching hold of the edge of her cloak and opening it to reveal the disarray of her gown and her barely-covered breasts. She tried to pull away, but he caught her around the waist and tipped up her chin so she could see the glitter of his eyes through the holes in his mask.

'Don't leave just yet – it's been a long time, more's the pity, and seeing you last night after so long made me hot for you again.'

She wrenched free, looking at him with loathing.

'There'll be snowdrifts in hell before I ever let you touch me again,' she said icily. 'Stay away from me and those I love or I swear you'll be discovered in a back alley one night with a bullet through your heart.'

She gathered her cloak around her and swept from the room.

TWENTY-ONE

To Julia's surprise, Isabel suddenly became enthusiastic about visiting Bath and immediately began to make preparations. Julia thought that it hadn't taken her cousin long to start missing Captain Moore, but as she herself had never visited the city she was quite happy with the notion of staying there for a time.

'Perhaps Richard would like to accompany us,' Isabel suggested, contemplating the numerous gowns in her closet as she tried to decide which ones her maid should pack.

Julia wasn't sure she wanted him to go with them and demurred, but Isabel brushed aside her objections saying, 'You will need Richard to keep you company while I entertain Captain Moore and anyway, it will be safer to travel with a man.'

As Isabel never travelled without an entourage of armed outriders, Julia felt that Richard's protection would be somewhat superfluous.

'It may not suit him to leave London at the moment,' she protested.

'I think it will suit him to be wherever you are,' was Isabel's airy rejoinder.

Julia was still feeling rather cross with Richard, but he called on her that morning and presented her with a pretty posy of flowers and a book she'd expressed an interest in. She was touched by the gifts and felt herself better disposed towards him.

Isabel came to join them and immediately invited Richard to accompany them to Bath.

'When do you propose to go?' he asked.

'At the end of the week,' Isabel told him.

'I'd love to come, the only problem is that my father wishes me to travel to Yorkshire on business on his behalf, so my time is not mine to command until I've performed this service for him.'

'When does he wish you to leave?' enquired Julia.

'The day after tomorrow, but I could join you in Bath as soon as the business has been successfully executed. Unfortunately I have no way of knowing how long it will take.'

Isabel had to be content with that and left them alone together while she went to write to Captain Moore to tell him of their impending visit and to ask him to bespeak rooms for them at Bath's finest hotel.

As soon as she'd quitted the drawing room Richard took Julia's hand. 'As you weren't at the reception last night, am I to understand that you haven't forgiven me for my behaviour at your party? I admit it was churlish in the extreme. Tell me that it has made no difference to the way you feel about me.'

Touched, she hastened to assure him that was the case and that her absence from the reception was not significant. He squeezed her hand gratefully before continuing, 'It was most unfortunate that Varsey singled you out for attention, but I'm sure everyone will understand how it was – that you felt constrained to dance with him. My only fear is that he'll attempt to take advantage of the situation by forcing an acquaintance which can only be distasteful to you – not to mention doing untold harm to your reputation. It's a great relief to me that you're leaving London and will be safely out of his way.'

Julia's emotions at this speech were mixed. However much she might dislike Lord Varsey, she didn't want Richard – or indeed anyone – presuming to tell her how she must feel about him.

Something of this must have showed in her face because Richard went on, 'His relentless pursuit of any female who takes his fancy is well known in certain circles and his intentions are never honourable. Sadly, women's heads are so easily turned by flattery and admiration. I want you to give

131

me your word that you will have nothing to do with him in the future.'

'What has he done that makes you speak of him in this way?' she asked, trying to conceal her annoyance.

'Nothing I wish to impart to you. Trust me to have your best interests at heart and make me this promise.'

Julia's lips set in a mutinous line. 'You seem to have very little trust in my discretion.'

'You're an innocent – you know nothing of the world or of men.'

Julia felt it really was too much to have first Isabel and then Richard warn her off Lord Varsey, without proffering any valid reasons, just making dark allusions to his past.

She withdrew her hand and rose to her feet.

'You have no right to ask me to make any such promise,' she pointed out.

'I have the right of someone who loves you and doesn't wish to see you come to harm.'

'I assure you I will come to no harm from Lord Varsey.'

'Promise me!' he urged her, getting to his feet and seizing both her hands.

'I will not,' she replied with determination.

'Then I will know what to think.'

'You may think what you please,' she retorted. His face set in petulant lines, he picked up his hat and cane before turning back to face her.

'I can mean nothing to you that you treat me this way,' he told her.

'And I can mean nothing to you that you treat me as though I were a child, instead of your equal in years.'

Much vexed, she turned her back on him and after a few moments' silence heard him leave the room. The sound of him talking to Isabel in the hall did nothing to assuage her annoyance and she swept out intending to tell them that if they wanted to discuss her, they could do it in front of her.

But Isabel had already ushered him into the library and closed the door and Julia felt it would be an intrusion on her part to join them and instead decided to go riding until her anger had passed.

She sent word to the stables and then went upstairs to change. When she came back down and went outside, her horse was waiting for her. The groom helped her into the saddle and then prepared to follow her at a discreet distance as was his usual custom.

'I won't need you today,' she informed him.

'You can't ride alone, Mrs Calvert,' he protested, 'not in London.'

'Of course I can.'

'Lady Marchmont has told me to accompany you on your rides.'

'Has she indeed?' snapped Julia, wondering why everyone thought they had the right to tell her what to do. 'But not today, thank you.' She urged her horse into a walk and rode off without looking back.

It was a hot, humid day, with some heavy clouds gathering in the west. Julia felt oppressed and wondered how much of it was to do with the weather. Her life suddenly seemed very complicated and she had to blink hard to keep back a tear which threatened to fall as she wished that things were back the way they were when she and Charles had been living an idyllic life at Cumberley.

But she wouldn't think of Charles – it would do no good, it would only serve to make her feel much worse.

She entered the park and made for the quietest part, unwilling to encounter anyone she knew and have the burden of conversation thrust upon her.

There was no one else to be seen as she rode along a narrow path under the trees, her hand going to her neck to loosen her starched white cravat in the gathering heat.

For once there didn't seem to be any birds singing – they obviously felt as oppressed as she did. She reined in her horse and tethered it to a branch, before wandering through the trees and inhaling the scents of moss and bark gratefully.

She came to a fallen tree trunk in a grassy clearing and taking off her hat sank down onto it, thinking what bliss it was to be alone. In London solitude was hard to come by.

She turned sideways and lifted her feet onto the trunk, then rested her chin pensively on her knees. Was she wise to

133

go to Bath with Isabel? Perhaps she should return home to her solitary existence.

But somehow the idea didn't appeal. Before, when she'd been awaiting Charles' return on a daily basis, there had been comfort in anticipating their reunion, but now she'd been forced to confront the truth, she wasn't sure she wanted to go back to her secluded existence.

She closed her eyes and thought about Lord Varsey. There was no denying that the night of their party had been exciting and that somehow the danger had added spice to the encounter. Dreamily, she re-lived it, pressing her thighs together as she remembered the way he'd used his lips and tongue to pleasure her.

She was still ashamed of having watched Elizabeth and Thomas make love, but playing voyeur had undoubtedly fuelled the fire of her arousal.

The sound of a twig snapping as loudly as a pistol shot made her head jerk round to see Lord Varsey sauntering towards her.

TWENTY-TWO

The sight of the man she'd just been having such carnal thoughts about brought a hectic flush to Julia's cheeks. What was he doing here?

He was impeccably dressed as usual in a long-tailed bottle-green coat, skin-tight fawn riding breeches, gleaming black boots and a high-crowned beaver hat.

Fleetingly she wished she'd allowed the groom to follow her, but it was too late for such thoughts now.

Lord Varsey took off his hat and swept her a mocking bow.

'The beautiful Mrs Calvert in idyllic woodland setting – what a sight to delight the eyes.'

'Is this encounter a coincidence or have you been following me?' she asked, determined not to be thrown off balance by his sudden appearance.

'I confess I spotted you from a distance and thought I'd . . . er . . . pay my respects.' He lifted her hand, peeled the kid leather glove from it and pressed his lips to the palm. A shiver of sheer carnal pleasure rippled down Julia's spine, but she snatched her hand away.

'Well now that you've paid them perhaps you'd go and leave me to my reverie.'

'And waste an opportunity to taste the intoxicating delights of your delectable body – you mistake my character if you believe that.'

He sank onto the tree trunk beside her and wound a wayward ringlet of her golden hair which had escaped its pins around his finger. He used it to gently turn her face towards him and then kissed her softly on the lips. Instantly she was on fire and hated herself for it, but not as much as she hated him. She tried to pull away but his hand slipped around to the back of her neck and held her still.

His mouth was warm and persuasive on hers, seeking – or rather demanding – a response. Her senses reeled and she found herself kissing him back, while perspiration, formed in equal parts from the day's sultry heat and her own fast-mounting arousal, gathered in her cleavage.

She wanted to insist he go away and leave her to her thoughts – how could she try and make sense of the situation which had arisen while he was making love to her? She knew from past experience that his desire was an unstoppable force that wouldn't be denied and which had the power to arouse her to equal heights of passion.

Against her conscious will, her lips parted in treacherous response and his tongue flickered between them to touch her own. Her eyes fluttered closed and she kissed him back, suddenly hungry for the pleasure she knew he could give her.

They kissed for a long time, his hand tracing lazy arabesques on her back, smoothing over the velvet of her riding habit. Deftly, he undid her jacket and drew it from her arms and then unbuttoned her white lawn blouse to reveal her slip. He drew out her breasts, which were already aching for his touch, and took one rose-pink nipple in his mouth.

She closed her eyes as he circled it with the tip of his tongue, then sucked gently. The heat and moistness of his mouth made her senses reel and she moaned softly as he turned his attention to her other smooth-skinned orb, which like the first, immediately hardened under his touch.

When both breasts had been licked, sucked and nuzzled until her nipples were pebble-hard, he toyed with the puckered peaks with his gloved hands, making her feel as if there must be a direct line from her nipples to her sex because his caresses were already fanning the embers of the other night's passion into leaping flames.

He removed his gloves and coat and lifted her from the tree trunk, then undid the voluminous skirt of her riding habit, allowing it to fall to the grass around her booted ankles. He reached for the ribbon holding her pantalettes closed but she stopped him.

136

'Someone might come,' she murmured.

He ignored her and his hand slipped between her thighs to massage her vulva through the fragile cotton of her undergarment. She knew that the damp fabric revealed immediately how aroused she was and stepped back, closing her legs, unwilling to let him know how much his practised caresses affected her.

His other hand went behind her to clasp her buttocks, holding her in position as he lazily stroked her belly and mound with a seductive circular movement. He ran his hands caressingly up her thighs and over her buttocks and hips, moulding her taut flesh.

It was as if they were in the middle of the countryside, not in a park in the centre of the bustling metropolis. The only sound was a faint humid breeze stirring the leaves and the whinny of Julia's mare a few hundred yards away.

Her groin burnt with a slow fire which made her reckless. She tried to keep her thighs firmly together but her knees trembled with the effort of doing so and she felt as though the throbbing knot of her clitoris was about to explode.

He slid a finger into her moist, tingling delta and she moaned and parted her legs for him. He found the blunt point of her most sensitive part and stroked it.

A sensation akin to that of a firework going off in her brain sent a tingling wave of heat shooting through her slim body, drenching her in a dew of perspiration. His fingers moved knowingly over her bud and she had to clutch at his shoulders to stop herself sinking weakly to the floor.

'Aaaaaaaah,' she cried as a heady climax rippled throughout her, leaving her faint and breathless. He lifted her and laid her on the ground, swiftly pulling her pantalettes to her knees. They caught on her boots and he ripped them impatiently from her so she was naked below the waist except for her riding boots.

He lay down and pulled her over him so she was on her knees straddling his face, the lewd position sending her into hectic confusion. He was looking directly up into her vulva and began to glide his forefinger over the soft folds of her labia.

'Your sex reminds me of a deep-pink peony opening on a warm day,' he murmured. 'I can see the petals of your sex-lips slowly unfurling when I touch you. They're already dripping with your female nectar, waiting open and ready for me.'

His words made even more warm moisture form and trickle stealthily downwards. A drop gathered on the blunt point of her clitoris and he raised his head to lick it off, sending a shudder of carnality through her slender frame.

He pulled her downwards so her sex was close to his face, clasped her pale thighs and began to explore the slick folds and furrows with his tongue.

Lord Varsey traced the rim of her labia with his tongue, pausing to plunge it deep into her female core. Her hips began to move in languid circles as his tongue continued to thrust in and out of her, before eventually finding her clit and stimulating it until she gasped and moaned, her head falling back on her shoulders.

He took her bud between his lips and began to suck, drawing it into the warm velvet of his mouth. Julia was dizzy with sheer, unadulterated desire as he stabbed at it rhythmically with his tongue. She came in a sudden engulfing wave of heat, her back arching and her whole body shuddering into an ecstatic release.

The heat seemed to be intensifying and she was as hot as if she were running a fever. Her sex-juices were trickling down her thighs, mingling with her sweat until she felt drenched, both inside and out. There was a sudden flash of lightning followed a few seconds later by a distant crack of thunder, neither of which she really registered.

He slid out from where he had been lying between her thighs and knelt behind her, his hands finding her small, firm breasts and stroking them. She could feel the swollen end of his member nudging between her thighs and along her moist cleft until he located the entrance to her quim.

One determined thrust and he was inside her, his entry triggering another less intense climax which had her internal muscles rippling around his shaft.

Julia was so absorbed in her pleasure that she didn't notice that the sky was darkening rapidly, with glowering graphite clouds gathering overhead. It was only when huge drops of water began to spatter down onto her that she realized they were about to be caught in a rainstorm.

But she was too far gone to care and the idea of stopping and going in search of shelter didn't occur to her. Within a few seconds the water was torrenting down, drenching them both instantly.

To Julia the cooling rain felt wonderful, gurgling arousingly over her naked breasts, running in rivulets over her firm buttocks to surge around her heated vulva where Lord Varsey's member was penetrating her so satisfyingly.

They seemed to be kneeling there endlessly with hot, urgent pleasure washing upwards through their bodies while the rain washed downwards over them. At last his hands tightened over her breasts and he plunged his phallus in and out of her to a fast, staccato rhythm as he erupted with the force of a long dormant volcano.

Still entwined, they sank sideways to lie on the sodden ground, her bottom nestling against his groin. It was several minutes before she began to feel chilled, her white blouse sticking clammily to her skin.

She eased herself free and stood up, while Lord Varsey got to his knees and adjusted his clothing, ruefully examining his mud-stained breeches.

'My servants will assume I took a tumble from my horse,' he observed. 'The mortification of it will be beyond anything.' Julia was examining her ruined habit with horror – she would have had to have been dragged behind her horse for about a mile to have inflicted this sort of damage on her clothing.

'Whatever will I tell Isabel?' she said aloud, wondering how she could have been so lost to propriety and the possible consequences of her actions yet again. He glanced at her grass-stained, muddied attire.

'If you wish you can return with me to my house – I'm sure I can find you something else to change into,' he told her.

Julia turned to him. 'Garments one of your discarded mistresses left behind? And what would I tell my cousin when she enquired why I had left the house in one set of clothes and returned in another? Thank you, but no.'

He grinned at her. 'Tell her the truth. She's not your guardian and she doesn't – as far as I'm aware – hold your purse strings.'

'No, but I am a guest in her house and my behaviour reflects on her.'

'Lady Marchmont's own behaviour wouldn't stand close scrutiny,' he pointed out. Thinking that Isabel's affair with Captain Moore was her own business and nothing to do with Lord Varsey, Julia ignored him and stepped into her ruined habit, as the rain continued to pour down on them both.

She didn't need a mirror to tell her that she looked terrible. She wiped her face with a sodden handkerchief and pinned her hat into position and then retraced her steps to find her horse.

He followed her and she found his black stallion tethered near her mare. He helped her into the saddle and then she glanced down at him saying, 'Do not, I beg you, follow me. Take the path in the opposite direction and leave the park on that side. No one must see us together looking like this, or our folly will become common knowledge.'

She urged her mare into a trot, half expecting him to follow her, but thankfully there came no sound of horse hooves in pursuit.

Luckily the park was deserted but she attracted several curious glances as she rode along the streets back towards her cousin's house.

She'd hoped to reach the privacy of her bed-chamber without meeting anyone. It would be too much to hope that Isabel wouldn't hear that she'd returned from her ride covered in mud and soaked through. Julia knew how much servants gossiped and she was certain that the grooms would tell the indoor staff and that Isabel would receive a full report from her maid. Her cousin probably already knew she'd been out without a groom.

But unfortunately Isabel was crossing the hallway as Julia came in.

Isabel's hand flew to her throat in shock, making Julia

think she must look even worse than she imagined.

'Are you hurt? Have you been attacked?' asked Isabel faintly.

'No on both counts – I merely took a fall from my horse,' Julia told her, trying to edge round her to gain the stairs.

'But that mare is so placid and you're an accomplished horsewoman.'

'My attention wandered and a rabbit running across the path startled her,' elaborated Julia, ashamed of lying.

Isabel pulled herself together, hurried into the drawing room and tugged the bell cord. A footman appeared through the green baize door leading to the kitchens.

'Have water heated for a bath for Mrs Calvert,' Isabel bade him. 'And send her maid up to her room immediately.'

After Julia had bathed, Isabel insisted she lie down on her bed and alternately scolded her for going out without a groom and fussed over her, afraid that Julia's fall and drenching would bring back her illness.

By early evening Julia felt so unbelievably guilty that she'd caused Isabel such a lot of trouble and anxiety that she pretended she was going to have an early night so she could be alone.

She was so affected by it that she almost resolved never to see Lord Varsey again.

TWENTY-THREE

Their journey to Bath was undertaken in a procession of carriages holding what seemed to Julia to be a disproportionate number of servants and which was accompanied by several outriders.

'Won't the hotel have staff?' she asked, puzzled when she saw how many of her employees Isabel was taking with her.

'I would certainly hope so, but I wouldn't care to rely on them for my comfort,' was Isabel's airy reply.

Julia thought that her cousin must be the only person in the country to consider a stay at Bath's most luxurious hotel as threatening privation beyond belief. As well as her clothes, Isabel had had several changes of bed linen packed along with her own towels, tablecloths and napkins.

The hotel turned out to be very comfortable and the rooms allocated to them spacious and well appointed, but Isabel complained about the colour of the curtains in her bed-chamber and the fact that their sitting room was above one of the public rooms and they could hear a certain amount of activity below.

The rooms were filled with flowers, courtesy of Captain Moore, and he'd also arranged for a lavish bowl of fruit to be supplied. They had been there but half an hour and Isabel was supervising the unpacking of her possessions when word was sent up that Captain Moore had arrived to call on them.

'I can't see him yet,' exclaimed Isabel in dismay. 'I need time to rest, bathe, change and then have my maid dress my hair.'

'You can't send him away without seeing him,' objected Julia. 'The poor man would be devastated. He's undoubtedly been counting the days to your arrival.'

'Then you go down and see him. Tender my apologies and tell him that I'll be delighted to receive him this evening and that we'd like him to dine with us.'

Julia was perfectly happy to do as Isabel suggested. Pausing briefly to tidy her hair she descended the stairs to see him leap eagerly to his feet and then look over her shoulder in obvious expectation of seeing Isabel.

'I'm afraid I have to disappoint you,' Julia told him. 'Isabel has decided that the journey has wreaked such havoc on her appearance that it will take until tonight to repair the damage.'

His face fell, causing Julia to laugh and say, 'How very unflattering that you think me such a poor substitute.'

'I'm pleased to renew our acquaintance – really I am,' he hastened to assure her. 'But I've been awaiting the moment of seeing Isabel again so eagerly.'

'She asked me to invite you to dine with us if you don't have a previous engagement.'

'If I had I would cancel it without compunction,' he returned gallantly. 'As she isn't ready, perhaps you'd like me to take you for a walk around Bath and perhaps a visit to the Pump Room.'

'I'd love to. I'll just go and tell Isabel and put on my bonnet and spencer.'

Julia ran lightly upstairs and found her cousin lying on her bed, a rose-scented paste on her face. She had no objection to Julia going out with Captain Moore, but merely urged her to return in time to perform her evening toilette.

The hustle and bustle of Bath was almost as pronounced as that of the metropolis. Julia thought it a most elegant city and enjoyed her brief tour. They went to the Pump Room and Captain Moore procured her a glass of the water which was deemed to have many medicinal properties. She took a sip and grimaced at its taste, and nothing – not even her companion's teasing – would induce her to finish it.

'It's good for you – drink it up,' he urged her.

'Thank you, but I'm in excellent health,' she retorted. 'I don't need the curative powers of a glass of mineral water, whatever claims are made for it.'

'You mustn't waste it – every drop is precious,' he told her. She passed him the glass.

'Then you finish it,' she retorted sweetly. He grinned and declined to do so and instead took her to an inn for a refreshing pot of tea.

'Will Richard be joining us in Bath?' he asked as she tried to make the difficult decision between the many different cakes and fancies on offer.

'You want Isabel to yourself,' she accused him, laughingly.

'Not at all,' he protested. 'What man wouldn't want two beautiful ladies to escort? I'll be the envy of all Bath. And besides – at every ball, party or concert we attend, there'll be men clamouring for your attention. My fellow officers will offer me all manner of bribes for an introduction.'

'Richard hopes to join us in a few days. He has had to go into Yorkshire to perform a service for his father.'

'He's taking a big risk that your affections won't be usurped by someone in his absence. Let me press you to another cake.'

'I'm apprehensive that we shall find the ball in the Assembly Rooms rather dull compared to the ones we're used to in London,' said Isabel as they waited for Captain Moore to come and escort them to such a ball several evenings later.

'I'm sure it will be most enjoyable,' returned Julia. 'Are you not enjoying our stay here?'

'Yes, but I fear the amusements on offer will soon pall. So many people here are in their dotage that I suspect we'll both be doomed to dance with septuagenarians tonight.'

'If you mean Mr Ludlow, he's absolutely charming and I don't believe him to be a day over fifty-five.'

To Isabel's amusement, Julia had caught the eye of a regular visitor to the Pump Room who had managed to gain an introduction to them and somehow turned up everywhere they went. He was taking the waters for his gout, but that didn't stop him from pursuing Julia vigorously.

Julia herself was feeling rather listless, but was at great pains to conceal the fact from her cousin. She didn't want

Isabel to feel she had to return to London on her behalf, when the older woman was clearly enjoying Captain Moore's sexual attentions again.

The ball was rather dull. Other than one dance with Captain Moore, Julia didn't stand up with a single man under forty. She was just taking a refreshing turn in the corridor after the country dance when her heart suddenly leapt in her chest and she felt dizzy when she realized who was approaching her – Lord Varsey.

What could he be doing in Bath?

His appearance was so unexpected that she had great difficulty masking her confusion, but as he made his bow and she her curtsey she willed her heart to stop pounding so violently.

'Lord Varsey – this is an unexpected encounter indeed,' she greeted him, trying to speak casually and as if his presence was not causing an unnerving little twitch of sheer lust high up in her sex. 'Are you here to take the waters?'

'Hardly,' he replied. 'I'm here because you are.'

His blunt admission took her by surprise.

'How did you know I was in Bath?'

'It wasn't difficult to find out. An enquiry by one of my servants was all that it took.'

'Should I be flattered?'

'You may be anything you wish as long as you have the next dance with me.'

Julia hesitated. Her cousin had made her opinion of Lord Varsey very plain and Julia was unwilling to antagonize her by ignoring her advice to have nothing to do with him. But it was her own life to live as she saw fit and dancing with a man still in his sexual prime rather than her previous elderly partners would be a pleasure indeed.

Isabel and Captain Moore had vanished somewhere together and it was possible they wouldn't even see her with Lord Varsey. What harm could one dance do and, after all, no one in Bath really knew her.

Lord Varsey's close proximity as he waltzed her around the floor made her body respond in its usual way, so that within minutes the twitch in her sex had become a demanding pulse

145

which told her beyond a shadow of a doubt that she was as hungry for him as he obviously was for her.

'What do you think of Bath?' he asked, the prosaic question at odds with the pressure of his hand on her waist and the lascivious gleam in his eyes.

'Pleasant but . . . well . . . staid.'

'You think so, do you? What would you say if I told you that there's another aspect to Bath, a much more exciting one.'

'I wouldn't believe you. The city's reputation is well known.'

'I'll show it to you if you wish.'

'Really? When?'

'Tonight.'

'I'm afraid I can't leave the ball with you. Isabel will expect me to return to the hotel with her when it's over.'

'Isabel need know nothing about it. I'll collect you from your hotel at midnight and take you to a party being held in the Roman Baths.'

Julia was intrigued. Who held parties which started at midnight? If the truth were known she craved some excitement after several days attending rather dull concerts and other sedate amusements. And anyway, once Isabel was closeted in her bed-chamber with Captain Moore she wouldn't know Julia had slipped out.

'Very well,' she agreed after some hesitation.

'I'll be waiting outside the hotel for you in my carriage – don't fail me and you shall taste pleasure such as you have never known before.'

A little frisson of licentious anticipation feathered down her spine and she trembled in his arms.

The waltz came to an end, he bowed, kissed her hand and vanished into the crowd.

TWENTY-FOUR

Leaving the hotel was a simple matter. A large party of guests was just returning from their evening's entertainment and were milling around the lobby as she slipped down the stairs. There were so many people there that one solitary woman passing through the doors occasioned no comment.

With her cloak drawn tightly around her Julia paused in the road, then the door of a carriage drawn up a few yards away swung silently open and she hurried towards it. She peered nervously inside to make sure it was Lord Varsey's carriage and not that of some stranger.

The sight of his silver-streaked dark hair reassured her and she hastened to get in. As soon as the door closed on them and they were alone he pulled her into his arms and kissed her.

The swaying of the carriage as it jolted along the road seemed to transmit itself to her female core. She was very aware of one of his muscular thighs pressed against her and the faint masculine scent of him made up of equal parts cologne, leather and smoke aroused her all the more.

He freed her breasts from her bodice and caressed them lazily, bending his head to press hard kisses on her cleavage, branding her with his passion. The journey was over all too soon and she straightened her clothing and pulled her cloak closed again as they drew to a halt outside the building.

No flambeaux or liveried doormen indicated that there was a party underway. No procession of carriages waited to let the occupants out in turn amid conversation and laughter; instead all was dark and silent.

'Are you sure there's a party being held here?' asked Julia

doubtfully as he opened the carriage door. It crossed her mind that he'd merely brought her here so they could be alone together. Perhaps he'd bribed a caretaker to let them in, but her desire for him was so strong that she didn't really care.

'I assure you that inside that building men and women are enjoying themselves in ways you won't have imagined in your wildest dreams.'

At that moment another carriage drew up behind theirs and a couple of shadowy figures slipped silently out and in through the door of the building which opened just wide enough to allow them to enter.

'Discretion is the watchword for a party such as this,' Lord Varsey told her, helping her to alight.

Inside was dimly lit, the air scented and steamy. He led the way down a long corridor between sconces of flickering candles to where a woman stood outside a door.

She was a delicately built brunette with large hazel eyes and an innocent expression. She was curiously attired in a simple white shift which only came down to her knees and left one breast and shoulder bare. Julia had seen similar clothing worn by Roman matrons in a book once, except that in those pictures the shifts had reached the ground and were more modestly draped to cover both breasts.

'First we must part company for a time, while you enjoy the pleasures of the ladies' steam room – the attendant will take good care of you. We'll meet again in the baths,' Lord Varsey told her. He walked off and left her feeling rather taken aback and not sure that to expect.

'Welcome,' said the attendant. 'My name is Anna. Please follow me.'

She led the way into a large, marble-floored room where steam hung densely in the air wreathing itself around the dozen or so women present, most of whom were naked or partially covered by a towel. Some lay on thick folded towels on marble tables and were being rubbed with scented oil, others lounged on benches set against the wall, sipping wine from silver goblets.

Julia was shocked to see two members of her own sex

embracing, the slender hand of one gently caressing her companion's bare breast.

Down three steps at one end of the room was a shallow pool in which a nude woman was being bathed by an attendant in a white shift similar to the one Julia's companion was wearing. The woman's breasts were above the water level and her pert nipples peeped from beneath a covering of suds, as one arm was gently lathered with a soapy sponge.

The heat, the steam eddying around smooth naked limbs like flimsy scraps of gauze, and the pervading air of sensual enjoyment made Julia feel warm, breathless and filled with anticipation.

'Come, let me help you undress,' Anna invited her. She led her into an antechamber to one side of the room and relieved her of her cloak, then moved behind her and began to unhook her gown. When Julia was naked and her clothes carefully hung up, Anna gave her a towel and Julia wrapped it around herself under her arms, feeling exposed, vulnerable and excited, all at the same time.

Anna led the way back into the main room and indicated that Julia should lie on one of the marble tables on her stomach. She climbed onto it, grateful for the folded towels between her and the cold, unyielding marble.

Anna loosened her towel so her back was exposed down to her waist and then picked up a silver flagon and poured some jasmine-scented oil into the palm of her hand. She began to rub it into Julia's left hand, working her way slowly up her arm to her shoulder.

It was an incredibly sensual experience and Julia closed her eyes and relaxed. When one arm was glistening with oil Anna turned her attention to the other, then worked her way across her shoulders and down her back. Julia felt like purring with delight and briefly wondered whether it would be possible to teach her maid, Jenny, to render the same service.

Her feet were next, each small toe, then her soles and heels massaged into squirming ecstasy, followed by her ankles and calves.

It was when Anna began to stroke her thighs that Julia became aware of a subtle change in her own reaction. Initially she had just felt deliciously pampered, but now Anna's ministrations began to reignite the heat in her groin evoked by Lord Varsey's earlier caresses.

She found herself furtively pressing her groin downwards in search of further stimulation and, as Anna's hands skimmed over the lower slopes of her bottom, she had to stop herself from pushing it demandingly upwards.

When she felt Anna parting the towel so her derrière was exposed she held her breath, then sighed with pleasure as a trickle of warm oil was poured into the cleft between her buttocks.

Anna massaged it in with firm, arousing strokes, coating the pert globes and letting her fingers slide into the glistening fissure between them. With each stroke she pulled them a little further apart and Julia felt her thighs opening slightly to allow Anna greater freedom of movement.

Her own honey was forming in her inner chamber and beginning to trickle onto her vulva to join the scented oil which had dribbled down there.

When Anna's fingers brushed over the outermost fronds of pale pubic floss, Julia felt an erotic tingling sensation feather into the highest reaches of her sex and make her yearn for a yet more intimate caress.

It seemed her wish was to be granted, because Anna turned her attention to Julia's inner thighs, her fingers sliding over the soft skin and just skimming over her damp pubic fuzz. Julia couldn't help herself, she spread her thighs in a blatant invitation and had to suppress a moan as Anna delved into the soft folds of her vulva.

Her outer labia were drawn gently apart and massaged until she could feel the blood pulsing urgently through her swollen tissues. Her inner sex-lips were similarly stroked until they ran with slippery moisture and were spread open around the throbbing bud of her clitoris.

Occasionally, Anna brushed lightly over the sensitive sliver of flesh and made Julia long for more sustained stimulation. The frustration was almost more than she could bear. She was aching with lust, her entire sex burning up with a heat that soon spread to her belly.

She ground her pubis against the towel beneath it, wishing there was nothing between her and the hard table top so she could bear down and stimulate herself on the cold marble until she came.

When Anna rubbed the pads of her first two fingers backwards and forwards over the throbbing bud, Julia nearly cried out. The fingers began to move rhythmically, sending hectic tinglings of hot, urgent pleasure coursing through Julia's veins.

She'd forgotten that she was in full view of a dozen or so other women being touched intimately by a member of her own sex in such a public way, forgotten even that Lord Varsey was somewhere in the building perhaps enjoying similar ministrations, all she was aware of was her own rapidly mounting pleasure.

She came in a sudden ecstatic series of spasms which rippled through her again and again and left her covered in a fine film of perspiration as well as a residue of the scented oil.

She seemed to lie there, her eyes closed, her cheek pressed against the towel, for an eternity until gradually her consciousness of the here and now returned and then a fiery blush spread through her body as she realized she'd just allowed herself to be manually stimulated to orgasm by one woman while presumably being watched by several others.

'Drink,' Anna's soft voice urged her. 'You must be thirsty.' Julia's eyes fluttered open to see the attendant offering her a goblet of wine and she took it, her eyes downcast, and drank deeply of the cooling liquid.

When at last she ventured to glance upwards, she saw that that, amazingly, none of the other women seemed to be taking the slightest notice of her and were all concerned with their own pleasure.

A couple of them were being similarly massaged, three more were in the pool entwined in an erotic embrace which made it difficult to tell who was touching whom where, and the couple who'd been lounging on a bench were now lying facing each other, their hands busy between each other's thighs.

Anna had crossed the room and was refilling the flagon of oil from a larger vessel, biting her lower lip in concentration.

She returned carrying a sponge and a bar of rose-coloured soap to say, 'Now I shall bathe you.' Julia gathered her towel around her and followed Anna to the pool, where she allowed the towel to slip to the floor and then sat on the steps with her feet in the water. It was pleasantly warm and she waited while Anna rubbed the cake of soap over the sponge to work up a rich lather.

She soaped Julia's arms and shoulders before gently sponging her breasts and belly, then her back. It was a pleasantly languid experience to be treated in such a way, with nothing to do but sit back and enjoy it.

Anna covered her in foam, pausing to run the sponge over Julia's mound in an arousing circular movement which had Julia aching to open her thighs as wide as she could.

When her entire body was covered in suds she slipped into the pool and immersed herself up to her neck. When she emerged, Anna patted her dry with a clean towel, then helped her into a sleeveless silk shift which only fell to her knees.

'If you're ready, I'll conduct you to the party,' she said.

Her knees trembling with anticipation, Julia followed her from the room.

TWENTY-FIVE

Julia was unprepared for the sight which met her eyes when she entered the room. Naked and semi-naked men and women were in and around the pool in couples and groups, sipping from goblets of wine and conversing just as if they were at a more conventional social gathering.

Except that at more conventional social gatherings women didn't display their female charms with such a shocking disregard for modesty and men didn't stand around with erections like drawn swords.

It was all a bit much for Julia and she sank onto a marble bench in the shadows just inside the door. An attendant glided over and silently proffered her a goblet of wine. She took it and gulped some gratefully down, wondering what she was doing here.

From her vantage point she recognized a couple of people whom she'd seen earlier in the assembly rooms when they'd been behaving with the usual decorum and restraint she was used to seeing in Bath society.

Now in complete contrast, the woman who'd been sitting sedately with the chaperones idly surveying the dancing through her lorgnette, was perched on the edge of the pool wearing only a thin silk shift which the water had rendered totally transparent.

It clung to her breasts, accentuating their lush roundness, her vermilion nipples pushing against the fabric like ripe autumn berries. Her thighs were lasciviously splayed to reveal a thick thatch of dark pubic hair and a man standing in the water had his face buried between them.

An admiral Julia had noticed at supper, a man of

commanding presence, was now caressing the naked breasts of a haughty beauty in a royal-blue velvet turban, his huge erection slapping against his belly. Oddly, he was wearing his admiral's hat at a jaunty angle, as if keen to retain the dignity of his rank even in such incongruous surroundings.

She caught sight of Lord Varsey in the centre of the pool, his broad shoulders and naked chest with its sprinkling of dark hairs glistening with drops of water. One of the women he was talking to pulled his head down and kissed him, making Julia bristle with indignation.

How dare he bring her to a party and then stand in a blatant embrace with another woman right in front of her?

He must have felt the force of her scrutiny because he looked up, caught sight of her and then said something to the woman who released him with what was obviously some regret.

He swam over to the edge of the pool and hoisted himself out, magnificent in his nakedness. It was the first time Julia had set eyes on him without his clothes and the sight made her mouth go dry.

'I didn't see you there,' he greeted her.

'Obviously not,' she retorted. 'A past mistress? Or is she still current?'

He grinned down at her. 'Jealous?' he enquired.

'No, I leave such primitive emotions to you.'

He scooped her up and sat down on the marble bench with her on his knee.

'You're the only woman who interests me at this moment,' he told her.

She could feel his erection hot and hard under her and was unable to stop herself wriggling on it. It was directly beneath her sex and she was very aware that there was only a fine film of silk between it and the heated tissues of her vulva. His hand closed on one of her breasts and caressed it through her shift.

'I like you wearing so little,' he murmured, his touch sending bolts of red hot desire shooting directly to her quim. With a huge effort of will she pushed his hand away.

154

'Not in front of all these people,' she murmured. He threw back his head and laughed.

'Look around you – what do you see?'

'Licentious behaviour the like of which I've never seen before.'

'Do you really think anyone's interested in what we're doing? They all have their own pleasure on their minds.'

It was true that things seemed to be hotting up. Two women, one a naked brunette and one a redhead in a pair of soaked muslin pantalettes, led a man to some cushions against the wall and encouraged him to lie down on his back.

The redhead straddled his groin and took his semi-erect manhood in her hand. She caressed it into full tumescence, while she stroked one of her own pert breasts with her other hand.

The brunette watched while kneeling behind the man's head and running her hands over his chest, her eyes on her companion's breasts.

The redhead used the man's burgeoning manhood to stimulate herself through her pantalettes. She stroked herself slowly and rhythmically, letting the swollen glans slide over the sodden material.

He reached up to clasp the opulent breasts of the woman kneeling behind him, kneading and squeezing the ample globes fervently. She bent down and kissed him on the mouth, her voluptuous bottom thrusting towards Julia and Lord Varsey. Her buttocks were candle-white, the skin smooth and satiny, the cleft between them well delineated.

The redhead began to lower herself onto the man's straining member, but as she was still wearing her pantalettes his entry was limited. Julia watched curiously as the fine muslin was stretched to its fullest extent.

He thrust his hips impatiently upwards with the obvious intention of breaching the fabric, but he thrust in vain; it didn't tear. The redhead smiled at him tauntingly and moved her pelvis in an erotic circular motion.

He leant forward, grasped the pantalettes in two hands and wrenched a gaping hole in them, then grabbed her by the hips and jammed her downwards. Her gasp was audible across the room, seeming to echo from the walls. She began to rise and fall on the phallus piercing her so determinedly, her breasts bobbing alluringly.

The brunette adjusted her position so she was kneeling astride the man's face. Julia caught a glimpse of his tongue, then he plunged it into her and began to lick his way over the intricate folds of her vulva.

They seemed completely unconcerned that there were other people in the room; they might have been alone for all the notice they took of anyone else.

Julia was reminded of the night she'd spied on Elizabeth and Thomas making love on her bed and found that her reaction was much the same.

Warm moisture began to gather in her quim and she felt the first stealthy trickle of it dampening her silk shift. She hoped that Lord Varsey wouldn't notice and draw the correct conclusion that she was finding being a voyeur exciting.

While she was engrossed in the lewd scenario being played out in front of them, he slipped his hand up her skirt and caressed her bare thighs.

It seemed pointless to stop him. The trio who'd claimed her attention were enacting only one of a number of carnal encounters taking place and most people were participating rather than observing.

When she felt the tips of his long fingers brush over her pubic floss she shivered with barely suppressed desire. He eased her thighs apart and toyed with the soft flesh of her vulva, exploring her hidden furrows and overlapping folds.

He tickled her clitoris with the tip of one finger, instantly turning her into a bubbling cauldron of anticipatory passion. There was now no hiding the fact that her juices had soaked through her shift and dampened his thigh.

He slid one finger slowly inside her, moving it so it pressed against the walls of her slippery, velvet inner chamber. It aroused her without satisfying her and she felt a desperate, aching urge to have his member inside her.

She shifted position to bear down on it and he drew her shift up to her waist and lifted her so she was straddling his thighs. She held onto his shoulders and raised herself while he positioned his member at the dripping entrance to her quim.

She took it inside her an inch at a time, revelling in its satisfying length, feeling herself stretched to capacity. He weighed her breasts in his hands, the pads of his thumbs circling her nipples, while she moved above him.

The unusual position made her feel penetrated to her very core and she enjoyed the sensation of being in control. The unreal quality which pervaded the night imbued their love-making with a dream-like languor.

It seemed to go on a long time and then Lord Varsey slipped his hand between her thighs to stimulate the deliciously tingling bud of her clit. Hot waves of pleasure washed through her and she quickened her movements on his throbbing rod. She came in a shuddering surge of release, her back arching and her head dropping back. He grabbed her by the hips and thrust strongly upwards, then came himself with a loud groan.

When Julia came back to reality she glanced around the room somewhat shamefacedly to see if anyone was watching them, but by now most of their fellow guests were involved in their own licentious activities and no one appeared to be looking their way.

She slid from his knee and pulled her shift down to conceal their mingled juices trickling down her inner thighs.

'I must go,' she murmured.

'Go?' he repeated. 'But the evening has only just begun.'

TWENTY-SIX

Lord Varsey took Julia's hand and led her to the pool.

'Now we shall swim,' he announced.

'I don't know how,' she admitted, wondering how many women he knew who could swim – it didn't usually form part of a female education.

'Then I won't take you out of your depth,' he promised, 'but you must taste the delights of amorous dalliance in water, while we're here.'

She allowed herself to be persuaded, a flicker of libidinous sensation in her quim indicating that her carnal appetite was not yet fully satisfied.

The water was warm and felt like satin against her bare limbs. It weighted the fine silk of her shift so the flimsy garment moulded itself to her slender form, emphasizing the swell of her breasts and hips.

It was rendered transparent so her rose-pink nipples were barely veiled and she hurried to submerge herself up to her neck rather than exhibit herself to all the men present.

But Lord Varsey had other ideas. He lifted her in his arms and held her so she felt as though she was floating on the surface of the water. She was very conscious of the way her breasts and mound formed three erotic islands and hoped no one else had noticed. Beneath her one of his hands caressed her bottom and the rear reaches of her private parts, arousing her all over again.

They were joined by one of the most beautiful women Julia had ever seen.

'This is Estelle,' Lord Varsey introduced her. 'Estelle, this is Julia.' As it wasn't possible to curtsey, Julia inclined her head, feeling faintly ridiculous and wondering if the other woman was another of Lord Varsey's mistresses, past or present.

Estelle's striking Titian hair was piled up in an intricate style threaded through with pearls. She had long, slanting dark eyes, high cheekbones and a full, rosebud mouth.

Only her bare shoulders were visible above the surface of the water and they were white and seductive below the slender ivory column of her throat. Julia could smell her perfume, a heady and exotic scent which floated around her in the steamy atmosphere.

'I'm delighted to meet you, Julia,' Estelle greeted her, her voice soft and husky. 'Lord Varsey has spoken of you to me.' Her eyes roamed the length of Julia's body where she lay in the water. 'How young and lovely you are. Tell me – have you been shocked by what you've seen tonight?'

The unexpected question took Julia aback and she wasn't sure what to reply. Eventually she said, 'I didn't expect to find such a gathering in Bath.'

Estelle ran her long, beautifully manicured nails down Julia's cheek and then slowly along her arm. Her touch made Julia shiver, but it wasn't a shiver of repugnance – far from it, in fact.

'Some people find that normal society doesn't answer their needs, they require more – much more,' said Estelle. 'Are you such a person?'

'I . . . I don't know,' Julia answered honestly.

'Some of them like to attend a party or reception where they behave according to the conventions, knowing that a couple of hours later they'll be enjoying a very different type of social event. The dullness of one heightens the pleasure of the other. Here you may act according to your desires with no fear of censure. Have you ever had another woman bring you to orgasm before tonight?'

Julia blushed to the roots of her guinea-gold hair. She felt at a disadvantage lying on the surface of the water while conversing on such a subject, particularly as Lord Varsey hadn't ceased his arousing caresses. Clutching his shoulders, she let her feet sink to the bottom and stood upright.

'Were you watching?' she asked.

Estelle laughed and shook her head. 'No, but it was part of tonight's entertainment that all the ladies should be pleasured thus on arrival. I was myself. Women are very adept at pleasing each other – after all, we know what we enjoy ourselves.'

Lord Varsey signalled to one of the attendants and the girl brought over a tray holding three goblets of wine. The three of them stood in the warm water incongruously sipping their drinks.

'Has Lord Varsey told you that there are men here tonight from whom you may request any form of gratification that you desire?' continued Estelle.

Julia shot a startled glance at him, but he merely looked amused.

'No, he hasn't. Is he one of them?'

Estelle laughed out loud, her head falling back on her slender neck to exhibit the smooth lines of her throat. Her laugh was low and musical and rippled gently over the surface of the water.

'No – or at least not to my knowledge,' she said at last. 'The men in question are the ones in the loin cloths.'

Julia had noticed that several men were thus attired, but hadn't realized that this was to distinguish them from the other males present. 'Lord Varsey is always more intent on gratifying his own desires,' added Estelle.

Julia's suspicion that the other woman had at some stage been Lord Varsey's mistress was instantly confirmed. Was this still the case?

'I'm desolated by your opinion of me,' he said. 'I'd always assumed that I was gratifying both of us.'

'You were,' agreed Estelle, shooting him a sultry look from under her thick lashes, 'but that was incidental. It isn't in your nature to put anyone's pleasure before your own. When I suggested that you make love to another man while I watched, and then you both make love to me, you declined.'

'You were asking me to go against my most fundamental nature,' he protested. 'Anyway, these men are being well paid to do whatever is asked of them.'

'You mean you would have done as I suggested if I'd offered to pay you?' Estelle raised one perfectly arched brow, her narrow eyes dancing with amusement.

'Certainly not – I'm a wealthy man and have no need of payment.'

'But your purpose in introducing me to Julia tonight was undoubtedly in the hope of persuading us to both make love to you at the same time.'

Julia's jaw almost dropped open and she wondered how many more times tonight she was going to be shocked. Was it true? Her eyes flew to Lord Varsey's face, but his expression was unreadable.

'Is that what you had in mind?' she demanded of him.

'Possibly,' he returned, unperturbed by the accusatory expression on her face.

'Perhaps Julia would like to engage the services of one of the male attendants,' purred Estelle, turning to her. 'If you don't wish to have an audience there are rooms here where you may be private, although many people find being observed adds greatly to the excitement. Imagine the joy of having a man who'll do anything – anything at all – to pleasure you. These men are all well trained, they can keep a woman in ecstasy for hours. And their stamina is matchless, they can perform all night if necessary. Wouldn't you like to experience such sexual pleasure at least once in your life?'

Her husky voice was hypnotic, hinting at untold carnal delights. Julia felt her sex flesh quickening at the lewd suggestion and hoped her excitement didn't show on her face.

'I've requested one myself,' Estelle went on. 'Would you like to watch us?'

The idea made Julia horribly conscious that warm honey was dripping out of her into the water lapping so sensually at her body. Her mouth was too dry to reply and she had to swallow and then clear her throat.

'W . . . watch you?' she stuttered, then felt like a complete fool for not managing to say anything less idiotic.

'Mmm – watch us. Then you can decide for yourself whether you wish to do the same.'

The idea of paying a man for his sexual services was a

completely new one to Julia. She knew there were women for whom sex was a financial transaction, but she'd never suspected that there were men who treated it in the same way.

She felt as if she was in a foreign country where the customs were completely strange to her and she was struggling to make sense of the simplest things.

But disturbingly, her innate response was one of intense arousal and a prurient desire to witness Estelle's coupling with her paid lover. Something of her feelings must have shown on her face because Estelle smiled and murmured, 'Come.'

She waded slowly towards the edge of the pool, leaving Julia staring after her and then glancing back at Lord Varsey in total confusion. He gave her an impassive look which merely added to her uncertainty.

Estelle ascended the steps from the pool revealing that her only covering was a silk slip which fell from her waist to her ankles and which, like Julia's, was totally transparent after its immersion in water.

Her derrière was a stunning sight, full and heart-shaped, swaying seductively as she left the pool. Like a woman in a trance Julia followed her, dimly aware that Lord Varsey was just behind her.

Estelle led the way to a room off the pool room where the only furniture consisted of two piles of large cushions, one in the centre of the marble floor and the other pile against the wall.

On the cushions in the centre of the room lounged a beautiful young man with curling brown hair and a strong, muscular body, wearing a loin cloth which barely concealed his private parts. Dark hair covered his chest and belly and arrowed down from his navel as if signposting his manhood.

Estelle stood with her hands on her hips surveying him, then turned towards Julia.

'This is James. He's beautiful, isn't he?' she said softly. Julia saw her breasts for the first time and marvelled at their voluptuous lushness. The coral-tipped orbs were large, firm and ivory-skinned and jutted proudly above Estelle's narrow waist, making Julia feel that her own slim figure was child-like in comparison.

James obviously found them as alluring as she did because to her embarrassment she distinctly saw his member rearing up beneath his loin cloth until the cotton garment was bulging impressively.

Her cheeks were suffused with hot colour which deepened when she saw that Lord Varsey too was paying tribute to Estelle's loveliness with a similar shifting of virile flesh, but as he was naked his was even more apparent.

'Why don't you two make yourselves comfortable over there?' Estelle invited them huskily, indicating the cushions against the wall.

She sashayed seductively over to James who rose to his feet and kissed her hand, then kissed his way up her arm to her mouth. It was a long embrace which had Julia holding her breath. James caressed Estelle's back and shoulders, stroking her smooth white skin; then, still kissing her, he lifted her in his arms and laid her on the cushions.

His hands glided arousingly over her body, moulding her breasts, toying with her coral-tinged nipples until they hardened to terracotta points. He stroked her thighs and bottom over the damp silk. One hand found the swelling of her mound with its covering of dark red hair and massaged it gently, making her sigh and close her eyes.

His lingering exploration had the effect of making her look like a contented, petted cat. He continued to massage her mound until gradually, an inch at a time, she parted her thighs. He delved gently between them and stroked her vulva through the veil of silk.

Julia was aware of a throbbing itch high up in her own sex and wished it was *her* vulva James was touching with such sensitivity. He began a rhythmic stimulation of Estelle's clitoris, rubbing it with two fingers while she began to move her hips in time to his touch.

Watching Estelle approach orgasm made Julia feel faint as she imagined the sensations the other woman was experiencing. She had to fight the urge to touch herself in the same way as a delicate flush tinted Estelle's pale skin and then she let

163

out a long, low moan and her body convulsed into a climax.

James withdrew his hand from between Estelle's thighs and removed her slip so she was lying there completely naked. Julia expected him to strip off his loin cloth and thrust into the Titian-haired beauty, but instead he began his gentle stroking of her body again, until the last throes of her orgasm had long died away.

He arranged her with her legs wide apart and her knees bent and then knelt between her thighs. He lowered his head so only his curling brown hair was visible and began an oral exploration of her private parts which had Julia squirming on her cushions wishing he was ministering to her in such a way.

She cast a sidelong glance at Lord Varsey, who was lolling back on the cushions drinking his wine, his erection still rearing up huge and hard between his thighs.

James took a long time to bring Estelle to another climax using his lips and tongue, his hands busy on her body, arousing her with infinite skill. She came again and this time after the last spasms of pleasure had died away he stripped off his loincloth to reveal a magnificently swollen phallus. He entered her in one long slow thrust and bent his head to cover her glorious breasts with kisses.

Lord Varsey put down his glass and turned to Julia. Without a word he arranged her on her hands and knees. It was a few moments before she realized he planned to take her in that position and was about to protest that she didn't wish to make love with Estelle and James watching them. Unexpectedly he slid two fingers deep inside her in a lewd, carnal gesture of possession which made her gasp and the words catch unuttered in her throat.

She could tell that she was running with honeyed juices which flowed down his hand. She felt rudely skewered, particularly as he moved his fingers carelessly around inside her, making her moan with wanton need.

He pulled them from her with an obscene plopping noise, grasped her hips and plunged into her with no further preliminaries.

On the cushions in the centre of the room James was thrusting in and out of Estelle to a sensual, languid rhythm, but Lord Varsey's rough penetration of Julia was followed by a vigorous coupling which blotted out all consciousness of the other couple.

He fondled her breasts with one hand while the other went between her legs and found her clit, which he rubbed swiftly and without finesse.

Julia was assailed by powerful waves of raw sexuality which made her moan out loud and work her hips to meet each thrust. She felt shameless in her need and the force of their movements made her blonde hair come loose from its pins and tumble around her shoulders.

It was a fast and furious coupling which reduced her to the level of a rutting animal. Her wrists and fingers tingled and then went numb as a wave of libidinous heat swept over her and she came. Her internal muscles clutched at Lord Varsey's rock-hard member and his hand continued its determined stimulation of her clitoris. But the pressure felt painful on her over-sensitive bud so soon after a climax and she tried to push his hand away.

He resisted her attempts and rubbed harder. She came again with a low-pitched moan wrenched from the depths of her being, then again, crying out as her body was racked with convulsions so strong she felt she couldn't stand another moment of them.

He pumped inexorably in and out of her, grabbing her by the hips to stop her collapsing weakly onto the cushions. She felt like a rag doll in his firm grasp, her limbs without strength, her body a tingling throbbing mass of carnal sensation.

She lost track of time and couldn't have said with any certainty whether it was minutes or hours before Lord Varsey erupted into her, his juices boiling over into her like a long-dormant volcano.

When at last he withdrew she collapsed weakly onto the cushions, her eyes closed, her breathing ragged. She was only dimly aware that in the centre of the room James and Estelle were still moving together.

When eventually she forced open her eyes she knew she had to return to the hotel as quickly as possible before she slipped into an exhausted sleep and woke up at goodness knows what time.

It was all she could do not to doze off in the carriage and she was so desperate to reach her room that she didn't spare a thought for what it must look like to the hotel staff to have one of their female guests return alone just before dawn, a sated glaze in her eyes and her hair tumbling around her shoulders in disarray.

TWENTY-SEVEN

It was almost noon when Julia awoke the following day, yawning and still sleepy but with a feeling of languorous contentment. She found Isabel in their sitting room flicking through a periodical.

'You must have been tired,' Isabel greeted her. 'I've never known you to sleep so late.'

'Perhaps the journey here caught up with me at last,' replied Julia, aware that she was heavy-eyed.

'Shall we descend to the dining room for some lunch? Or shall we see if we can procure you some breakfast?'

'I'll forego breakfast in favour of lunch.'

'I have a hankering after a new bonnet and perhaps another parasol, so I thought we might see what Bath has to offer in the way of milliners.'

'That's a good idea,' said Julia absently, aware of a languid ache in her sex and a certain tenderness of her clitoris.

'Are you feeling well?' enquired Isabel, looking concerned.

'Yes, quite well, thank you. Why do you ask?'

'You seem abstracted. Is it that you're missing Richard?'

In fact Julia had barely given Richard a moment's thought since their arrival in Bath.

'Perhaps. Shall we go down to lunch – I must confess I'm hungry,' she prevaricated.

Two hours later they strolled through the centre of Bath examining the bonnets on offer in the windows of the fashionable shops. Isabel spotted a chic creation adorned with emerald green ribbons and they went inside so she could try it on.

Once inside she found another two bonnets which took her fancy and she spent a considerable amount of time trying them and discussing their various merits with the woman serving her.

Slightly bored, Julia wandered to the door which had been thrown open to allow the afternoon sunlight and warm breeze into the shop. She stood in the doorway, gently swinging her reticule and allowing her mind to wander back over the events of last night.

'Hello, Julia.' She started when she was hailed by a husky voice. Looking up she saw Estelle was sitting in an open carriage which had drawn up a few yards away.

'Estelle – good afternoon.' Blushing a little at her last memory of the other woman, Julia went over to her. Estelle looked ravishing in a gown of aqua watered silk worn with a tight-fitting spencer of French blue. She was holding a parasol of matching aqua silk to screen her ivory complexion from the sun's coarsening rays.

Estelle smiled down at her. 'Did you enjoy yourself last night?' she asked.

Julia's blush deepened and she looked down at the ground before replying.

'Very much,' she murmured.

'You went before trying out one of the attendants,' continued Estelle. 'Were you not tempted to follow my example?'

Julia looked hastily around to see if anyone was within earshot, but thankfully no one was.

'I was too tired,' she admitted.

'Lord Varsey can be very fatiguing,' she agreed. 'All vigour but very little subtlety.'

'Have . . . have you known him long?' asked Julia.

'Years,' Estelle informed her. 'More years than I care to remember.'

'*Julia*!'

Looking round Julia was taken aback to see Isabel standing in the shop doorway, an expression of horror on her face.

'Your companion awaits you,' said Estelle, looking amused. 'We must meet again soon. Drive on,' she added to her coachman.

Puzzled by Isabel's reaction Julia hurried over to her.

'Are you out of your mind?' hissed Isabel, taking her arm and leading her in the opposite direction to the one taken by Estelle.

'Whatever's the matter?' asked Julia, puzzled.

'What can you possibly be thinking of to engage the most notorious courtesan in England in conversation in the middle of the street?'

Estelle a *courtesan*?

'Perhaps you'd be good enough to tell me where you made her acquaintance, because it certainly wasn't through me or any of my friends.' Isabel's tone was icy in the extreme.

Julia struggled for a reply, but nothing was forthcoming.

'Well?' demanded her cousin.

'I . . .'

At that moment Lord Varsey rounded the corner just in front of them and took off his hat before sweeping a low bow.

'Lady Marchmont. Mrs Calvert. How delightful to encounter you like this.' Had Lord Varsey been a man of any sensitivity Isabel's look would have withered him in his tracks, but he appeared impervious to it, as he continued, 'May I have the honour of escorting you to your destination?'

'You may not,' retorted Isabel in a tone which would have frozen tea poured boiling from the spout of a teapot. 'Come, Julia.'

Not daring to look at him Julia hastened to follow her cousin who remained ominously silent all the way back to their hotel. As soon as they were alone in their sitting room, Isabel wrenched off her bonnet and threw it viciously onto a chair.

'You little fool!' she cried. 'I warned you not to have anything to do with that man, but you've obviously not paid the slightest heed. If anyone saw you talking to . . . that woman, your reputation will be in tatters. Don't deny that he introduced you to her because I can't think there's any other way you could have met her. Where did he take you?'

'A party late last night,' admitted Julia.

Isabel sank into a chair and covered her eyes with one hand.

'I blame myself, I'd rather have let you rot in the country than have this happen. How long have you been seeing him?'

'For some time,' Julia confessed.

Isabel looked up, her heavy-lidded grey eyes full of concern.

'He'll break your heart and ruin you into the bargain. How deep are you in with him?'

'Pretty deep.'

Isabel rose to her feet and crossed the room. Taking one of her cousin's hands in hers she said, 'Give him up, I entreat you. Promise me you'll never speak to him again or have anything to do with him – all may not be lost.'

'I can't,' Julia replied, withdrawing her hand and turning away. She paced the room with agitated steps. 'Besides which, I don't see why I *should* give him up or what it has to do with you or anyone else.'

'I'm simply trying to save you from the consequences of your own folly.'

'Well don't.' Their eyes locked and Isabel opened her mouth to speak when there was a knock on the door.

'Who is it?' she called impatiently.

'It's Richard,' came the reply. 'May I come in?'

'I can't see him,' said Julia in a low voice.

Isabel paused and then said in an undertone, 'You may take a few minutes alone in your room to compose yourself, but then you should come back and be pleasant to Richard, as simple courtesy demands when it's you he's come to see.'

Julia hurried into her bed-chamber without another word. As she closed the door she heard Isabel open the one leading to the corridor and say, 'Richard! How wonderful to see you. Why didn't you let us know when you would be arriving?'

Alone in her room Julia sank onto the bed and closed her eyes. Why was life so unbearably complicated? She suddenly felt as though Richard was the last person she wanted to see. The situation was complex enough without his unexpected arrival.

But Isabel was right, she owed him the courtesy of greeting him pleasantly. She washed her hands and face and then sprinkled cologne on a handkerchief and dabbed her wrists and forehead. She examined her reflection in the looking glass and then took a deep breath and opened the door into the sitting room.

'Richard,' she greeted him. 'We weren't expecting you. How was your trip to Yorkshire?'

'Tedious, but I was able to conduct my father's business very quickly and make haste to join you here. What do you think of Bath?'

Had he always looked so young and callow? Compared to Lord Varsey he seemed a mere boy, lacking in assurance. She had thought his features sensitive, but today they looked weak and the set of his mouth sulky.

Somehow Julia got through the next hour exchanging pleasantries and then Richard rose to his feet.

'I must go – I have several things to do before tonight. Would you join me for dinner at my inn? I'm putting up at the Crown and I'm assured they serve a tolerable meal. Captain Moore too, of course.'

Isabel looked towards Julia who forced herself to say, 'Thank you – I can't speak for the others but I'd be delighted.'

'You may count on me and I know I speak for Captain Moore too,' Isabel assured him.

TWENTY-EIGHT

Dinner seemed interminable even though Captain Moore, undoubtedly primed by Isabel, excelled himself by keeping up a flow of lively, inconsequential conversation.

Julia was barely able to eat, weighed down by the knowledge that she was going to have to tell Richard it was over between them. Somehow her feelings had undergone a change and she knew she no longer wished to continue their affair.

It was a lowering reflection to acknowledge to herself that she'd become so enamoured of Lord Varsey that he was the only man she could bear to have make love to her and that she no longer desired Richard's caresses. How ever was she going to tell him?

At the end of the meal, Richard suggested they adjourn to the assembly rooms, where he'd been told that dancing would be in progress.

A flicker of alarm passed over Isabel's face.

'It's so comfortable here, it seems a pity to move,' she announced, obviously afraid of whom they might meet there. But Julia felt so constrained that she jumped at the chance.

'I'd love to – I yearn to dance,' she told the others, aware that the dictates of the day meant that Richard would only be able to claim two dances with her and the rest of the time she'd be able to escape his attentions. Isabel acquiesced reluctantly and they summoned the carriage.

Julia accepted Richard's invitation to join a set forming for a country dance and replied abstractedly to his conversation. The assembly rooms were no place for the difficult talk she needed to have with him – it would have to wait until tomorrow.

Their dance came to an end and they were leaving the floor when her heart leapt as she saw Lord Varsey strolling towards them. Richard saw him a few moments before he reached them.

'If that fellow has the effrontery to ask you to dance, just decline and keep walking,' he told her.

How dare he tell her what to do and decide whom she could and couldn't dance with? Julia was fuming at his high-handed manner.

'My dear Mrs Calvert,' Lord Varsey greeted her. 'Evening, Wortham.' Richard nodded coldly and would have continued walking but their way was barred. 'I believe the next waltz is ours,' he continued to Julia. She hesitated and felt Richard stiffen beside her.

Before she could reply Richard said, 'Mrs Calvert doesn't wish to dance with you.'

'Really?' He raised one eyebrow quizzically and held out his arm to her. She felt rather than saw Richard's disbelief when she took it.

He grabbed her hand and said urgently, 'If you dance with him I'll leave Bath tonight and it'll be over between us.' Julia was aware that people were looking at them. How could Richard put her in this position by behaving so possessively?

'I'm sorry, Richard,' she said in a low voice. His face went pale and he looked at her steadily for a few moments as if he couldn't quite believe what was happening. Then he turned on his heel and stalked off.

Julia caught sight of Isabel's shocked face on the other side of the room and then she allowed Lord Varsey to lead her onto the floor.

'It appears I've been put to a lot of trouble for nothing,' he commented.

'What do you mean?' she asked, puzzled.

'When young Wortham returns to London he'll discover that he's just been offered a coveted post to travel to Portugal as the secretary of the new ambassador.'

'Did you arrange it?'

'Certainly I did. It's a wonderful opportunity for a young man with his way to make in the world. His knowledge of the language and country from his stay there with his father will prove invaluable to the new ambassador. When I suggested it to him he wondered he hadn't thought of it himself.'

Julia felt a surge of sheer fury at his effrontery. It was one thing that she'd decided to end her affair with Richard, it was another that Lord Varsey should have tried to end it for her.

'He wouldn't have gone,' she informed him, as they twirled around the floor.

'He wouldn't have had any choice.'

'Of course he would.'

'You mistake the matter. Wortham doesn't have a guinea of his own, his father would have cut him off without a penny if he'd refused to take such a wonderful opportunity to begin a diplomatic career.'

At that moment Julia would gladly have stuck her embroidery scissors into Lord Varsey's leg if they'd been to hand. His arrogant assumption that his scheme would have worked and Richard be so easily detached from her, left her feeling insulted and degraded. A faint suspicion that Isabel was right merely served to infuriate her more.

They passed the rest of the dance in silence and then when it finished Julia sketched the barest curtsey and hurried back to Isabel who was talking with great animation to a stately-looking woman in a purple brocade gown.

Isabel glanced swiftly behind Julia and a brief expression of relief flitted across her face when she saw she was alone.

'May I present my cousin, Mrs Calvert,' she said to her companion. 'Julia, this is Lady Leicester. We were friends when we were girls, but have met rarely since she married and went to live in Scotland.'

Julia did her best to conceal her agitation and said pleasantly, 'I'm delighted to meet you. Which part of Scotland do you live in?'

'We no longer reside there – my health has become indifferent so we've moved to warmer climes and have a house in Gloucestershire.'

They chatted for a few more minutes and then Lady Leicester took her leave, having arranged to call on them the following day.

'Can we go?' Julia demanded of her cousin as soon as the other woman had gone.

'Certainly,' replied Isabel. 'Captain Moore is dancing with the wife of one of his fellow officers but we can depart as soon as the dance ends. What has happened – I take it you've told Richard that you no longer wish to see him?'

Julia nodded, her eyes downcast.

'I wish you hadn't. He was good for you and I believe he cared for you. Lord Varsey cares for no one but himself and if you think otherwise you're deluding yourself.'

'I've quarrelled with him,' admitted Julia.

'But you still won't give him up?'

Julia shook her head.

'He has you in his sexual thrall,' observed Isabel shrewdly. 'You're the latest in a long, long line and once he has you totally subjugated to his will he'll move on to the next one, leaving you with a broken heart and unable to hold up your head in society.'

'That can't happen,' retorted Julia.

'How can you be so sure?'

'Because my heart is already broken.'

It was a hot summer night and Julia lay with the window of her bed-chamber open, tossing and turning in the humid air, plagued by dreams which both disturbed and aroused her.

She dreamt she was sitting in an open carriage next to a man, but she wasn't sure who it was. She was unable to see his face because for some reason she had to look straight ahead and her bonnet prevented her from glancing sideways to ascertain his identity, but she could see his thighs, lean and well-muscled in his close-fitting breeches.

They were being driven along a country lane, passing under the spreading branches of a row of chestnut trees. The fields on either side of them beyond straggling hawthorn hedges were strewn with wild flowers and she could hear the muted humming of bees.

The man beside her put his leather-gloved hand on her knee and she shot a look of consternation at the driver's back, hoping he wouldn't glance behind him and see what a liberty was being taken with her. The gloved hand caressed her knee carelessly, then began to ease her skirt gradually upwards until the tops of her kid half-boots were revealed, then her calves in their silk stockings, then her garters and finally her bare knees.

She reached out and tried to pull her skirt down, but the man caught her wrists, pulled them behind her and secured them with the ties of her reticule.

Unable to prevent him, she could only watch as he raised her skirt to her waist to expose her pale thighs and ivory silk, loose-legged drawers. He pulled aside the crotch of the flimsy garment and examined the golden triangle of her silken fleece, making her face burn with shame.

She could feel the warm breeze wafting over her private parts, a strange and unaccustomed sensation. He hooked his fingers in the crotch of her drawers and yanked hard, tearing the silk and leaving her mound completely exposed to his gaze.

He pushed her thighs apart and traced the folds and furrows of her vulva with one finger with the impersonal interest of a botanist examining a rare species of flower.

When he touched the pink bud of her clitoris she jumped because a jolt of devastating carnal sensation shot along her nerve endings and made her feel hot and feverish. He slid a finger inside her and moved it slowly in and out of her hidden cavern until she was shifting on the seat, not sure whether she was trying to expel the finger probing her so rudely, or get it deeper inside her.

There was something unspeakably lewd about his treating her in such a way in an open carriage while the driver's back was to them and he was oblivious to what was taking place just behind him.

A wayward lick of lust assailed her loins and she was aware that her private parts were softening and moistening, while somewhere high up in her sex a pulse beat at a hectic rate.

When at last the man beside her removed his hand his leather-covered finger was slippery with her juices. He shouted a command and the driver pulled the horses to a halt in the leafy lane.

To Julia's chagrin he turned around in his seat and she saw it was Richard. She wasn't sure what he was doing driving a carriage dressed in servant's livery, or why he gave no indication that he'd ever seen her in his life before.

Instead he let his eyes roam over her wantonly parted thighs and brazenly displayed vulva, then to her horror he took his whip and ran the handle over her mound, parting the blonde floss and touching her most intimate folds.

The man beside her grasped the neckline of her dress and with a sudden rough gesture ripped it downwards, tearing it to the waist and leaving her breasts naked and vulnerable. Richard drew the whip over them and circled her nipples with it, while the man beside her resumed his exploration of her quim.

She felt completely at their mercy, unable to prevent them handling her in any way they chose, subjecting her to the most degrading caresses.

Richard climbed into the back of the carriage with them and the two men lifted her so she was kneeling on the seat, facing sideways. The man beside her unbuttoned his breeches and drew out a huge, erect phallus, heavily knobbed at the end.

With a crude gesture he indicated what he wanted her to do. Her bound hands making her awkward, she bent forward and took the glans between her lips. She ran the tip of her tongue over it and felt it throbbing, then commenced a diffident sucking.

His deep groan indicated that he was enjoying her ministrations and she sucked harder. His hands found her breasts and fondled them, squeezing them and toying with her nipples.

Richard seized her by the hips from behind and the next moment he threw her skirt up to her waist so her bare bottom was exposed to the sun and warm breeze. She was aware that there was a trickle of hot moisture on her inner thigh and hoped he hadn't noticed it.

She felt his manhood nudging determinedly between her legs and she parted them wider to facilitate his movements. He entered her in two jerky thrusts and then moved rapidly in and out of her, his thighs against her backside making a smacking noise which seemed out of place among the usual sounds of the countryside on a summer's afternoon.

She lost track of time as she continued to use her lips and tongue on the phallus of one man and enjoy the vigorous shafting of another. To her shame she felt her arousal mounting until she trembled with an overwhelming desire to climax.

Richard suddenly quickened his strokes and dragged her back against him hard, before erupting into her with three last staccato thrusts. She was almost there and the slightest touch on her tingling bud would have sent her toppling over the brink, but he pulled out of her immediately with an obscene sucking sound.

The other man lifted her head from where it was bent between his thighs and she knelt up again, biting her lip with frustration, wishing she'd managed to attain her own satisfaction. She wondered what they were going to do with her next as she was bent forward over the seat.

Richard used the handle of the whip to trace the cleft between her buttocks and then to delve into her sticky delta. He drew it smoothly back and forward over her clitoris, rubbing the swollen bud with a firm, insistent pressure.

The stimulation made her gasp and her breathing became rapid and shallow. It was only as she neared the point of no return that she was seized by the absolute conviction that as soon as she climaxed he'd use the horse whip to spank her across her bare bottom.

The dreadful notion made her clench her internal muscles and try to hold back, sure that if she didn't come she'd escape this humiliating punishment. But he just laughed softly and increased the pressure. She tried to jam her thighs together, but the other man held them apart and even worse, bent his head and began to nibble her right buttock, his mouth warm and persuasive on her skin.

She held her breath as she felt the warm wave which signalled her climax begin to break over her. With a loud, choking cry she came, and great rippling surges of pleasure swept through her slender body leaving her weak and trembling.

The handle of the whip slid an inch or two inside her and pressed on the front wall of her inner chamber. For some reason this prolonged her pleasure and she was panting and gasping as though she'd run a race when he withdrew it again, just as the last trembling convulsion receded.

Richard stood up behind her and she felt the whiplash trail across her bottom as he measured his stroke, while the other man held her still. She heard the whistling sound it made as it slashed through the air and then heard her own scream . . .

Julia woke up and sat upright in bed, drenched in perspiration, her heart beating so loudly she was sure everyone in the hotel must be able to hear it.

She threw the covers back and went over to the open window, breathing in the cool night air and holding her nightgown away from her damp skin.

Oh, Charles, she called silently to the breeze. Why did you have to leave me?

TWENTY-NINE

While Julia and Isabel were waiting for Lady Leicester to pay her promised morning call the following day, Julia told Isabel that she intended returning to London as soon as she could make travelling arrangements. She outlined her intention of opening up her own town house, sending for some of her servants from Cumberley and engaging others.

Isabel's expression was a study in consternation.

'But why?' she asked. 'I thought you were happy staying with me.'

'I am, but it isn't fair to you to remain under your roof while carrying on a liaison you've made it clear you disapprove of.'

'I'm only thinking of your welfare,' murmured Isabel defensively.

Julia leant forward and took one of her cousin's hands. 'I know and I'm grateful, but I can no sooner stop seeing Lord Varsey than I can stop the sun rising in the east. If I'm your guest, my conduct will reflect on you and while I'm prepared to risk a scandal myself, I have no right to embroil you in one.'

'Please, Julia, stop and consider your proposed course of action. You can't live alone and without the chaperonage of a respectable older woman – you are not yet twenty.'

'You live alone,' pointed out Julia.

'I'm older than you and a widow.' As soon as the words were out of her mouth Isabel bit her lip, obviously wishing she could take them back. 'I'm sorry,' she said. 'I spoke without thinking.'

'Oh Isabel, I'm well aware that I'm neither a wife nor a

widow. Don't try to dissuade me from what I plan to do – I can't stay with you and you know that every time I leave to meet Lord Varsey I'm causing you untold anxiety.'

'Better that than this reckless behaviour. If you're determined to return to London I shall take you; your own house can't possibly be ready for you to live there until it has been cleaned and aired.'

'You can't leave Bath so soon after arriving. Imagine Captain Moore's disappointment. I wouldn't dream of imposing on you in such a way – I shall hire my own conveyance.'

Their conversation was interrupted by the arrival of Lady Leicester. Julia was grateful for the fact that the conversation centred on the other two women's shared memories, so she herself need only nod and smile occasionally.

While Lady Leicester was there a servant entered with Lord Varsey's card on a silver tray. Isabel took one look and directed the servant to tell him that Mrs Calvert was not receiving visitors.

This was exactly what Julia herself would have said, given the opportunity. She might admit her inability to break off her liaison with Lord Varsey, but she planned to keep him at arms' length for a while to punish him for his unwarranted interference in her affair with Richard.

Nevertheless she had great difficulty restraining her anger at her cousin's high-handed manner. As soon as Lady Leicester had taken her leave, Julia went into her bedroom and came out tying the ribbons of her bonnet.

'Where are you going?' asked Isabel.

'For a walk,' retorted Julia, and left the room before Isabel could say another word.

She didn't notice in what direction she walked or the fact that her furious pace had her skirts swirling around her ankles in a flurry of lilac silk. She only knew that she was angry with everyone – Isabel, Richard and Lord Varsey. Why were they all so hell-bent on imposing their wills on her as if she didn't have a mind of her own?

It had also occurred to her that she wasn't altogether sure how to go about hiring a carriage to take her back to London.

Such a necessity had never arisen before. She supposed she could enquire at their hotel, but she was aware that it might occasion some comment as Isabel's various conveyances were in the hotel's coach house.

The sound of rapid footsteps just behind her didn't penetrate her consciousness. It was only when he drew level with her and caught her arm that she became aware that Lord Varsey had been right behind her.

'My dear Julia, please, I beg you, slow down. This pace is unbecoming for a man of my stature.'

'Then walk at your own pace and leave me to walk at mine,' she snapped, trying to shake off his restraining hand, but he merely tightened his trip.

'Was it your decision to deny me, or your redoubtable cousin's?'

'What difference does it make?' she asked coldly, stopping and turning to face him.

'A great deal.'

'It was mine.'

'And why, may I ask, did you not wish to see me? I thought we had reached an understanding.'

'Why on earth would you have thought that?'

'Because every time I touch you, you become instantly ready for dalliance. Your cavern runs with honeyed moisture, and your thighs splay ready for my entrance.'

The colour rushed to Julia's pale cheeks and she had to suppress a strong desire to slap him.

'I don't see that the fact I respond to you physically means that you have to interfere in my life,' she blazed.

'Ah – that's it,' he said thoughtfully, his sloe-dark eyes amused beneath their thick lashes. 'I told you that I wouldn't share you – or at least not unless I choose to for my own gratification. Most women would be flattered to have a man go to so much trouble on their behalf. Look upon it as a service I rendered you and think more kindly of me.'

It suddenly occurred to Julia that he might be the very person to tell her how to go about hiring a carriage to take her back to London. She could then repair immediately to her own house, and closet herself away until she was ready to

182

face the world again on her own terms.

She began to walk again, but at a much slower pace this time.

'There is a service you could render me which might go some way towards appeasing me,' she told him.

'Name it, but I warn you that if it involves keeping away from you, you'll ask in vain.'

'I wish to return to London before Isabel. Where should I enquire about hiring a carriage?'

'Surely Lady Marchmont will let you use one of her conveyances?'

'I don't wish to impose on her.'

'When do you want to travel?'

'As soon as possible.'

'Then, if you wish, I'll escort you back to your hotel and pick you up there, shall we say in an hour?'

'Will you take me to where I may speak to someone about hiring a carriage?'

'No, I'll carry you back to London in mine.'

Julia was completely taken aback and not sure what to say. Her immediate reaction was to refuse. He was one of the people she was trying to get away from, but a few seconds' reflection indicated that the scheme had many things in its favour.

She could leave at once, thus limiting the amount of time Isabel had to expostulate, and her safety would be assured with him to protect her, far more so than if she hired outriders. Once established in her own house she could do as she chose without having to answer to anyone. She would just have to be careful that no one saw her getting into the carriage with him.

'Very well,' she told him. 'I accept your kind offer.'

Isabel, as Julia had predicted, was practically beside herself when Julia confessed her intention. As Jenny hurried to pack her mistress' clothing, Isabel tried every argument in her power to persuade her cousin that such a course of action was reckless, but Julia was not to be swayed.

'Discretion is everything – please don't pursue such a

foolhardy course of action,' Isabel beseeched her.

'It's not foolhardy, I'm merely taking up residence in my own house,' Julia pointed out.

At last, when Julia showed no sign of listening to her, Isabel played her final card. 'Very well – you may see Lord Varsey under my roof,' she conceded and sank onto a sofa as if the effort of making such a concession had exhausted her.

Julia sat next to her and kissed her on the cheek.

'I'm well aware what it must have cost you to say that,' she murmured. 'But really, Isabel, I wouldn't be comfortable with the situation. This way you may wash your hands of me and disclaim any responsibility for my behaviour.'

At last her bags were packed and a porter summoned to carry them downstairs. As there was no room for Jenny in the carriage, Isabel offered to bring her back when she returned in a few days.

As Julia picked up her cloak, Isabel said, 'Should there be any problem with your house, or you decide that it isn't habitable, go at once to Marchmont House and send me word.' The cousins kissed and then Julia hurried downstairs to meet Lord Varsey.

THIRTY

Julia half expected Lord Varsey to begin some form of amorous dalliance in the carriage, but instead, much to her amazement, he stretched out his long legs in front of him and fell asleep.

She studied him for a while, her eyes lingering on his broad shoulders under his waisted navy-blue coat and the powerful muscles of his thighs in his fawn breeches. Even asleep his body held a mesmerizing sexual menace that made her aware of a sneaky little lick of lust in her sex which she struggled to damp down.

He was a man obviously well versed in the highways and byways of sexual dalliance and at this particular point in her life she was ready to experience them all, anything rather than focus on the emptiness of a life without Charles.

But no sooner had the memory of Charles presented itself than she forced herself to think of something else and began to consider all the things she would have to do to render the town house habitable after it had been empty for so long.

She felt ill qualified for the task ahead. True, she had been mistress of Cumberley these last two years, but the servants had all been there a long time and the house ran like clockwork, with or without her.

It would probably be best to send word to the housekeeper and butler that they should journey to London with as many of her staff as they deemed necessary and leave it up to them to hire any others. She knew there was a caretaker living in the basement, but he was unlikely to be of much help to her, other than to let her in.

The journey seemed interminable and she tried unsuccessfully to doze, wishing she had something to occupy herself.

Around dinner time they stopped at a posting house to change horses and order a meal. Julia wasn't hungry and only managed a glass of wine and a piece of chicken breast with some peas, then reluctantly allowed her travelling companion to press her to a small slice of glazed fruit tart. He consumed a substantial amount of food washed down by several glasses of wine, then eyed her speculatively.

'Perhaps we should put up here for the night,' he suggested. 'You look tired.'

Julia wasn't about to throw caution to the winds quite so recklessly.

'On no account,' she said. 'I don't care how long after nightfall we arrive in London, I won't stay here.' Rather belatedly it occurred to her that if he refused to travel any further there was very little she could do about it. But happily he seemed prepared to continue with their journey and they returned to the carriage.

Shortly after nightfall she fell asleep and awoke some time later to find her companion leaning back opposite her, studying her as carefully as she had studied him earlier. Moonlight streaming in through the window caught the silver streaks in his hair and the gleam of his dark eyes. Something in his expression alarmed her and for a few moments she wondered how wise she'd been to trust him to deliver her safely to her destination.

The feeling that all was not as it should be made her glance downwards and to her shock she saw that he'd unbuttoned her gown to the waist and drawn her breasts from her tightly-laced bodice so that they were completely exposed. With every jolt of the carriage they bobbed up and down and it was on her twin ivory orbs that his gaze was fixed.

In a swift reflex reaction she pulled her gown closed but he said in a tone of voice that made her shiver, 'Leave it.'

'I can't—'

'Leave it or I'll rip it off you and throw it from the window,' he promised her.

His threat had the usual effect of half-enraging, half-exciting her and she hesitated. He lifted his cane and used it to pull the silk of her gown free from her clutching hands.

'Such a dull journey needs enlivening,' he commented. 'Caress your breasts for me. Make your nipples as hard as berries and perhaps I'll reward you.'

She didn't want to obey such a cavalier order, but somehow she found her hand gliding over the firm curves of her satin-skinned peaks. She circled one jutting nipple with her forefinger, then clasped both breasts and lifted them, pushing them together to form a deep cleavage before toying languidly with her nipples again.

It was a strange and heady feeling to be stimulating herself in such a manner while he watched her, his gaze unfaltering. She wasn't sure whether it was her own caresses which were lighting a fire in her groin, or the knowledge that he was watching her avidly. But whichever it was she could feel her pantalettes becoming damp and her breathing ragged.

'Keep stroking your breasts with one hand and lift your skirts with the other,' he directed her. Trembling, she obeyed him. He frowned when he saw her pantalettes.

'I think it's time you stopped wearing undergarments,' he said. 'I'm tired of having to rip them from you. In future I want to find you naked beneath your skirts so I may see you or touch you whenever I please.'

He leant forward and wrenched them from her with one savage movement. A moment later they fluttered through the window, leaving her face burning in the darkness and her mound exposed to his scrutiny.

'Touch your quim,' he told her. 'Stimulate yourself until the sweet honey drips from your sex.'

Without making any conscious decision to do so, she found her hand dropping between her thighs and sliding over the slippery tissues of her outer sex-lips. The atmosphere in the carriage was thick with sexual ether, wrapping itself around them and drawing Julia into his erotic thrall.

She let her fingers glide around the entrance to her hidden chamber and then into the furrow between her outer and inner labia. She allowed them to drift over her clitoris and a

187

dark, heady jolt of sensation shot outwards from the sensitive nub and made her nerve-endings tingle.

She delved into her own private parts and slipped two fingers in as far as she could, marvelling at the way in which her channel felt like velvet. She could tell that she was already wet and getting more so by the moment as she explored the yielding, clutching folds.

She could feel her juices trickling onto her fingers as she swivelled them around and then slowly withdrew them. She began to work the head of her tingling bud between her finger and thumb, drawing back the hood and then letting it slip back again. She became so immersed in the hot waves of pleasure her own touch was provoking that she almost forgot Lord Varsey was watching her intently.

Her other hand continued to stroke her breasts, enjoying the firm, full softness of them in contrast to her thimble-hard nipples. She could tell that her climax was close and worked the hood of her clit faster.

Lord Varsey reached across and caught her wrist, preventing her from attaining her satisfaction. Slowly, his eyes on hers, he drew her dripping fingers into his mouth and sucked them clean, winding his tongue around them and making her catch her breath at the sheer eroticism of the gesture.

He released her hand, dropped to his knees and parted her outer sex-lips with his hands. She gasped as he used his tongue to probe her quim, delicately circling her internal membranes and then plunging it into her as far as it would go.

She wriggled forwards on the seat to give him greater access, biting her lip as he withdrew his tongue and flickered it tantalizingly over her swollen bud.

He licked his way along her valleys and then slowly ascended each and every ridge, tasting and pleasuring until she was almost delirious with delight.

At long last he took the plump point of her clitoris between his lips and sucked, tugging gently and stabbing at it rhythmically with the tip of his tongue.

'*Aaaaaah*!' Her cry of satisfaction echoed over the sound of the horses' hooves and the wheels jolting along the rutted road.

She buried her hand in his hair and jammed his face into her vulva as she came, writing on the seat as she welcomed the waves of carnal pleasure washing over her.

At last she closed her eyes and leant back as he got to his feet, dusted the knees of his breeches and sank back into his seat. He mopped his damp face with a pristine white lawn handkerchief and then unhurriedly undid his fly. His member sprang out, hard and ready.

'Come,' he invited her. She rose to her feet, holding her skirts around her waist and he turned her so her back was to him and helped position her over his phallus.

She steadied herself by holding onto the strap on one side of the carriage, but then the conveyance hit a particularly deep hole in the road and she sat down with far more force than she'd intended and cried out as she was pierced to her very core.

The rocking and jolting of the vehicle added vigour to their movements as he grasped her by the hips and she rose and fell on his engorged rod.

Julia wondered briefly if the driver or the groom sitting next to him on the box had the slightest idea that their employer was engaging in sexual congress as they drove through the night.

It was a heady sensation and added a dimension of wantonness to their coupling. It was impossible to control their rhythm or to slow down and all too soon Julia felt another climax approaching.

Lord Varsey suddenly dragged her down hard and she felt the bucking of his hips beneath her as he spurted his hot fluid into her sheath, then clasped her breasts and rested his head on her shoulder.

Eventually she stood awkwardly up and tidied her clothing before returning to her own seat. She must have dozed off because the next thing she was aware of was a cool draught on her face and the realization that they'd stopped moving.

Blinking blearily, she saw that the carriage had drawn to a halt outside an elegant house in a quiet London crescent.

'Are we here?' she asked, rubbing her eyes and looking quickly down to make sure he hadn't rearranged her clothing

189

again. But thankfully she was decent, though her gown was now crumpled enough to look beyond salvation.

He helped her alight, annoyingly looking as though he'd just come from the hands of his valet, then stood staring at the darkened house while the driver and groom unloaded her luggage.

'Is anyone expecting you?' he asked.

'No, I'll have to wake the caretaker.' She hesitated, suddenly not sure she'd been wise to arrive in the middle of the night with no warning. The caretaker would in all probability be alarmed to be woken at this time. She looked doubtfully at the bell, reluctant to pull it and half wishing herself back in Bath with Isabel.

Lord Varsey obviously had no such reservations because he seized it and pulled it vigorously. She heard its resounding jangle echo through the house and waited nervously for an irate servant to appear in his nightgown.

What if he didn't recognize her? She'd only met him once and that was some considerable time ago. He might refuse to let her in and then what would she do? There was no sign of life from within the house despite two more vigorous yanks on the bell.

Sighing, Lord Varsey handed her his hat and then descended the steps to the basement.

'What are you doing?' she asked nervously.

'Gaining entrance,' he replied.

'Don't—'

She spoke too late; her words were interrupted by the sound of shattering glass and then some fumbling and a door being shoved open. She glanced back at the carriage and saw both the driver and guard standing silently waiting. She had the distinct impression that nothing their master could do would surprise them.

She was glad of their presence, otherwise she would have been frightened to be waiting on the pavement alone at this hour. It seemed an eternity before she saw a dim, wavering light appear through the glass above the door. A few seconds later it opened to reveal Lord Varsey, a lighted candle in a candlestick in one hand and a candelabra in the other which he placed on the hall table and lit.

'Bring those boxes in,' he called to the two men and then stood back so she could enter.

'I don't think there's anyone here,' he told her. 'The basement's deserted, but I'll take a look in the servants' quarters.' He vanished up the dark staircase while she breathed in the depressing smell of stale air, now wishing with all her heart that she hadn't been so impetuous. All the furniture was covered with white dust sheets, which looked ghostly in the flickering light from the candles.

She looked into the drawing room while the two men carried in her luggage and piled it in the hallway. Just as in the hall, the furniture was all shrouded in white, but everything looked clean and she didn't see the thick layer of dust she'd been half expecting.

When at last Lord Varsey returned he said, 'There's no one here at the moment, but someone's been in residence fairly recently because there are some vegetables and other food in the kitchen.' Julia's heart sank, she hadn't bargained for being here completely alone, but she was determined not to let it show.

'Thank you so much for bringing me here,' she said politely, 'and for gaining entrance.'

'I can't leave you here on your own – anyone could get in through the basement door.'

'Would it be possible for one of your men to secure it?' she asked. He stepped outside and spoke to the guard who vanished obediently into the kitchen regions.

'Do you want me to stay with you until daylight?'

'Thank you, but no,' she returned politely.

'Then why don't you come and pass what's left of the night in my house, where there will be servants to prepare food and a bed for you.'

'You must know I can't, but thank you for the offer.'

They heard banging coming from below them and after a few minutes the guard reappeared, wiping his hands on his breeches.

'It's secured,' he told them and went back outside.

Lord Varsey pulled Julia into his arms and kissed her, his

body lean and hard against hers, his lips demanding. By the time he released her she could feel the rigidity of his erection against her belly.

She felt that the slightest encouragement on her part would have resulted in him taking her again on the floor of the hall but she suddenly felt weary and ready to get what sleep she could.

'Good night,' she said, stepping back. He left the house silently, pulling the door shut behind him.

THIRTY-ONE

When Julia awoke the next morning, much to her surprise it was almost noon. She'd been too tired the night before to do much more than remove her gown, pull the dust sheet from the bed in the master bedroom and roll herself in the coverlet.

She lay there looking around the room and noticed there were moth holes in the royal blue velvet curtains and that the paintwork was a little dingy, but other than that the room was in reasonable repair and had obviously been cleaned fairly recently.

A thick Turkish carpet covered most of the floor. It was woven in shades of dusky-blue and old rose on a cream background. The colours were slightly faded, but it was a beautiful carpet and its hues were echoed in the satin coverlet, currently wrapped around her like a cocoon.

She stretched and got out of bed, wishing she could ring the bell and have a maid appear. More than anything she wanted a warm bath, but had to content herself with a wash in cold water.

She opened one of her valises and pulled out the first day dress that came to hand. She had difficulty hooking it up and it was sadly crumpled after the journey. Although she spent ages trying, she was unable to arrange her hair in anything approaching a passable style and she wished fervently that she'd brought Jenny back with her.

She made her way downstairs, glancing into other rooms as she passed them and noticing that, like the master bedroom, they were all reasonably clean. Arrangements had obviously been made for someone to come in and look after everything, because there were only the finest traces of dust here and there and the floors had been recently swept.

She threw open several windows to let in some fresh air and then sat down to write a letter to the housekeeper at Cumberley. She was just about to put on her bonnet to go and post it when there was a knocking at the door.

When she opened it she was mortified to find Lord Varsey standing there. She was aware he'd never seen her looking so badly groomed and her hands flew to her hair which was already escaping from its pins. Behind him was a man in butler's livery waiting at the bottom of the steps holding what appeared to be a picnic hamper.

'Good afternoon,' Lord Varsey greeted her, walking past her into the hallway without waiting for an invitation to enter. 'Bring the hamper in, Scholes.'

Once in the hall, the door closed behind him, he said casually, 'I'm lending you Scholes for the day. Just tell him what you need in the way of staff and he'll arrange it – won't you, Scholes?'

Scholes bowed. 'It will be my pleasure, my lord.' He had a coldly handsome, expressionless face, but there was a knowing look in his pale-grey eyes which made Julia uncomfortable. She wondered if he knew that she was Lord Varsey's mistress and suspected that he did.

She could imagine the maids and other female household staff working with him finding him very attractive and vying for his attention. If he followed his master's example he was in all probability an accomplished seducer.

'Set Mrs Calvert's lunch out in the dining room, will you please.' The man bowed again and vanished down the hall. Lord Varsey turned to Julia. 'I can't stay, but I'll pick you up tonight at ten and take you out.'

'Where?'

He moved close to her and said, 'Somewhere you may experience pleasure of an intensity you have only ever dreamed about.'

Something in his tone made her shiver and she swallowed as her stomach lurched with anticipatory lust. She knew she should refuse, she had after all fled to London so she could be alone, but the lure of the heady pleasures of the flesh proved too strong for her and she remained silent. He turned and strolled back to the door.

She followed him saying, 'Thank you for lending me your butler – it's very kind of you.'

'It isn't kindness that motivates me. It wouldn't be in my interests to have you living here without servants – I like my women to be beautifully dressed, coiffed and perfumed and I dare say you've never dressed yourself before today in your entire life.' He cast a disparaging glance at her imperfect toilette as he spoke, then departed.

His words stung – how dare he refer to her as one of "my women" and be ungentlemanly enough to indicate that she was looking less than her best?

Scholes appeared behind her in the hall. 'Luncheon is served, madam,' he announced. She had a fleeting impression that his eyes flickered over her body, but when she looked directly at him, he was turning away.

He'd removed all the dust sheets and set a single place at one end of the massive oak dining table. A lavish selection of cold meats, fruit and crusty fresh bread was laid out, the very sight of which made her mouth water. He helped her silently to a large plateful and then left the room.

When he returned half an hour later he asked her how many staff she wished him to engage. Once again, she found his presence made her uncomfortable, but she told herself impatiently not to be so foolish.

'I'll leave it up to you,' she said, not sure how many were needed. 'I've written to my housekeeper at Cumberley asking her go come and bring staff from there, but it will be a few days before they'll be here. Take on as many as you think necessary to run a house of this size efficiently until then. Oh, and I must have an experienced ladies' maid by late afternoon.'

'Very well, madam.' His tone was respectful enough, but she thought she sensed a faint contempt emanating from him. As he left the room she hoped it wouldn't be long before her own household arrived to look after her.

★ ★ ★

Julia spent the afternoon exploring the house, a painful process because everywhere she looked there were reminders of Charles. The wardrobe in the master bedroom was full of his clothes and she took some of them out and buried her face in them.

She found his old toys in the nursery and sat examining them, trying to imagine him as a little boy. In the library she found a portrait of him that had been painted when he was twenty-one and which reduced her to tears as she gazed at it. She had a miniature of him which he'd presented her with on their engagement, but this picture had captured his likeness much more effectively.

She pulled a chair under it so she could see it at close quarters, then pressed her lips to the painted ones with tears streaming down her cheeks.

When she'd decided to move in, she hadn't considered that being there might have such an effect on her and cursed herself for not thinking the scheme through.

In recent months her primary aim had been to put Charles from her mind because of the grief her memories provoked. Far better to dwell on the wanton carnal pleasures Lord Varsey had introduced her to, than mourn for something she could never have back.

Her current lover might be a man for whom she had no real regard, but as long as he could effectively distract her from the loss of her beloved husband, she would let him lead her along the well-trodden path of debauchery.

A knock at the library door had her scrambling hastily down from the chair and dabbing her eyes with her handkerchief before she called, 'Come in.'

Despite her reservations about him, Scholes was obviously a miracle worker because he brought in a middle-aged woman with a plain but pleasant face and introduced her as Susan, her temporary ladies' maid.

Glad of the distraction she took the woman up to her bed-chamber, indicated her boxes and valises and asked her to unpack and press her clothing.

Determined to keep a grip on herself she went from room to room making notes of anything that required refurbishment.

Some of the curtains were shabby and several of the carpets threadbare. Although all the furniture was fine and costly and she knew that much of it had been in the family for years, she disliked some of it and thought she might buy some more to her taste for a couple of the rooms.

It would help fill her days to embark on a long-term plan to have the house redecorated. She would enlist Isabel's help; her cousin had excellent taste. Perhaps she should do one of the rooms in the fashionable Chinese style, with lacquered furniture and hand-painted silk hangings.

Julia managed to keep herself occupied until late afternoon and then went back to her bed-chamber to begin her preparations for the evening, determined to look her best.

She wasn't sure what to wear, but after Lord Varsey's jibe she eventually chose a stunning ballgown of jade-green silk with a lavishly embroidered train.

Susan helped her bathe and wash her hair, then dressed it in glossy ringlets which cascaded around her face to frame it becomingly. Into the golden curls the maid pinned two sweetly scented roses plucked freshly from the garden and then helped her apply a little discreet make-up.

Emeralds and a generous sprinkle of rose-scented French perfume added the finishing touches and, as she pirouetted in front of the looking glass, Julia was well pleased with her appearance.

Let Lord Varsey find anything amiss with her now.

THIRTY-TWO

When his carriage arrived to collect her, she deliberately kept him waiting twenty minutes. She'd hoped to infuriate him, but when she descended the stairs in a rustle of silk she found him sprawled in a chair in the drawing room, drinking a glass of wine and talking to Scholes, apparently unruffled by her tardiness.

He rose and kissed her hand.

'A vision of delight,' he greeted her. 'Does Mrs Calvert not look beautiful, Scholes?'

'Indeed, my lord.'

'But is she as obedient as she is beautiful? What do you think, Scholes?'

'I really couldn't say, my lord.'

'Well let's see, shall we?'

Julia was puzzled by the strange turn the conversation had taken. What did he mean, obedient? Also, she didn't think it altogether seemly for him to be discussing her with a servant as if she wasn't there.

'Lift your skirts,' he directed her. Julia thought she must have misheard him. Even Lord Varsey couldn't be so lost to decency as to make such an outrageous proposal in front of his butler.

She looked at him, saw the lascivious anticipation in his eyes and then glanced swiftly at Scholes, whose face was as expressionless as usual, but in whom she thought she detected a suppressed excitement. She hesitated, wondering whether to dismiss the man and demand of Lord Varsey whether she'd heard him correctly.

'Lift your skirts,' he repeated, proving beyond a shadow of

a doubt that he'd taken leave of his senses.

'You may go, Scholes,' she said swiftly, intending to tell Lord Varsey in no uncertain terms that she wouldn't tolerate such behaviour from him. But much to her surprise, instead of leaving the room, Scholes merely remained where he was, looking towards his master.

'This bodes ill, Scholes. She doesn't *seem* inclined to be obedient, does she?'

'Indeed not, my lord.'

Julia simply couldn't believe this was happening, particularly not when Lord Varsey bent down and took hold of the hem of her gown. Furiously, she slapped him across the face, turned on her heel and would have left the room, but at a nod from his master Scholes seized her by the arms from behind.

Her immediate reaction was to struggle, but she checked herself, unwilling to lose any more of her dignity than she already had.

'Tell him to release me,' she said through clenched teeth.

'That chair, I think,' said Lord Varsey, and to her horror, the butler dragged her over to an upright chair with a chintz seat and forced her to sit in it. Lord Varsey passed him a silk scarf and he tied her hands to the back of it so efficiently that Julia found herself wondering, even in her fury, how many other women he'd accorded similar treatment.

'Do you remember what I said to you on our journey here last night?' Lord Varsey asked her. She stared at him mutely, not sure what he was talking about.

'I told you that in future I wanted you to dispense with lingerie so that you might always be accessible to me,' he reminded her.

Julia's flushed cheeks became an even brighter shade of pink that he should speak to her so in front of someone else.

'We shall see if you've obeyed me.'

He bent down and raised her skirt to her waist to reveal her pretty white muslin pantalettes threaded through with pale-green ribbon.

He shook his head and murmured, 'I feared as much. Do you have a knife, Scholes?'

The butler moved in front of Julia and passed his master a

pocket knife. Her eyes widened as slowly and deliberately, Lord Varsey slid it under the waistband of the offending garment and began to slice his way steadily through the fine fabric so that it fell open to reveal first her belly, then her mound and finally her thighs.

She hung her head and thought she must be about to die of shame. How dare he treat her like this, stripping away every iota of self-respect along with her pantalettes? The two men stood and looked at her as if she were some sort of whore paid to display herself to their lewd gaze.

Lord Varsey took hold of one side of the ruined lingerie and pulled it from underneath her, before letting it flutter to the floor.

'Mrs Calvert has such a lovely fleece, soft as silk and pale as flax,' he remarked conversationally to his butler. 'She has a quim as beautiful as the rest of her too. Would you like to see it?'

'Very much, my lord.'

When she realized his intention she pressed her thighs together as hard as she could, but he forced them wide apart and displayed the intricate pink folds of her sex with the geniality of a horticulturist exhibiting a particularly fine species of flower to a fellow enthusiast.

Scholes studied her private parts at length, while Julia willed the earth to open and swallow the two men up, preferably in some hideously painful manner. She could scarcely believe she was sitting tied to a chair in the drawing room of her own town house, being forced to participate in this depraved erotic game.

'Is it not beautiful?' Lord Varsey released her and strolled to the sideboard where he refilled his glass from the decanter there. Julia closed her thighs so swiftly that they made a loud slapping sound which echoed obscenely around the room.

'Keep your legs apart so we may admire you,' he ordered her.

'Let me go at once!' she hissed, raising her head and glaring at him, thinking that as soon as she was free she'd take the poker from the fireplace and lay about him with it.

'Tsk, tsk. Your lack of obedience grieves me and I think I

shall have to punish you for it. Tie her ankles, Scholes.'

The butler produced two more silk scarves and knelt in front of her. Julia kicked out as hard as she could and caught him on the chest, sending him sprawling, but it availed her nothing except a fleeting satisfaction. He merely grunted, grabbed her feet and secured first one and then the other to the chair legs.

'Not only does Mrs Calvert have a beautiful quim, but it moistens at the slightest touch until it glistens with the sweetest honey.' Lord Varsey's voice was so dispassionate that he might have been describing the finer points of a horse. 'Would you like to see that?'

'I certainly would, my lord.'

It was possibly the worst moment of Julia's life as Lord Varsey took a sip of his drink, put his glass down, than ran his forefinger over the outer petals of her labia. The butler watched, his face wooden, as his master caressed every inch of Julia's vulva, toying with her sex-lips, parting them to expose the flaccid point of her clitoris and circling the entrance to her hidden chamber.

Scholes cleared his throat and licked his lips while Julia stared straight ahead and vowed revenge on her tormentor at the first possible opportunity.

When he brushed over her clitoris she was mortified to feel a hot little lash of excitement snake through her. She summoned every ounce of self-control, determined not to add to her humiliation by becoming aroused under such demeaning circumstances.

But it seemed that her body was in league with her lover against her, because however hard she struggled to remain cold and unmoved, his touch had its usual devastating effect and against her will, she felt herself becoming wet.

She bit her lip and tried to think about something else to distance herself from the proceedings, but he squeezed her clitoris with such careless expertise, working it between his finger and thumb, that it rapidly hardened to a plump point and her treacherous juices trickled stealthily from her body as if ashamed of their own part in the lewd scenario.

She couldn't bear to see the satisfaction on his face or the impassive concentration on that of the butler so she closed her eyes.

Perspiration gathered on her cleavage as her arousal mounted to the point where she could scarcely breathe. Despite the fact that the windows in the drawing room had been open all day, it felt stifling and airless.

Hot, urgent pleasure was coursing through her and every nerve-ending was tingling in wayward anticipation. When she felt the simmering sensation in her loins that indicated her climax was imminent, she bit her tongue so hard in an attempt to stop it that she could taste her own blood.

Her low moan of pleasure sounded as though it had been dragged from her as she spasmed into a climax which seemed to go on forever, before she spiralled slowly back to earth. She wanted to sob with humiliation that the butler had witnessed her degradation, but pride made her control herself.

She opened her eyes to see Lord Varsey drinking his wine, watching her idly. He took out a gold pocket watch and glanced at it before saying, 'There's still a little time before we have to leave. Would you like to see Mrs Calvert's breasts, Scholes?'

'It would be a great pleasure.'

'Perhaps you'd like to open her gown for her.'

'Certainly, my lord.'

Julia looked him in the eye and said icily, 'Don't you dare touch me,' but he ignored her and unfastened the front of her gown and exposed her pink-tipped breasts. Her face burned afresh at the way in which he devoured them with his eyes.

Lord Varsey sat on the edge of a table and stretched his long, booted legs in front of him.

'You may touch them if you wish,' he invited the butler casually, as if he had every right to make such an offer.

'Thank you, my lord.'

Julia inhaled sharply when the butler's cool hands lifted her breasts as if assessing their weight, then rolled her nipples between his finger and thumb. He spent a long time toying with the ivory-skinned orbs, savouring the feel of them and teasing her nipples to pebble-hard points.

She stared unseeingly ahead, trying to ignore the renewed trickle of moisture his touch was arousing. She felt as though someone had kindled a piece of tinder in her very core and it lay smouldering inside her, ready to burst into flames at any moment. Jagged darts of lust kept lancing from her breasts to her sex, even while she hated herself for finding the degrading scenario so shamingly erotic.

Rubbing her nipples with his thumbs, the butler glanced over his shoulder at his master.

'My lord.'

'Yes, Scholes?'

'I wonder if I might fondle her sex and bring her to a climax?'

'I think that after you've organized her household so efficiently, you deserve a reward,' Lord Varsey replied after a pause. 'But we have to leave in about ten minutes – is that long enough?'

'It should be, the nectar is dripping from her like juice from a ripe peach.'

'Very well.'

Scholes knelt in front of her and parted first her outer sex-lips and then her inner ones. Holding her open with one hand, he slid his forefinger inside her and tickled the wet satin of her sheath so that Julia couldn't help but squirm on the chair. His touch provoked the most delicious sensations which were as arousing as they were unwelcome.

She could feel her internal muscles clenching around the finger, eager for something more substantial inside her. She couldn't stop herself shifting further forward on the seat to allow him greater penetration. He tickled her relentlessly, turning her quim to molten lava and making her moan out loud.

When she felt she couldn't bear it a moment longer, he turned his attention to the swollen kernel of her clitoris which was standing proud from the overlapping folds which usually concealed it, obviously eager for more stimulation.

He stroked the shaft, making her quiver and grit her teeth as she willed him to rub it harder and give her the satisfaction she craved so much.

Lord Varsey took out his watch and glanced at it again and Julia was suddenly afraid that he would call a halt to the proceedings before she'd come, leaving her high and dry. Scholes quickened his movement, rubbing the hard little nub with the same rhythm she imagined he employed when polishing silver.

'*Aaaaaah*!' The cry was wrenched from her as her body was racked with spasms of sheer lascivious pleasure. Scholes plunged two fingers into her and moved them rapidly in and out, prolonging the agony and ecstasy of the climax.

He rose to his feet and dried his hand on a handkerchief, then used the same handkerchief to dab fastidiously between Julia's thighs, mopping up her copious juices.

Lord Varsey drained his glass of wine and levered himself to his feet.

'Time we were going,' he said pleasantly. 'Just one thing before we leave.'

He plucked the two white roses from her hair, ran his fingers over the stems as if checking for thorns, then slowly slid them inside her so that only the blooms were visible, nestling incongruously among the pink folds of her vulva. 'This will serve to remind you that in future I expect you to obey me and remain naked beneath your gowns. You may untie her, Scholes.'

Julia was now in such a state of trembling excitement that her earlier intention of wreaking bodily harm on his broad-shouldered person was forgotten. When Scholes released her she rubbed her wrists dazedly and rose unsteadily to her feet. Her skirts feel back around her ankles and she could feel the velvety petals of the roses against her own velvety petals and it aroused her all the more.

With trembling fingers she fastened the front of her gown, horribly aware that if Lord Varsey unbuttoned his fly and wanted to take her right there in front of the butler, she would have opened her legs to him with depraved eagerness.

Or if Scholes suggested bending her over the highly polished table and thrusting his phallus into her, her desire for sexual gratification would in all probability have been stronger than her sense of what was fitting.

'You may go, Scholes,' Lord Varsey directed him. 'Please return to your usual duties in my house.'

'Very good, my lord. Have a pleasant evening – you too madam,' he said, before bowing and withdrawing as if he'd just served them wine and cakes instead of tying the mistress of the house to a chair and making free with her most intimate parts.

When the door closed behind the butler, Lord Varsey turned to Julia and said, 'If you want to call a halt to the evening, now is the time to say so and I'll wish you good-night. I warn you that if you come with me you must do whatever I ask without question.'

Julia hesitated, but a libidinous bubbling inside her told her that her body had already made that decision.

'I'll come,' she said.

THIRTY-THREE

Lord Varsey ushered Julia out of the house and into his carriage, where he produced the same silk scarf Scholes had tied her hands with.

'You must be blindfolded until we arrive at our destination,' he told her. Remembering his earlier words about obedience, Julia refrained from protesting and let him bind it around her eyes.

When eventually the carriage drew to a halt and he helped her alight, she didn't have the faintest notion where they were. With his arm around her waist guiding her, she took a few hesitant steps and felt rough grass underfoot, then heard the creak of a door or gate. A moment later she was walking along what was obviously a path through a garden or park because plants and shrubs caught at her skirt and she could smell the heady scents of honeysuckle and sweet peas.

She stumbled a couple of times but he steadied her and after several minutes they stopped and she heard him knock on a door. Once inside it was noticeably cooler than the balmy night air outside and when she stretched out a hand it encountered cold, rough stone.

'Wait here a moment,' he told her and then she heard him conversing in a low voice with another man.

When he returned she felt his hands on the sash around her waist and then he raised her skirt at the front and tucked it into the sash. She wasn't sure if the man she'd heard Lord Varsey talking to was still in the room, but if he was she wondered what he thought about the fact that she had two roses nestling among the damp floss of her pubic fleece.

Lord Varsey took her arm and led her forward. She had the

impression that they passed through another door, because her skirts wafted against something on either side of her. The floor underfoot was hard and slightly uneven and her satin slippers made a faint slapping noise as she made her uncertain way over it.

She strained to hear the sounds of other people, half convinced that she was being paraded past a room of men, all staring at her exposed mound and the lewdly placed roses.

After her recent experience in her drawing room she felt beyond embarrassment and the idea that she was being silently observed added to her state of excitement.

'We're going to ascend a flight of stairs – stop and feel for the first step,' her companion directed her. She inched her foot cautiously forward and found it, then stumbled when she misjudged the height and stubbed her toe quite painfully. A moment later she felt herself swept into Lord Varsey's arms and he strode up the stairs carrying her easily.

He didn't put her down when they reached the top and she found being borne along in his arms much less anxiety-making than walking blindfold, afraid of falling.

Suddenly into the silence came a piercing shriek which made Julia's hair stand on end.

'What was that?' she gasped, clutching at the lapels of his coat. Another shriek followed the first and then a loud groan.

'Nothing that need concern us,' he told her, not even breaking stride.

'But it sounded like someone in terrible pain.'

He didn't reply and she was suddenly filled with dread. Perhaps she hadn't been wise to come here – what if he intended to beat her the way Lord Westbourne beat Elizabeth? She knew that some men enjoyed inflicting pain and fervently hoped he wasn't one of them.

So far he'd shown no inclination to hurt her, but perhaps Isabel's warnings had been intended to convey something more sinister than she'd imagined. But he could have done that just as easily in her drawing room as here. He could have had Scholes bend her over a chair and used his cane on her bare backside and there wouldn't have been a thing that she could have done about it.

He stopped and put her down then took her arm and led her through another door. She wished he'd remove the blindfold, she didn't know where they were or who else was present and it was unnerving her.

He pulled her arms above her head, then secured her hands to something which must be hanging from the ceiling. Now she felt totally vulnerable, unable to move and with her sex on display. He – or anyone else – could do with her as they chose and she'd be unable to stop them.

She heard the rustle of silk and realized another woman had entered the room, then a hand caressed her fleece, making her start and jerk away as far as her bonds would let her. There came a husky laugh and Julia smelt a heady exotic scent which she thought she recognised, but it took her a few moments to realize who it was – Estelle, the beautiful Titian-haired courtesan from the Roman Baths.

The same soft hand glided over her fleece again and she relaxed slightly, remaining still when the back of her gown was tucked into her sash too, so she was naked from the waist down except for her stockings, garters and satin slippers.

Caressing hands stroked her bottom, thighs and belly, soothing her jangled nerves and reminding her of the sensual massage she'd enjoyed two nights ago.

She thought she heard the sound of clothing being removed but couldn't be sure. Were there just the three of them in the room, or were there others present watching, perhaps waiting to join in?

Every nerve-ending felt highly sensitized and she was aware that high up in her quim was a pulsing itch which she knew would only be assuaged by the entry of a bone-hard phallus.

Was Lord Varsey now naked and erect, ready to steady her by the hips and thrust into her while Estelle continued to caress her? Would he take her from the front or behind and would Estelle watch enviously, wishing it were her being penetrated?

The roses were withdrawn from her quim one at a time and then she felt their scented petals brush against her cheek. Her thighs were parted and she waited breathlessly until warm lips pressed against her own sex-lips and kissed them.

She was sure it must be Estelle, the mouth felt so sweet and delicate as it moved over her vulva, the tip of a tongue flickering intoxicatingly over her slick, satiny folds.

Julia gave herself up to the heady delight of being pleasured in such a way and only half registered that someone – presumably Lord Varsey – was unfastening the front of her gown to expose her breasts.

He fondled them carelessly in complete contrast to the languorous oral exploration of her private parts, but somehow it only added to the pleasure she was experiencing. He pinched one nipple, making it harden to a swollen point, and then massaged both orbs, clasping them and covering them with his hands.

Estelle, meanwhile, had taken the throbbing knot of Julia's clitoris between her lips and was exerting a subtle pressure which made Julia push her hips forward eagerly. The pressure increased and she felt a heady rush of tingling heat just before she came in a glorious wave of pleasure.

She moaned softly and felt the warm mouth buried in her vulva withdrawn, to be replaced by the smooth, hard end of a phallus nudging between her labia from behind. She parted her thighs as widely as she could and he grasped her by the hips before thrusting smoothly into her.

It was a hot and breathless coupling which made her moan and writhe as she felt the unbearably urgent itch in her core abating. He caressed her breasts and belly, his other hand sliding down to cup her mound and stroke her clit as he moved urgently in and out of her honey-slick delta.

Julia wasn't sure what had happened to Estelle, but she soon forgot the other woman as she felt herself being worked towards another heady climax. For a long time the room seemed full of the scents and noises of raw, animal sex as she shoved her bottom back to meet each lengthy plunge.

He held her still as he changed the tempo to a series of swift, staccato thrusts which pierced her to her very core and made her cry out. Three last urgent movements and he discharged himself into her, sending her toppling over the edge into a dizzying valley of erotic sensation.

Her blindfold slipped slightly and she saw that they were in a bare stone chamber, furnished with only a deep cushioned sofa and a rough, rustic table. Several flaming torches burned in metal sconces set in the wall, casting a much more dramatic light than that of wax candles.

Estelle, the upper part of her face hidden behind a black velvet mask, was seated on the sofa with the skirts of her shimmering fuchsia-pink gown thrown up to her waist, her hand busy between her own milk-white thighs.

On the table were a curious array of objects which included several lengths of silk cord, a riding crop, a bunch of ostrich feathers, a leather belt with a heavy buckle and a chunk of marble carved in the shape of a phallus. There was also a flagon of wine and several goblets.

But she was only allowed a brief glimpse of her surroundings before the blindfold was pulled back into position and then Lord Varsey withdrew from her, replacing his member again with a single white rose. A few moments later she heard the sound of them both leaving the room and was sure she was alone.

It made her uneasy to be in such a vulnerable position and she hoped they'd return very soon. She hadn't heard the door close and hoped that it was at least pulled almost shut or she'd be visible to anyone passing. Twice she heard footsteps, but they went past without a pause, making her breathe a sigh of relief.

She was just mentally reliving the delicious sensation of being filled to capacity by her lover's huge phallus, when a noise from the direction of the door made her head jerk round, then a male voice drawled, 'Now there's a pretty sight.'

'Shh,' said another male voice from the same direction. 'Remember the rules.'

'Forgot – sorry,' returned the first voice and then there was the distinct sound of a hiccup. Julia was almost certain she knew the speaker, but wasn't sure where from.

She prayed that if it *was* someone she was acquainted with, he wouldn't recognize her, blindfolded as she was. She felt at such a disadvantage, unable to see the two men, while she was sure she could feel two pairs of eyes burning into her naked breasts, bottom and sex.

She heard booted feet crossing the floor and flinched as a rough hand squeezed her breasts and another was thrust between her thighs, pawing at her quim.

'You'll get us barred,' hissed the second voice.

'I don't care – it's too good an opportunity to miss – she's dripping wet.'

Julia was horrified to hear the distinct sound of him fumbling with his buttons and when she felt him brushing against her she raised her knee and rammed it as hard as she could where she guessed his groin to be.

She was rewarded by a yelp of pain and then he exclaimed, 'You vicious little bitch!'

She opened her mouth and screamed as loudly as she could and was relieved to hear the other man say urgently, 'We'd better go before someone comes.'

She heard the sound of them hurrying down the corridor and then there was the swish of silk and Estelle's husky voice saying, 'What on earth's the matter?'

'Two men came in and one of them handled me roughly,' she told her, 'but I thrust my knee where I thought it might do most damage. Please untie me.'

She felt Estelle pulling at her bonds and then mercifully her hands were free. She dragged her blindfold off and rubbed her wrists, only then noticing for the first time that they were almost numb.

Estelle went to close the door and then led her to the sofa.

'No one should have touched you,' she said. 'It's strictly forbidden and I shall have to report it. There are rules which must be adhered to and someone has broken them.'

'Where are we?' asked Julia, pulling her skirts free of her sash and fastening the front of her gown.

'You are not allowed to know that unless you become a member in your own right – you're here as Lord Varsey's guest.'

'Where is Lord Varsey?'

'He had something to attend to in another part of the mansion. Here, let me pour you some wine.'

She handed Julia a goblet of ruby-coloured claret and poured one for herself. The evening's events must have unnerved Julia, because she forgot her usual reserve and found herself asking, 'Is it true that you're a courtesan?'

Estelle laughed softly. 'Yes, it's true.'

'Then why do you come here?'

'You mean because I spend my time in carnal dalliance anyway?'

Julia blushed and nodded.

'My profession means that most of the time I have to accommodate men's whims and caprices, here they have to accommodate mine.' She smiled a sultry, alluring smile. 'And I have some very specific whims and caprices.' She ran the tip of one elegant forefinger around the top of her goblet and her long, slanting eyes glittered through the holes in her black velvet mask.

Julia suddenly felt exhausted and lay back against the cushions, murmuring, 'Will Lord Varsey be very long, do you think? I feel the need to seek my bed.'

'I think he has plans for you later.' It occurred to Julia that he might be pleasuring some other woman even as they spoke and the idea annoyed her.

'Is there any way I could return home now?' she asked.

'My carriage can take you, if you wish.'

'Will he be angered to find that I've left?'

'In all probability.' Their eyes met in perfect understanding.

'Then I'd be happy to accept your kind offer.'

THIRTY-FOUR

Several days later Julia was delighted to receive a call from Elizabeth. Her friend was in particularly good looks, her eyes sparkling and her cheeks touched with delicate pink.

'But how did you know I was here?' Julia asked, embracing her.

'My housekeeper told me – she's friendly with the woman you've taken on as your temporary ladies' maid. I probably know more about your household than you do. Are you aware that your caretaker has just returned from visiting his married daughter in Brighton?'

'No,' she admitted, marvelling at the ways in which gossip got around and hoping that any talk about her was restricted to her domestic arrangements.

'Was your stay in Bath agreeable?' Elizabeth wanted to know.

'Yes, very pleasant, thank you.'

There was a pause and then Elizabeth said, 'Is it true that Richard is to travel back to Portugal?'

'I believe so,' replied Julia.

'Then it's all over between you?'

'Sadly, yes.'

Elizabeth toyed with the locket hanging around her neck. 'I have some news of my own,' she murmured.

'Good news, I hope.'

'Yes indeed. Lord Westbourne had been appointed special advisor to the new ambassador to Portugal. He sets sail there tomorrow with the rest of the entourage.'

'Do you go with him?'

'No, the ambassador's wife is increasing and she's unable

to contemplate the rigours of such a journey until she's recovered from the birth. The ambassador has convinced my husband that I should wait here so that I may accompany his wife when she's ready to travel, which will not be for some considerable time.'

'Good news indeed,' said Julia, hugging her.

'Thomas swears that he will find a way for us to be together permanently. It has become harder and harder to prevent him from forcing a quarrel on Lord Westbourne on some pretext and calling him out. I feared for him, but now anything may happen in the next few months.'

Julia hoped that a freak wave would wash the objectionable Lord Westbourne overboard, or that he would be attacked by brigands while out riding, but whatever happened Elizabeth would be spared his brutality for a considerable time.

'Do you go to the Miltons' party tomorrow?' asked Elizabeth as she prepared to take her leave.

'I don't know if I'm invited. Any invitation would have gone to my cousin's house and she's still in Bath.'

'I feel sure you must be. Why not send a servant round to collect your post? We could go to the party together if you like.'

Thinking this a sound idea Julia despatched one of the footmen after Elizabeth had left. Her post included that particular invitation and several others as well as a letter from Sir Henry Bartrum, stating his intention of visiting London and of calling on her and Isabel.

It would be good to see him again and she hoped Isabel would think so too. Perhaps her neighbour from the country might go some way towards consoling Isabel for the loss of Captain Moore from her bed.

Julia was just about to go out for a walk when Richard was announced. She felt she owed him what would obviously be a final meeting, but hoped he hadn't come to make a scene.

However, when he was shown in he seemed perfectly composed, kissed her hand and said, 'I didn't wish us to part on bad terms after all that has passed between us. I leave for Portugal tomorrow and I wanted to see you one last time before I went.'

'I'm glad you came,' she assured him. 'Your friendship meant much to me and helped me through a very bad time in my life.'

'I'm sorry it ended the way it did, but I think perhaps it was for the best. I know that you didn't love me the way you did your husband and I would never have been happy to be second choice.'

They chatted on neutral subjects for several minutes and then he rose and picked up his hat and cane.

'Take good care of yourself,' he urged her. 'I earnestly hope that you don't have cause to regret your liaison with Lord Varsey.'

'So do I,' she admitted. 'I wish you a safe journey,' she added, rising on tiptoe to kiss him on the cheek.

When he'd gone she felt a sense of relief that they'd cleared the air and hoped that in Portugal he'd meet some woman who was more deserving of his love.

She felt restless that evening and, as she dined alone, she wondered how long it would be before Isabel returned from Bath. After dinner she tried to settle down with a book, but found she couldn't concentrate and put it to one side.

There had been no word from Lord Varsey since she'd left the mansion several evenings ago. Estelle had blindfolded her again and then she'd been escorted to the other woman's carriage by an unknown man who spoke only to warn her of obstacles in her path.

As soon as the carriage had set in motion she'd ripped off her blindfold, but it had been too dark to see where she was, although she could tell from the direction they'd driven back into London that the mansion must be somewhere in the vicinity of Chiswick.

Was Lord Varsey punishing her by keeping his distance? Did he expect her to send him word she was anxious to see him? He'd wait a long time before she'd do that.

She hoped that the party the following evening would be enjoyable, she needed the distraction.

THIRTY-FIVE

Isabel's return to London was earlier than she'd planned. She'd parted from Captain Moore with great regret and had almost given in to his pressing arguments that she prolong her stay in Bath.

But she was worried about Julia and had decided to return and do anything in her power to save her cousin from heartbreak and social ruin. Isabel had conceived a scheme for Julia's social salvation which she hoped would meet with her approval.

The two cousins had a mutual aunt, who lived a quiet and retiring life in a cottage owned by Isabel in Sussex. Aunt Amelia had been left virtually penniless when her husband, a clergyman, had died many years previously. Isabel had offered her the cottage rent-free and paid her a generous allowance to allow the elderly woman to live out the rest of her days in comfort.

If Julia could be persuaded to invite Aunt Amelia to stay with her for a while, it would put an end to any gossip about her setting up house on her own.

Isabel only hoped that Julia's memory of their aunt was imperfect, because the less appealing aspect to this scheme was that she was not only rather deaf, which made communication difficult, but she was also extremely voluble and could keep up a non-stop stream of inconsequential chatter for hours.

Even at her most charitable Isabel had to admit that Aunt Amelia was wearing on the nerves and she herself would not have wished to spend much time in her company. But hopefully, Julia could barely remember her and could be talked into issuing the invitation.

If her cousin was determined to continue seeing Lord Varsey, she must do so in secret and not appear in public with him. It was a great advantage that he was not received in many respectable houses in London, so if Julia could be persuaded to attend parties and balls where he was not present, her name would be less likely to be linked with his.

If she absolutely had to see him, she could receive him in her own house when Aunt Amelia was safely closeted in her room taking a nap or chattering to her maid.

It afforded Isabel a not inconsiderable amount of amusement to imagine the scenario if their aunt ran across Lord Varsey in her niece's home. She estimated that it would take less than five minutes for Amelia to drive him from the house with her well meaning, but ceaseless conversation.

'Aunt Amelia?' said Julia, furrowing her smooth brow as she poured Isabel a cup of tea. 'I did meet her once, but I was only a child. She brought me a rag doll she'd made which I became very fond of. Why do you mention her?'

Isabel stirred her tea and chose her words carefully.

'In her last letter she said how much she'd like to see us again and I was thinking of inviting her to visit me for a while. But it occurred to me that she could stay with you and provide you with a chaperone which would put paid to any gossip.'

Julia regarded her cousin steadily. 'I don't need a chaperone,' she replied.

'My dear Julia, I've been out in the world much longer than you have and I wish you'd believe me when I say that you do. Your circumstances are so unusual that you have to be particularly careful. Why run a serious risk of being socially ostracized when you don't have to? You would be doing an old lady a kindness and keeping your reputation intact. If you don't like the idea, you could always move back in with me.'

'Thank you, but I imposed on you for long enough. If we're speaking plainly then I feel I should point out that she'll be rather in the way when Lord Varsey pays me a visit.'

'I don't think you need worry about that. If you establish her in a comfortable room on the second floor and make sure that she's well supplied with refreshments, she'll probably rarely venture downstairs. She'll want to bring her maid, Myers, who's been with her for years and knows exactly how to look after her, so all you'll have to do is pop in and see her from time to time. Oh and she's deaf too, so she's unlikely to even know Lord Varsey is in the house when he calls.'

Julia settled back in her chair, indecision on her delicate features. Knowing that her cousin had a kind heart, Isabel continued, 'It would be such a treat for her to visit you. She lives a quiet and retiring life in the country with only her maid for company – the change would do her a great deal of good.'

'Very well – I'll write to invite her,' said Julia reluctantly.

'Write the letter now,' commanded Isabel. 'There's no time to be lost. I'll send it with my carriage and several servants – they should reach her before nightfall and can bring her back tomorrow.'

Julia was dismayed by the prospect of a house guest, but could think of no reason to delay things. She still hadn't heard from Lord Varsey and was beginning to think it was over between them, a possibility that filled her with dread.

'Very well,' she said, going over to the writing desk. 'I'll have my staff prepare a room this afternoon.'

While Julia was putting pen to paper, Isabel decided that as soon as she reached home she would write a letter of her own to accompany her cousin's. She had a shrewd suspicion that Aunt Amelia would really rather not visit London – telling Julia that the old lady had expressed such a wish had been a complete fabrication on her part.

She planned to tell her aunt that Julia was still mourning her husband and would benefit from the companionship and solace that the widow of a clergyman, who had experienced her own loss, could bring her.

Julia was just finishing her letter when the butler announced the arrival of Sir Henry Bartrum. Her own staff from Cumberley were now established in the house and the butler and Sir Henry knew each other well. They were exchanging words as her neighbour was ushered in.

'Sir Henry,' Julia greeted him, taking both his hands in

hers. 'This is a pleasure indeed. You remember my cousin, Lady Marchmont?'

The warmth of his expression indicated that he remembered her very well and as he bent over Isabel's hand he squeezed it gently before kissing it with the utmost gallantry.

Julia invited him to be seated and rang for more tea. They chatted animatedly until it was time for him to take his leave.

'Sir Henry has arrived most opportunely,' Isabel commented. 'I hope we can prevail on him to escort us to the Miltons' party tonight.'

'I wasn't expecting you back from Bath so soon,' said Julia, 'so I've arranged to go with Elizabeth Westbourne. But perhaps Sir Henry could take you and we could meet there.'

This scheme met with everyone's approval, then her two visitors left and Julia rang for her housekeeper to tell her she was expecting a guest for an indefinite stay.

THIRTY-SIX

Julia had very little expectation of seeing Lord Varsey at the Miltons' party because Mrs Milton moved in the first circles of respectability and was the mother of two pretty daughters of seventeen and eighteen.

It was therefore a surprise to see him appear in the drawing room doorway half-way through the evening, survey the gathered throng briefly and then saunter over to greet his hostess.

The sight of him made Julia's mouth go dry and caused a faint fluttering sensation somewhere between her sex and her belly. She lost track of what Elizabeth was saying to her as she gazed over her shoulder to watch what happened.

It was immediately obvious that his entrance was an unwelcome surprise to Mrs Milton and that her husband, standing just behind her, looked self-conscious and uncomfortable.

For a moment Julia thought that Mrs Milton was going to ask him to leave, but before she could speak her husband stepped forward and said, 'Varsey – didn't expect you to make it, but we're glad to see you all the same.' His voice rang with unconvincing heartiness as he spoke, then he took Lord Varsey's arm and led him back towards the door. 'We're just setting up another card table in the library – come on through and have a game.'

It was his obvious intention to take him away from most of the other guests and get him ensconced in the male-dominated sanctum of the library as swiftly as possible.

Lord Varsey's eyes met Julia's and he raised one eyebrow at her quizzically, before turning his attention back to his host.

'So good of you to invite me when we ran into each other this afternoon,' he said, allowing himself to be led from the room.

Julia wondered how he'd managed to get an invitation out of Mr Milton and from the expression on his wife's face didn't envy him having to explain that very thing to her.

It was over an hour later when she was helping herself from the array of food laid out for supper in the dining room that her lover came strolling in and greeted her.

'My dear Mrs Calvert, what a surprise to see you here.' He moved around to join her on the far side of the table and helped himself to a prawn from her plate. She glanced hastily around, hoping no one had seen him, worrying that such an intimate gesture might betray them.

'A surprise?' she said, smiling sweetly. 'You didn't need a crystal ball to predict my presence here, as I'm sure you can't fail to be aware that Mrs Milton is a friend of my cousin.'

'I see the ubiquitous Lady Marchmont is present too, and with a new admirer,' he continued. 'I have to admire her stamina. I don't recognize the fellow – who is he?'

'My friend and neighbour from the country, Sir Henry Bartrum.'

'Hopefully her obvious fascination with him will prevent her from interesting herself over much in your affairs,' he commented. He moved closer to her to say softly, 'I was unhappy to discover you'd left the other night. You missed out on a great deal of pleasure.'

'Then perhaps you should have stayed with me rather than leaving to attend to other . . . business. I trust the lady was suitably appreciative.'

He was now standing so close that she was aware of the heat of his body and could smell his eau de Cologne.

'There's no reason why we shouldn't now take up where we left off,' he told her, his hand stroking her bottom. Julia tried to move away, but she was standing in a corner just behind the table and there was nowhere for her to go. She glanced swiftly around the room, but fortunately no one seemed to be looking at them.

'Take your hand off me,' she hissed, trying to smile pleasantly as if they were just exchanging commonplaces.

'I'm just endeavouring to ascertain if you're wearing pantalettes.'

Julia felt a warm tide of colour rise over her bosom, neck and face as she recalled how he'd humiliated her in front of Scholes. The flush was as much shame at the memory of her own wanton reaction, as it was from the way he'd debased her by making her a slave to her own desires.

For some reason she didn't care to dwell on too closely, she hadn't worn pantalettes since then and was now very conscious of the fact that she was naked beneath her skirts.

'So you're back are you, Miss?' The abrupt question interrupted the intimacy of their exchange and to her dismay, Julia saw Lady Berwick descending on them, her thick brows drawn together in disapproval. 'I heard you'd gone gallivanting off to Bath, spending my poor nephew's money,' she snapped.

Her son and one of her daughters were just behind her and Julia thought fleetingly that fate had dealt some cruel cards to the family in making them all so physically unprepossessing.

'Good evening, Lady Berwick,' she murmured, willing Lord Varsey to fill a plate with food and act as though his presence by her side were merely accidental.

Instead he smiled affably and bowed. 'What a pleasure to see you, Lady Berwick, and your charming daughter too. Evening, Berwick.'

He nodded at Gerald who nodded in return, while his mother ignored the greeting and stared at Lord Varsey through her lorgnette as if he were some sort of unpleasant insect, before saying to her daughter, 'Marie, go and join your sisters.'

The girl hurried off while Julia was horrified to feel Lord Varsey begin a stealthy raising of her skirt at the back and was so preoccupied by thinking wildly of how she might stop him, that she missed Lady Berwick's next words.

'. . . the most notorious libertine in London.'

'I'm sorry – what did you say?' she asked, when it became clear Charles' aunt was waiting for some reply.

222

'I said my poor nephew will be turning in his grave – if indeed he's in it – to know his wife is keeping company with the most notorious libertine in London.'

The table behind which she and Lord Varsey were standing came up to Julia's waist and was covered in a white damask tablecloth which fell to the floor. As long as she remained facing Lady Berwick and the other woman stayed directly opposite her on the other side of the table, she was unlikely to be able to see what Lord Varsey was doing.

But Julia found it small comfort as she felt her lover's warm hand on her bare backside, having successfully slipped it underneath her skirt.

The room suddenly seemed unbearably hot and her face was suffused with more colour as he caressed her covertly, smiling blandly as though Lady Berwick hadn't just rudely insulted him. Julia felt him trying to slide his hand between her thighs and clamped them together in an attempt to arrest his movements.

She felt as though she'd been struck dumb as she struggled to reply, but was spared the necessity when Lord Varsey drawled, 'Surely not, madam. Your own husband has a much greater claim to that title than I have.'

He managed to slip two fingers inside Julia who gasped and then hastily turned it into a cough as he moved them insidiously around inside her and she had to fight an urge to bear down on them.

'How dare you?' spluttered Lady Berwick. 'I'm amazed that Matilda Milton will have you under her roof. Decent women fear for their daughters when you're around.'

'I assure you, madam, that your own daughters need have no fear of me.' His jibe elicited a snort of laughter from Gerald Berwick, which he hastily suppressed as his mother turned to glare at him.

Julia could feel her juices covering Lord Varsey's fingers and rendering her inner chamber honey-slick. Her bud was throbbing urgently, eager for attention and she found that, unconsciously, she'd parted her thighs for him.

'I won't stay and bandy words with you,' snapped Lady Berwick. 'Come, Gerald.' She turned on her heel and stalked off, but instead of following her Gerald stood and stared at Julia, his loose mouth curling in an unpleasant, knowing smile. Then he too turned and left, his unsteady gait indicating that he'd imbibed more claret than he could hold.

Julia and Lord Varsey were alone in the room except for a party of people by the fireplace, all with their backs turned as they discussed a dreary painting of a horse.

'Take your hand from up my skirt,' she hissed at him, gulping as he slid his fingers over her clitoris.

'You don't really want me to, do you?' he returned, squeezing the hot little nub between his finger and thumb. His look of absolute certainty that she would allow him any liberty infuriated her and she tossed the contents of her glass of wine down his breeches.

His exclamation made everyone turn to look at them but it had the desired effect because he withdrew his hand and dabbed at his wet clothing with a napkin, a pained expression on his face.

'I'm so sorry – how clumsy of me,' she said sweetly. 'Do forgive me.'

'My valet will be inconsolable if I return with my breeches ruined. Excuse me, I must go and see what I may do to limit the damage.'

He left her and she glanced discreetly over her shoulder to check that her skirt had fallen back around her ankles before coming out from behind the table.

She chatted to various of her acquaintances and then wandered into the drawing room and over to the open window in search of a breath of cool air. She was joined by Gerald Berwick and felt a frisson of distaste as he openly ogled her bosom.

'You're in good looks tonight, cousin,' he complimented her, his mouth hanging open around his prominent teeth. Something about his tone of voice made her uneasy, but she wasn't sure why.

He was standing too close to her for her comfort and she moved away to where there was a large arrangement of white roses and ferns in a silver urn on a small table. She bent to inhale their sweet fragrance and then froze in that position as he said, 'Pretty, aren't they – but they'd look even prettier decorating your quim.'

Every nerve in her body jangled in alarm as the implication of his words sank in. She straightened slowly up and turned to look at him.

She felt the colour draining from her face as he continued, 'I thought I knew you from somewhere, but it was only tonight I realized that the golden-haired beauty with her hands tied above her head and her bubbies and cunt on display to anyone passing was my dear cousin Charles' wife. I haven't been able to get that image of you out of my mind since then.'

He leered at her as she felt her knees trembling and reached out a hand to the table to steady herself.

'I won't tell anybody,' he assured her. 'At least not if you give me what I want.'

'H . . . how much do you want?' she asked faintly, sure he was going to ask her for money to pay his gambling debts.

'Eh?' he exclaimed, then as he took her meaning he laughed unpleasantly. 'Oh no, it isn't money that I'm asking for, or at least that would be an added bonus. I want what you didn't choose to give me that night – the use of your fair white body, whenever I want it and for as long as I want it.'

'I'd throw myself into the Thames first,' she returned in a low voice.

'Oh, that's the way it is, is it? Well, you might have to because if you don't do as I say, I'll tell every man I know where you were and what you were up to. You won't be able to leave your house without being propositioned by every male you meet. All London will know what sort of angel-faced whore my cousin was married to.'

He put his face so close to hers that she could see every broken vein on his face and said threateningly, 'I hear you've moved into the Calvert town house. I'll pay you a cousinly visit tomorrow and you can either open your legs for me or I'll ruin you.'

He pinched her nipple hard through the silk of her gown and then lurched off, stumbling against Lord Varsey who had just come into the room and was standing right behind him.

Julia sank into a chair. 'This is all your fault,' she accused her lover. 'How could you leave me tied up like that so that I could be seen by anyone passing? You heard him – he'll ruin me.'

He shrugged and took a drink from his glass. 'He's known as a fool and a drunkard – no one will pay him any heed.'

'Is that all you have to say? You'd better think of some way of preventing him from doing as he threatened or I'll be forced to retire to the country in disgrace and you'll never see me again.'

There was a long pause before he said, 'Very well – I'll deal with it.' He sounded so certain that she lifted her head and looked at him.

'How can you be so sure? You heard him. Or is it part of your degenerate game that I should be forced to accede to his wishes?'

'I told you before that I wouldn't share you.'

'You let your butler amuse himself with me.' Her voice rose as she felt her self-control slipping.

'That was different. Resist the temptation to give way to hysteria – there isn't the slightest need for it and I can't bear hysterical women.'

His tone was cold and chilled her to the bone. Making a huge effort she took a deep breath and said in a steadier voice, 'How can you stop him from telling anyone who'll listen that I'm a whore?'

Lord Varsey made a minute adjustment to the wristband of his shirt.

'By having him thrown in Newgate tomorrow.'

'How can you do that?'

'He owes me a vast amount of money in gambling debts. I'll call in the notes which he won't be able to redeem and then set the bailiffs on him. There'll be no one in gaol for him to tell. When he's been there a few days I'll pay him a visit and offer to write off the debts if he promises to keep his mouth shut.' He sounded bored by the whole situation.

When he made to leave her side she said urgently, 'Will you call on me tomorrow to let me know if you were successful?'

'If I have time. I have several engagements and setting the bailiffs on him will take up time I can ill afford, as it is.'

THIRTY-SEVEN

After her upsetting conversations with Gerald and Lord Varsey, Julia could barely sleep. When she awoke the following morning she was almost beside herself with agitation and kept going to the window, dreading seeing Charles' cousin approaching the house.

Despite Lord Varsey's assurances that he'd deal with the situation, she was afraid that Gerald might elude the bailiffs and could even now be on his way here.

She was so caught up in her own troubles that it was only Isabel's arrival in the afternoon that reminded her she was expecting a house guest. Having to entertain her elderly aunt was the last thing she felt like and she heartily wished she hadn't let Isabel talk her into issuing the invitation.

She tried to chat to her cousin as if nothing were wrong, but Isabel was no fool and after watching her pace the drawing room said, 'Whatever's the matter?'

'N . . . nothing.'

'Has Lord Varsey upset you in some way?'

'No.'

'Was it Lady Berwick? I gather she was her usual obnoxious self. Incidentally, what was her repellent son saying to you? I saw him ogling you. How a delightful man like Charles came to be related to such a family, I really can't imagine.'

It was all too much for Julia, she burst into tears and sobbed, 'Gerald says he'll ruin me if I don't let him into my bed. He caught me in a . . . compromising position and threatens he'll tell every male acquaintance in London that I'm a whore.'

Much concerned, Isabel passed her a handkerchief and

slowly, between dabbing her eyes and twisting the handkerchief into a damp knot, Julia told her what had occurred.

'I was dreading Lord Varsey taking you to the mansion – I knew he would eventually,' said Isabel when she knew the whole.

Julia raised her tear-stained face. 'You know about it?'

'He took me there too.'

Julia let this sink in, her blue eyes round, before saying, 'You and he were lovers?'

Isabel nodded. 'I know I should have told you, but it's something I preferred to keep to myself because I'm not proud of the fact.'

'When was this?'

'Shortly after my husband died. I was grief-stricken and vulnerable. Lord Varsey sought me out and I believed erroneously that he cared for me and that some time in the future after a suitable period of mourning we would be married.'

'What happened?'

'At first I thought him a wonderful lover and in his arms I was able to forget my misery at the death of my beloved husband. But soon our love-making became more and more risky and debauched and it was with mixed feelings I discovered I had a taste for depravity.

'Several times our couplings were so public that we were almost discovered and I think I knew even then that it would have been a matter of indifference to him if I'd lost my reputation. He's a man and society is most forgiving of men's shortcomings, but sadly it is not so with women. It got worse. Gradually, a little at a time, he managed to get me to accept the presence and participation of other people in our love play until I became addicted to every sort of excess.'

Isabel paused and rearranged the folds of her garnet silk gown. 'I did many things to please him that make me hot with shame, even today after all this time. When he knew he had me totally subjugated to his will, he told me it was over. I lost my dignity and begged him not to end it, but he merely said that one of his friends would be glad to take me on, as if I were a housemaid or some other servant he no longer wished to employ. I have never forgiven him and it has upset me deeply to watch him leading you down the same path.'

There was a long silence before Julia said, 'I'm sorry that my liaison with him has caused you so much grief.'

'And I'm sorry I didn't tell you all this before, but it has been hard for me to admit to my own foolishness.'

They were interrupted by the sound of a carriage drawing up outside. Isabel rose and made her way to the window, her hips swaying.

'It's Aunt Amelia,' she said, looking out. 'My coachman made very good time.'

'I can't greet her like this – I must go and splash some cold water on my face,' said Julia frantically. 'I'll be back in a few minutes.' She ran hastily from the room while Isabel went into the hall to meet her aunt as she was helped up the steps by her maid, talking all the while.

'Aunt Amelia – how lovely to see you,' Isabel greeted her, kissing her on the cheek.

'Isabel, my dear . . . I came at once . . . poor dear girl . . . you should have written to me before . . . such a comfortable journey in your carriage . . . I've brought several of my favourite tracts . . . most uplifting . . . a delightful meal at an inn . . . the chicken perhaps a little tough but it doesn't signify . . . such a considerate coachman . . . his livery the same colour as the flowers in church on Sunday . . . Miss Beaton grows the sweetest smelling roses . . . greenfly this year have been terrible – have you been much troubled by them? Perhaps there aren't greenfly in London . . . such a lovely house . . . one of my neighbours has a sideboard like that – could it be the same one, do you think? No, of course it cannot . . . what a silly woman I am. Dear Isabel, and in such good looks too . . . What a hot summer it has been . . . is it the fashion to display quite so much bosom, dear? Perhaps a handkerchief tucked in your bodice would be more the thing . . . or some lace . . . Myers could sew you some in a trice. Myers – do you have your needle to hand?'

'Perhaps Myers would like to go up to your room to begin unpacking your clothes,' suggested Isabel hastily, but Aunt Amelia continued to talk over her as if she had not spoken.

'Myers fashions such delightful gowns out of the veriest

off-cuts of material . . . made this one in just a day . . . would be delighted to make some for you too, dear . . . London dressmakers so expensive, I imagine . . . I'm not sure your uncle would have approved of that gown . . . modesty in a woman is a most becoming trait . . .'

She continued to ramble on while Isabel felt her face beginning to ache from smiling and nodding. She tried a couple of times to proffer refreshment, but it was obvious that her aunt hadn't heard her. Where on earth was Julia?

By the time her cousin came back downstairs ten minutes later, Isabel was at screaming point as her aunt rummaged in her bag, saying, 'Handkerchief in here somewhere . . . cover your bosom . . .'

'Aunt Amelia, how lovely to see you again.'

Julia hurried over and kissed her aunt, who patted her cheek murmuring, 'Grown so much . . . would never have recognized you . . . but so pale and thin . . . calves' foot jelly is the very thing . . . Myers shall prepare some for you . . . build you up in no time . . . do you have a calf's foot in the house? Not to worry if you don't . . . my kind neighbour Mr Rimmington can send me one . . . no trouble at all . . .'

'I have to go, I'm afraid,' said Isabel briskly, pulling on her gloves and avoiding Julia's eyes the better to ignore her anguished expression. She kissed her aunt who remained in full spate, as Julia tried to get her to sit down and take her bonnet off.

'Mrs Swinton swears by pigeon livers . . . not as good at all . . . no doubt about it . . . so thin and peaky . . . tracts somewhere in my bag . . . such a comfort . . . read them together . . . has dear Isabel gone? Your uncle wouldn't have approved at all.'

A ring at the doorbell in the late afternoon made Julia jerk upright on the sofa and she strained to hear who it was over the sound of her aunt's ramblings. It was with considerable relief that she heard Lord Varsey's deep voice in the hall and a moment later the butler came in.

'Lord Varsey is here, Mrs Calvert.'

'Please show him into the library – I'll be there in a moment.'

'. . . to the boil . . . let it set overnight in a cool larder . . . is your larder cool dear? Skim off the fat . . . nothing better for a chesty cough . . .'

'Excuse me a moment, Aunt Amelia, there's something I must attend to.' Julia leapt to her feet and hurried from the room.

Lord Varsey was looking out of the window, but turned as she came in.

'Well?' she demanded agitatedly. He raised an eyebrow at her.

' "Well" is hardly the greeting I hope for after the considerable amount of trouble I've gone to on your behalf.'

'It was you who got me into this difficulty in the first place,' she flashed.

'I don't recollect dragging you to the mansion kicking and screaming.'

'Don't trifle with me – I barely slept last night and I've been waiting in for you all day.'

'If by "well" you mean, have I been successful in having young Berwick incarcerated in gaol, then the answer is, yes I have.'

Julia slumped onto a chair in relief.

'I'm very grateful,' she murmured.

'I'm pleased to hear it. I hope that in return you'll play hostess at a small party I'm giving for a few friends.'

'You know I can't play hostess for you – whatever would people think?'

He came to stand behind her and let his hand drift over her neck in an idle caress.

'This would be a very private party. No one would know except the people present.'

'And what would playing hostess consist of?'

His hand slid round to caress the soft skin above her breasts and then slipped lower.

'Endless pleasure. Four men to satisfy your every need and cater to your every desire,' he said softly.

Julia was deeply insulted by the suggestion. His meaning was plain – he wanted her to participate in some sort of degenerate orgy, allowing his friends the use of her body, presumably while the others watched. She tried to ignore the smouldering little squib of wayward lust which his words and touch were evoking and bit her lip as his hand closed over her breast inside the bodice of her gown.

'I think you should give me some small reward in recognition of my endeavours on your behalf,' he said, his hand going to his fly and unbuttoning it. 'Pleasure me with your lips and tongue.'

His phallus sprang out, hugely erect. He took her arm and guided her to her knees and then buried his hand in her golden hair as she took the head in her mouth.

It was warm and smooth and she could feel it throbbing against her lips as she commenced a delicate sucking that had him sighing with satisfaction. She strummed at the ridge running down from the glans, then wound her tongue around the rigid shaft.

She took it into her mouth an inch at a time, exerting a seductive pressure as it slid between her lips into the warm velvet of her mouth. She moved it in and out, sucking harder as she felt his arousal grow, her hand holding the base and directing his movements.

The only sounds in the peace of the library were the slight liquid squelching noise of her mouth on his phallus and the faint rumble of a passing carriage.

Suddenly the door opened and Julia froze in horror, wondering which of her servants had dared to enter without knocking, and bitterly regretting that yet again she'd been foolish enough to allow herself to be caught in a compromising situation.

'Julia my dear . . . wondered where you'd got to . . . didn't mean to interrupt your devotions . . . please carry on . . . just remembered . . . boiled brains supposed to be most beneficial for low spirits . . . or maybe gout, Myers would know. Boil them up for no less than two hours . . . lambs' brains best . . . pigs' brains are not as good . . .'

Lord Varsey had his back to the door and Julia was almost hidden from view as she knelt in front of him. He too had frozen as the door was pushed open and now she heard him make a faint sound of disbelief. Letting his member slip from her mouth as silently as possible, she glanced up and was nearly undone by the thunderstruck expression on his face.

Looking as if he couldn't believe this was happening, he made himself decent still with his back to the door, while Julia got to her feet. Aunt Amelia was standing just inside the room, peering myopically towards them, her vision impeded by the fact that the curtains were half drawn against the hot afternoon sunshine.

She came forward holding out her hand to Lord Varsey saying, 'My own dear husband a man of the cloth . . . so pleased to see Julia getting spiritual guidance . . . hope to see much of you . . . here to help my niece get over her sad loss . . . dear husband much troubled by gout . . . do you suffer from it yourself?'

He made his bow like a man in a trance, looking so bemused that it was all Julia could do not to burst out laughing as her aunt continued, '. . . different in London, I suppose . . . country clergyman a different matter . . . sober dress expected . . . those boots cannot help your gout . . . slippers much better for indoor wear. Myers shall make you some . . . some felt and a scrap of leather . . . shall look forward to hearing you on Sunday . . .'

He bowed again towards them both saying, 'It was a pleasure to meet you. Goodbye, Mrs Calvert – I may stop by tomorrow but if I happen not to find you at home I trust I shall see you on Thursday night at Astly House.'

'Yes, certainly – thank you for calling. Goodbye,' she managed to say, choking back her laughter with difficulty.

THIRTY-EIGHT

'I haven't had a moment to myself since she got here,' wailed Julia, pulling off her bonnet and tossing it onto the sofa in Isabel's blue drawing room a few days later. 'If I go up to my bed-chamber she follows me and if anyone calls she just talks and talks until they go away again. This morning I was still asleep when she brought me some absolutely vile brew Myers had concocted and said it would put the bloom back in my cheeks. It made me want to retch.'

'I'm sure she means well,' murmured Isabel, trying not to smile.

'I'm sure she does, but that doesn't make it any easier. Lord Varsey came to pay me a call this morning, obviously hoping to find me alone, and she immediately joined us, fell to her knees and invited him to lead us in prayer.

'Even if he had been inclined to do such a thing, he couldn't have got a word in edgeways because she just kept talking. It makes me wonder how her husband ever managed to conduct a service. I can see her in the front pew, her voice echoing relentlessly around the church as he tried to deliver a sermon.'

Julia looked so agitated that Isabel poured her a glass of wine.

'You said she'd stay in her room and talk to her maid,' Julia accused her. 'Far from it – she follows me around the house contradicting my orders to the domestic staff and urging me not to eat anything unwholesome which is just about everything I enjoy.

'She ordered coddled eggs for lunch. The chef's face was a picture, but I think he must be frightened of Myers, who seems to have taken over the running of the kitchen, because that's what appeared on the table – just that. I'm expecting him to give notice any day.'

'She has your welfare at heart.'

'Well, I wish she'd go back to Sussex and have it at heart from there. You did this on purpose, Isabel – don't deny it. You knew what she was like and that it would be impossible for me to entertain Lord Varsey while she was under my roof. You couldn't have hit on a more effective chaperone if you'd considered the entire female population of London.'

'Just out of interest – how did you escape from her to come here?'

'I waited until she went to call for Myers to come and measure me so she could make me a new nightgown. Aunt Amelia said that the ones I wear are unsuitable for a woman in my position and sent Myers out yesterday to buy some thick calico to make me a new one. As soon as she'd gone upstairs I grabbed my bonnet and reticule and fled from the house. I didn't even dare wait to call for my carriage – I had to walk here.'

Isabel burst out laughing while Julia regarded her fulminatingly.

'You're going to have to invite her to stay here instead – I can't stand another day of this.'

'I'll come and take her out for a drive, if you like,' offered Isabel.

'I don't want you to take her out for a drive, I want you to invite her to stay with you so she can make your life a misery instead of mine.'

'That would make it too difficult for me to entertain Sir Henry.'

Julia eyed her cousin narrowly. 'So it's fine for you to entertain your lover, but I'm being forced into celibacy because of your misguided attempts to safeguard my social position. I think I'd rather become a fallen woman than have Aunt Amelia spend one more day endeavouring to lift my spirits.'

'Never mind, it's the annual costume ball at Astly House tomorrow. Have you organized your costume yet?'

'I haven't been able to give it a moment's thought. Anyway, how am I going to be able to escape from the house? Aunt Amelia's notions of the amusements suitable for a woman in my position are very different from mine. She'd consider a costume ball on a par with devil worship.'

'Mmm – I'll send a carriage for her in the late afternoon to take her to Westminster Abbey or somewhere. You come here as soon as she's gone and I'll have a costume ready for you to change into. You can dine with me and Sir Henry can escort us both there. Tell your staff to inform her that you've gone to visit the sick or something equally worthy.'

Julia rose to her feet. 'If you don't get her to leave by the end of the week I'll take up residence in Lord Varsey's house,' she threatened.

Julia refused Isabel's offer of a carriage to convey her home and took a long detour on her way back, her footsteps dragging as she neared her destination.

A carriage overtook her but she didn't even notice it until it stopped and the door opened.

'Julia.' Lord Varsey leaned out. 'Get in.' Julia glanced around and saw two ladies of her acquaintance on the other side of the road.

'You know I can't,' she told him, 'not in a closed carriage.'

A look of annoyance crossed his face and he emerged and joined her, saying, 'Wait for me here,' to his driver.

'People are looking,' she told him. 'We'd better walk.'

'What the devil are you playing at?' he demanded angrily. 'I thought you were living in your own house so you could entertain me without interference. Instead I find that you've moved some elderly relative in who seems to be acting like a Mother Superior.'

'Isabel wished her on me,' she admitted.

'Aah! Your cousin will obviously go to any lengths to keep us apart. If I can't come to you – you must come to me.'

'You know I can't do that.'

They were just passing the entrance to a narrow, rubbish-strewn alleyway. Without warning he seized her arm and pulled her into it and then around a bend so they were

236

hidden from passers by on the main thoroughfare. A skinny cat went slinking by, sniffed contemptuously and carried on its way.

'Then I must take any opportunity that presents itself,' he growled, dragging her into his arms and kissing her hard on the mouth, pressing her against the wall with the length of his body.

She could feel the strength of his arousal against her belly and it excited her. She made no protest as he jerked her skirt around her waist and thrust his hand between her bare thighs. She hadn't worn pantalettes since the night he'd cut them from her with a knife.

The sensation of her silk skirts against her bare mound and derrière intoxicated her and reminded her of the aberrant pleasures he'd introduced her to.

He pushed two fingers inside her and moved them roughly around, then ripped open the buttons of his fly and jammed his organ into her in one forceful movement.

She gasped and pushed her pelvis forward as he commenced a vigorous thrusting which left her unable to do anything except cling to his shoulders and move against him.

He drew her breasts from the bodice of her lemon-yellow muslin gown and fondled them as he shafted her. The knowledge that they were copulating in an alleyway, close enough to the road to hear people walking by, imbued the proceedings with a hot, squalid excitement.

It didn't last long; with several final frenzied thrusts which flattened her against the wall, he erupted into her and then pulled out immediately.

'Tell me that your aunt won't be accompanying you to Astly House tonight,' he remarked as she pulled her bodice back up over her breasts and rearranged her skirts.

'She won't.'

'Then I'll see you there.'

THIRTY-NINE

Isabel had chosen a lovely sea-green dress in the style of that worn by the ancient Greeks for Julia's costume. It left her arms and shoulders bare and tied around her narrow waist with a gold girdle. There were gold thonged sandals for her bare feet and a gold circlet for her hair which Isabel's maid dressed in a deceptively simple style that matched the costume.

Isabel herself had chosen a regal, richly-embroidered cardinal-red gown of the type worn when the Stuarts were on the throne. It had a ruff which rose stiffly around her face which she claimed scratched her cruelly.

'I declare I don't know how they stood wearing anything so uncomfortable,' she said, struggling to loosen it a little.

'I can't tell you how much I'm looking forward to an evening without Aunt Amelia,' replied Julia, twirling in front of the looking glass so that the skirts of shimmering silk floated out around her bare ankles.

Sir Henry – obviously besotted by Isabel – arrived to escort them there and they all pulled on light silk cloaks and their black velvet masks.

The ball was one of the best attended events of the summer and the ballroom was already full of waltzing couples when they arrived. Julia accepted an invitation to dance with a Roman centurion, her eyes constantly skimming the dancers, looking for the tall, broad-shouldered frame of Lord Varsey.

What would he come as? She wished she'd thought to ask him, but was sure he'd find her eventually. She danced with Sir Henry, who was attired as Henry VIII, a pillow adding the additional girth to his burly frame needed to fill the over-large costume.

He talked only of Isabel, her beauty and her graciousness, confirming Julia's suspicion that he was completely smitten. He had too much delicacy to mention her other more earthy charms, but Julia was sure he was aware of them. Her heart leapt when she spotted Lord Varsey strolling around the dance floor with a glass of wine in his hand.

He was dressed as a highwayman, completely in black except for the white lawn of his shirt and cravat, a tricorne hat on his silver-streaked dark hair.

He sought her hand for the next dance.

'Have you rid yourself of that tiresome old woman yet?' he asked, holding her closer than the dictates of the day deemed proper.

'She's not a tiresome old woman – she's my aunt,' retorted Julia, for whatever she might have said to Isabel on the subject, she didn't care for the derisive way in which he spoke of Aunt Amelia.

'If you don't arrange for her to quit your house, I will,' he threatened.

'I suppose you'll pack her off to Portugal,' she said sweetly. 'Or will it be Newgate? I'm well aware of the lengths you're prepared to go to to rid my life of anyone who doesn't meet with your approval.'

'*You* begged me to get Berwick out of the way and you know it. Incidentally, his unpleasant mother has called on me three times this week. I'm amazed that the strength of her maternal feelings would lead her to sully her shoes on my doorstep. I told my servants to deny me, of course.'

'W . . . what do you think she wanted?' asked Julia, taken aback by the news.

'Either to pour imprecations on my head or to beg me to have her son released from prison. She doesn't have the money to pay his debts for him, so I imagine she thinks to move me with her abuse or her pleadings. What a pity she's not comely – I love to have an attractive woman beg a favour from me and to see what she's willing to grant me in return.'

His tone was so callous that Julia found herself wondering

exactly what sort of a man she'd allowed herself to become involved with. She herself had no affection for Lady Berwick, but she found she had to respect a mother's love which made her prepared to debase herself before a man she'd publicly insulted.

'I wish to be alone with you,' Lord Varsey murmured. 'I want to rip that alluring costume from you and take you naked except for the girdle, your jewellery and your sandals.' His words rekindled the heat which seemed to be ever-smouldering in her female core these days and she was unable to prevent herself from rubbing her mound against his thigh in a lewd, wanton gesture.

'There's a small orangery off the yellow sitting room at the back of the house,' he told her. 'I think we may be private in it for a little while. I'll meet you there on the hour.'

Their dance ended and she took to the floor with a corsair with a dashing moustache and a pleasantly flirtatious manner.

At around ten to the hour she made her way slowly around the dance floor, butterflies of sheer carnal desire fluttering in her belly. She'd paused to watch Isabel and Sir Henry deep in conversation as they danced together, when she became aware she was being closely studied by a man in a dark travelling cloak, which hid whatever he had on underneath.

Something about him made her heart lurch and she looked at him carefully, trying to decide what it was. She thought that she knew him, but couldn't put a name to his face, partially hidden behind a black satin mask.

He was as broad-shouldered as Lord Varsey but slightly taller. His face was tanned and his hair touched with gold, as if he'd recently been in the tropics, making her think he must be a naval man.

She shot him a slight smile, hoping he'd ask her to dance so she might discover his identity. He bowed in her direction, but made no move to approach her. She moved towards him, meaning to pass close by and see if closer scrutiny gave her any further clues, but he melted into the crowd.

Thinking it must be almost time to meet Lord Varsey, she put him from her mind and went to look for the yellow sitting room. She had to glance into several rooms before she located it along a corridor at the back of the house.

The orangery was entered through double doors and she had a moment's unease as she passed through them, knowing that yet again her carnal appetites were leading her to the most reckless of behaviour.

The air in the orangery was warm, moist and fragrant and she breathed in the heady scents of lilies, gardenia and freesia growing among potted palm trees and other hot house plants.

She wandered around, inhaling their sweet scents, wondering what was keeping Lord Varsey. She was eager for his touch and impatient for his arrival.

The sound of the door opening made her turn, a smile of anticipation on her lips. The smile faded when she saw the man in the travelling cloak in the doorway. He closed the doors behind him and she felt alarm rising within her as he approached.

'Sir, I must ask you to leave at once,' she said. 'You're compromising me by being here alone with me.'

He didn't reply, just stared at her steadily, his expression unreadable, before walking slowly towards her.

She retreated, wondering whether to make a dash for the door and cursing Lord Varsey for getting her into yet another difficult situation.

'*Julia.*'

Her name was spoken in a low voice which seemed to echo endlessly around her head, making her feel as though she'd suddenly emerged from a place of noisome darkness into the peaceful light. Her hand flew to her throat and she stood as still as a statue.

'Charles.'

She whispered the word in disbelief, certain that in a moment she'd realize she'd made a mistake and be plunged back into the abyss she'd lived in these last two years.

It couldn't be her husband – Charles was dead.

He raised his hand and in a moment that seemed to last a lifetime, he pulled off his mask and it dropped to the ground. Julia's bones turned to water and she would have slipped to the floor if he hadn't sprung forward and caught her in his arms.

'Charles,' she whispered again, gazing into his eyes, wondering if it was just a dream she'd wake from in a few minutes. 'Is it really you?'

He laid her tenderly on a small sofa in the shadows and knelt beside her, chafing her nerveless hands.

'Darling Julia. I've thought of little but this moment for two long years.'

She tried to raise her head from the cushions, but felt too weak and dizzy. 'W . . . what happened?' she managed to ask.

'It's a long story. I journeyed into the interior and was captured by natives. They held me prisoner for a long time, and for much of which I was ill with some tropical fever. When I eventually recovered I managed to escape but my journey back to the coast took forever and then I had to make my way to a port. All in all it took me until now to return to you.'

'How did you know I was here?' Her mouth felt so numb she could barely form the words.

'I went to the town house to see whether you were there or at Cumberley. I met your aunt who seemed to think you were visiting the sick – a curious notion. The butler told me you were here and I came at once, unable to wait another moment before being reunited.'

'I . . . I saw you in the ballroom,' murmured Julia, clutching one of his hands and holding it as if she would never let it go. 'But I didn't realize it was you. Your hair is much lighter and your skin so tanned. Why did you not make yourself known to me?'

'In front of all those people, unsure what your reaction would be? I followed you at a distance hoping to get you alone.'

He bent his head and their lips met in a tender kiss which almost immediately became more demanding and had the blood coursing feverishly through her veins.

'Let us return home at once,' he muttered, raising his head and devouring her slender body with his eyes. 'Or I fear I'll take you right now on the sofa and cause a terrible scandal.'

They were so occupied with each other that they didn't hear the door open and the first intimation that they were no longer alone was a woman's voice crying, 'You shameless little whore, dallying in debauchery with your lover while my son lies incarcerated in Newgate!'

FORTY

Julia looked over Charles' shoulder and was horrified to see that a small crowd had gathered behind Lady Berwick as she shouted her accusations.

'You foul, wanton slut!' she raged, advancing on them. 'How dare you behave with such a lack of decorum in public?'

Charles rose slowly to his feet and turned to face her.

'Good evening, Aunt Berwick,' he said coldly. 'I'm happy to see you're in such rude and strident health.'

The mottled colour drained from her face, leaving it the colour of a linen sheet.

'Charles!' she exclaimed.

'Indeed. And may I ask why you see fit to barge in on our reunion so rudely, bellowing unfounded accusations?'

'Unfounded are they? I'll have you know that your strumpet of a wife has been playing fast and loose with half the men in London during your absence, including frequently entertaining one of the most debauched libertines in England in the house which has been in our family for hundreds of years.'

Julia struggled to sit up, her face as pale as alabaster.

'She'd have difficulty doing that since our Aunt Amelia is currently residing with her.' Isabel's voice came from behind Lady Berwick as she stepped forward and embraced Charles.

'Dearest Charles – welcome home,' she breathed.

'No one's residing with her – she's set up house alone as anyone will tell you!' shrieked Lady Berwick.

'I've just come from the town house and seen my wife's Aunt Amelia,' Charles said haughtily. 'What mischief are you at now, Aunt? I know you always disliked Julia but this is beyond belief.'

'Julia lived quietly in the country until the spring,' Isabel informed him. 'I persuaded her to return to town and she stayed with me for a while. Now she has her aunt with her, so I'm baffled to hear Lady Berwick asserting otherwise.'

'Her lover had my son thrown in gaol because he threatened to expose her. There he is! Deny it if you dare!'

She pointed an accusing finger at Lord Varsey who was standing just inside the doorway watching the proceedings with mild interest.

'I certainly don't deny I had him thrown in Newgate,' he drawled. 'He lost vast sums of money to me he made no attempt to repay.'

'She was his whore!'

'*That's enough!*' roared Charles. 'I won't hear another word! You and your wretched family have been leeching off me for years and this is how you repay me – blackening the name of an innocent woman from sheer, vicious spite. If you ever repeat a word of this to anyone else, I'll sue you to recover every penny I've ever handed out to you. I'll have the roof from over your head and see you on the streets! Now get out!'

Lady Berwick quailed before his towering wrath. Her mouth opened and closed a couple of times and then she turned on her heel and left the room.

Charles helped a trembling Julia from the sofa. 'Let's go home.'

As he led her towards the door, Lord Varsey raised one hand briefly in an unobtrusive salute of farewell, a faint smile of regret playing around his lips.

Charles and Julia lay in bed hours later, their arms around each other, their bodies pressed together after a long and explosive bout of love-making.

'I have a confession to make,' he murmured, stroking her hair. 'I hesitate to make it because I don't want to grieve you, but I can't live with myself unless I tell you.'

'What is it?' she asked, propping herself up on one elbow

and tracing the hard line of his cheekbone with one finger.

'When I was very ill – near to death – I was nursed back to health by a native girl whose husband had been killed two years before. There was something about her that reminded me of you. Her gentleness and sweetness, perhaps. When I recovered – thinking I might never see you again – we became lovers. I don't expect you to forgive me just yet, but I hope that at least in some small way you'll understand.'

Julia hesitated. Should she make a similar confession? She had to admit that she was afraid to.

'Charles . . .' she said diffidently.

'Uum?' He gathered her back into his arms.

'I have something to tell you too.'

He put his finger to her lips. 'I don't want to hear it. Let's just pick up where we left off. If you've no objection I'd like to return to Cumberley as soon as I've reported on my mission and settled some other business.'

'I've no objection at all. That's what I'd like, above all else. What other business do you have to settle?'

'The Berwicks. I've put up with my aunt's behaviour too long because she was my mother's half-sister, but I'm damned if I'll tolerate it any longer. Gerald can make his choice between rotting in Newgate or joining the army – his gambling debts have been a thorn in my side for years. I'll make sure he joins a regiment which is due overseas and hope that's the last we'll see of him for years.

'I'm going to offer to pay my uncle's debts too if he and my aunt will go and live in the country where he won't be tempted to visit every club and gambling hell in London on a weekly basis. But before I do that I'll have a public apology from the old harpy. Still, don't let's dwell on that. There are more pressing things on my mind.'

He shifted position so he could stroke her breasts and the pert swell of her bottom, his lips meeting hers in a heart-stopping kiss.

He caressed every inch of her skin, lingering on her delicate curves and letting his fingers drift along her slender limbs. One hand closed on her breast and he dropped a series of kisses on her bare shoulder while he stroked her smooth-skinned orb, running his fingertips lightly over her puckered areola, making the nipple harden and push upwards.

He bent his head so he could flick her nipple with his tongue and take it between his lips. He sucked at it gently, sending tremors of sheer carnal desire through her slender frame and making her sex-flesh moisten and soften even more.

Julia bit back a moan of pleasure and shifted her hips on the bed. Her movement made her even more aware of how erect and ready he was again. She couldn't stop herself pushing her groin against him and felt an immediate answering pressure.

His hand glided down to trace the curves of her hip and belly, then his fingertips dabbled teasingly in her pubic fleece. He shifted position so he was lying to one side of her and his fingers dipped lower to rim her outer labia, provoking a further flood of moisture.

He touched her most secret places, tracing every undulation, before sliding down the bed and pressing his lips to the soft skin of her inner thigh. He kissed his way slowly up to her vulva and then swirled his tongue in a languid, lazy circle around the rim of her outer sex-lips.

Julia sighed and parted her thighs even more widely as he licked his way over every fold and furrow of her sex-flesh, turning her limbs to water and lapping eagerly at the renewed flood of moisture which his caresses provoked.

He introduced his tongue into her very core and explored every velvety crevice of her inner chamber that he could reach until she was squirming on the sheet, moaning with pleasure.

He slid back up the bed, propped himself on one elbow and rubbed the hot, smooth end of his phallus over her swollen quim.

She gasped and tried to get it inside her, but he moved it tantalizingly over her engorged clitoris until she thought she would pass out from sheer erotic pleasure. He rubbed harder and she clutched at his shoulders, her back arching and her head falling back on the pillow.

She spasmed into a climax which took her breath away, then cried out as he slid his member smoothly into her and her convulsing muscles clenched around it, prolonging her pleasure.

He moved above her at a slow, languorous pace, each stroke penetrating her deeply and working her further up the spiral of sheer ecstasy. She wound her legs around his thighs and savoured the sweet, heady delight of his love-making, she'd thought never to experience again.

He kept it up until she hovered on the brink of a release, then paused briefly, making her cry out in protest. He quickened his strokes until she spasmed into another long-lived climax which felt as though it had been wrenched from the deepest, most hidden part of her womb.

Charles groaned loudly as he erupted into her with the force of a dam breaching its banks and then collapsed by her side, his hand on her breast.

There came a rattling at the door and in the flickering light of the candle by the bed, Julia saw the handle turn fruitlessly.

'Is it locked?' she whispered.

'Yes,' he assured her.

'Julia, dear – are you ill? Or is it Charles with some unpleasant ailment he's brought back with him from foreign parts? I heard such a noise . . . the gripe can be a terrible thing . . . a poultice is the best possible remedy . . . or a purgative made from nettles . . . or is it dandelion leaves? Myers will know . . . I'll go and wake her . . . nobody knows better than . . .'

They heard the sound of Aunt Amelia pattering off down the corridor, her voice fading as she got further away.

'She's not coming with us to Cumberley,' said Charles grimly, his hand straying back between his wife's thighs.

Adult Fiction for Lovers from Headline LIAISON

SLEEPLESS NIGHTS	Tom Crewe & Amber Wells	£4.99
THE JOURNAL	James Allen	£4.99
THE PARADISE GARDEN	Aurelia Clifford	£4.99
APHRODISIA	Rebecca Ambrose	£4.99
DANGEROUS DESIRES	J. J. Duke	£4.99
PRIVATE LESSONS	Cheryl Mildenhall	£4.99
LOVE LETTERS	James Allen	£4.99

All Headline Liaison books are available at your local bookshop or newsagent, or can be ordered direct from the publisher. Just tick the titles you want and fill in the form below. Prices and availability subject to change without notice.

Headline Book Publishing, Cash Sales Department, Bookpoint, 39 Milton Park, Abingdon, OXON, OX14 4TD, UK. If you have a credit card you may order by telephone – 01235 400400.

Please enclose a cheque or postal order made payable to Bookpoint Ltd to the value of the cover price and allow the following for postage and packing: UK & BFPO: £1.00 for the first book, 50p for the second book and 30p for each additional book ordered up to a maximum charge of £3.00.
OVERSEAS & EIRE: £2.00 for the first book, £1.00 for the second book and 50p for each additional book.

Name ....

Address ....

....

....

If you would prefer to pay by credit card, please complete:
Please debit my Visa/Access/Diner's Card/American Express (Delete as applicable) card no:

Signature .... Expiry Date ....